Like many authors, Lesley started w............. chequered beginning, including jobs .... crew and nightclub DJ, she fell into .... including *Business Matters*, *Which?*, *Computing* and *Farmers Weekly*.

She progressed to short stories for the vibrant women's magazine market and, following a Master's degree where she met her publisher, she turned to her first literary love of traditional British mysteries. The Libby Sarjeant series is still going strong, and has been joined by The Alexandrians, an Edwardian mystery series.

Praise for Lesley Cookman:

'Nicely staged drama and memorable and strangely likeable characters'
Trisha Ashley

'With fascinating characters and an intriguing plot, this is a real page turner'
Katie Fforde

'Lesley Cookman is the Queen of Cosy Crime'
Paul Magrs

'Intrigue, romance and a touch of murder in a picturesque village setting'
Liz Young

'A compelling series where each book leaves you satisfied but also eagerly waiting for the next one'
Bernardine Kennedy

'A quaint, British cozy, complete with characters who are both likeable and quirky'
Rosalee Richland

Also by Lesley Cookman

Libby Sarjeant series:

Murder in Steeple Martin
Murder at the Laurels
Murder in Midwinter
Murder by the Sea
Murder in Bloom
Murder in the Green
Murder Imperfect
Murder to Music
Murder at the Manor
Murder by Magic
Murder in the Monastery
Murder in the Dark
Murder in a Different Place
Murder Out of Tune
Murder at Mollowan Manor
Murder in the Blood
Murder Dancing
Murder on the Run
Murder by the Barrel
Murder Most Fowl
Murder and the Glovemaker's Son
Murder and the Pantomime Cat
Murder Repeated
Murder on the Edge
Murder After Midnight
Murder by Mistake
Murder in Autumn
Murder by Christmas

Murder Most Merry: A Christmas Omnibus

The Alexandrians:

Entertaining Death
Death Plays a Part
Death Treads the Boards

Rosina Lesley Novels:

Running Away
A Will to Love

MURDER BY CHRISTMAS

Lesley Cookman

ACCENT

First published in 2023 by Headline Accent
An imprint of HEADLINE PUBLISHING GROUP

1

Cataloguing in Publication Data is available from the British Library

ISBN 978 1 0354 0568 8

Typeset in 10.5/13pt Bembo Std by Jouve (UK), Milton Keynes

Printed and bound in Great Britain by Clays Ltd, Elcograf S.p.A.

Headline's policy is to use papers that are natural, renewable and recyclable
products and made from wood grown in well-managed forests and other
controlled sources. The logging and manufacturing processes are expected
to conform to the environmental regulations of the country of origin.

HEADLINE PUBLISHING GROUP
An Hachette UK Company
Carmelite House
50 Victoria Embankment
London
EC4Y 0DZ

www.headline.co.uk
www.hachette.co.uk

*Dedicated to my daughter-in-law Carrie and
her parents, Ginny and Tom*

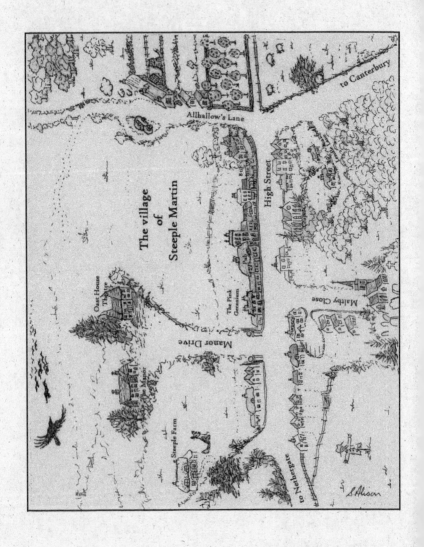

Character List

Libby Sarjeant
Former actor and part-time artist, mother to Dominic, Belinda and Adam Sarjeant and owner of Sidney the cat. Resident of 17 Allhallow's Lane, Steeple Martin.

Fran Wolfe
Former actor and occasional psychic. Owner of Balzac the cat and resident of Coastguard Cottage, Nethergate.

Ben Wilde
Libby's significant other. Co-owner of the Manor, the Oast Theatre and the Hop Pocket pub.

Guy Wolfe
Fran's husband and father to Sophie Wolfe. Artist and owner of a shop and gallery in Harbour Street, Nethergate.

Peter Parker
Freelance journalist, part owner of the Pink Geranium restaurant. Ben's cousin and Harry Price's partner.

Harry Price
Chef and co-owner of the Pink Geranium. Peter Parker's partner.

DCI Ian Connell
Local policeman and friend. Fran's former suitor.

Hetty Wilde
Ben's mother. Lives at the Manor.

Flo Carpenter
Hetty's oldest friend.

Lenny Fisher
Hetty's brother. Lives with Flo Carpenter.

Jane Baker
Editor of the *Nethergate Mercury*.

Reverend Patti Pearson
Vicar at St Aldeberge.

Anne Douglas
Librarian and Reverend Patti's friend and partner.

Edward Hall
Academic and historian.

Alice Gedding
Sheep farmer and friend of Edward.

Colin Hardcastle and Gerry Hall
Former Residents of Steeple Martin

Cassandra
Libby's cousin.

Mike Farthing
Owner of Farthing's Plants and partner of Cassandra.

Tim Stevens
Landlord of the Coach and Horses, Steeple Martin.

Mavis
Owner of the Blue Anchor café

Joe Wilson
Friend of Lenny, Flo and Hetty.

Simon Spencer
Manager of the Hop Pocket

Beth Cole
Vicar at Steeple Martin.

John Cole
Beth's husband.

Adam Sarjeant
Libby's son.

Ron Stewart
Retired pop star.

Maria Stewart
Ron's wife.

Barney
A dog.

Ricky Short
Barney's owner.

Debbie Pointer
Ricky's mother.

Linda Davies
Ricky's grandmother.

Chloe Vaughan
Elderly resident of Canterbury.

Judy Dale and Cyd Russell
Panto cast members.

John and Sue Cantripp
Friends of Libby.

Jemima Routledge
Landscape gardener.

Stella Black
Owner of Brooke Farm and riding stables.

Alanna
Stable hand.

George
Landlord of the Red Lion.

Philip Jacobs
Barrister.

Hannah Barton
Philip Jacobs' employee.

Dickie Marsham
CEO of Marsham's brewery

Roy Marsham
Dickie's younger brother.

Gina Marsham
Roy's wife.

Ruth Baxter
Dickie and Roy's sister.

Quentin Baxter
Ruth's husband.

Izzy
Manager of the Puckle Inn.

Lewis Osbourne-Walker
Owner of the Creekmarsh estate.

Edie Osbourne-Walker
Lewis's mother.

Sid Best
Landlord of the Poacher.

Richard Brandon
Panto cast member.

Pat Bailey
Manager of the George and Dragon.

Stan
Former landlord of the Fox and Hounds.

Sir Jonathan
Owner of Anderson Place.

Inspector Rob Maiden
Detective.

Rachel Trent
Detective.

Sandra and Alan Farrow
Friends of Libby.

Jenny
Landlady of the Bell and Butcher.

Trisha
Roy Marsham's ex-girlfriend.

Anthony Leigh
Dickie Marsham's old school friend.

John Newman
Son of the former licensee of the Hop Pocket.

Zack
Landlord of the Gate Inn.

Veronica
Dickie Marsham's ex-wife.

Kayleigh
Barmaid at the Red Lion.

Chapter One

It was quiet away from the main shopping streets in Canterbury. The moon appeared briefly from behind the clouds to reveal the huddled shape in the doorway, and an intermittent breeze blew a crisp packet to catch on the tarnished tinsel tucked in beside it. Then the darkness returned.

Chloe Vaughan stepped cautiously out of her front door and squinted into the semi-darkness. Two weeks to go until Christmas and it wouldn't be light for at least an hour, and even then, it wouldn't be exactly bright. Not that brilliant daylight was necessarily a good thing, as far as Chloe was concerned. Her eyesight was so poor these days she needed her stick for more than just her arthritis. But despite everything, she was determined to get out for her short walk every day. No longer to buy a newspaper – she couldn't read those – but to go to the Goods Shed to buy something nice for dinner, and perhaps have some breakfast while she was there. The people there were so kind, even if she did feel rather patronised sometimes. Small price to pay, though.

She stepped out carefully onto the narrow pavement, keeping her eyes down in case of trip hazards, and spotted one immediately. Only a pile of old clothes, though, and Chloe tutted to herself. People were so careless. Although this pile was at least festive, with a strand of tinsel fluttering slightly on top. Chloe smiled and used her stick to push the clothes aside.

Saturday morning, with only two weeks to go before Christmas, Libby Sarjeant and Ben Wilde were going to the Cattlegreen Nursery to collect a Christmas tree.

'Could have delivered it with the others,' Joe, the owner, said, when they arrived. The tree for Ben's family home, the Manor, and the huge one for the foyer of the Oast Theatre, which stood next door, had been delivered by Owen, Joe's son, the week before.

'This way we get a mug of Owen's special hot chocolate,' said Libby, smiling at the young man as he appeared from the back of the shop. 'How are the family, Owen?'

He beamed. 'Fine, thank you, Libby. And we're all singing in the choir on Christmas Eve. Will you come and hear us?'

Libby, a determined atheist, numbered, however, several Church of England vicars among her friends, including Bethany Cole, incumbent of the church in Steeple Martin. Her choir was a great success.

'Yes, of course – midnight service? Are the children allowed to stay up?'

'Oh yes.' Owen nodded earnestly. 'I'll go and get your chocolate.'

'Did you see they found one of those homeless people dead in a doorway in Canterbury this morning?' Joe asked, after his son had disappeared.

'No!' Libby frowned. 'Was it on the local news?'

Joe nodded. 'Thought you'd know, being involved with that group down in Nethergate.'

Libby could just about see the logic in that. 'No, no one's told us,' she said. 'That's so sad.'

'Well, you were trying to do something about it, weren't you?' said Joe, as Owen reappeared with two steaming mugs. 'Can't save everybody, Lib.'

'I'm not sure we actually managed to save anyone, Joe.' Libby shook her head. 'Oh well. The fight goes on.'

'Perhaps,' she said to Ben on the way home, 'I ought to see if the patrols are out in Canterbury.'

'What patrols?' Ben shot her a quick look.

'You know – those patrols they send out to look for vulnerable people. Street pastors – that's it.'

'They were for people who'd had a tad too much to drink, weren't they?' Ben brought the car to a halt at the crossroads.

'Don't they look after people in doorways, too?'

'I don't know. Ask your Nethergate group.'

He drew up opposite number 17 Allhallow's Lane.

'I'm not sure we've still got a group now,' said Libby, climbing out of the four-by-four.

A series of high-profile events in the area recently had prompted the formation of a group to fight the rise of homelessness and poverty. Fran Wolfe, Libby's best friend, and her husband, Guy, a well-known artist, had been part of it, and had co-opted Libby, but an equally high-profile murder had put rather a dent in the proceedings.

'It can't hurt to ask. You're usually only too keen to talk to Fran.' Ben hauled the Christmas tree out of the car.

'True,' said Libby, and opened the front door.

After the tree had been installed in the sitting room and soup put on to heat for lunch, Libby did indeed phone Fran, who sounded flustered.

'Libby, we are rather busy!'

'Oh – yes. Saturday two weeks before Christmas. I should have realised.'

Fran worked in Guy's shop and gallery a few doors along from their cottage in Harbour Street in Nethergate.

'I'll call later,' Libby went on. 'I just had something to ask you.'

'No – ask me now,' said Fran. 'We're going out with Sophie and her new man when we close here, so I won't have any time.'

'New man?' Guy's daughter Sophie and Libby's son Adam had been an item on and off for several years. This was the first Libby had heard of a new man.

'Ad didn't tell you, then.' Fran sounded amused.

'Oh dear. I wonder how he feels about that.' Libby pulled a face at Ben, who shook his head. 'Anyway, it was about a homeless person who was found dead in a doorway this morning in Canterbury.'

'Has it got anything to do with us?' Now Fran sounded puzzled.

'I don't know. That's why I was asking.'

A gusty sigh assaulted Libby's ears. 'Well, I don't know. When we get a moment, I'll ask Guy. Now I must go.' And the connection was cut.

After lunch, the tree decorations were hauled down from the loft and the ritual began, helped by Sidney the silver tabby, who was convinced his assistance was essential. Then, after tea in front of the fire and a hastily prepared chilli, they strolled down to the Hop Pocket, the small pub Ben had recently restored and refurbished, where they were to meet Judy Dale and Cyd Russell, two members of Libby's pantomime cast, who had today moved into their home for the next few weeks, another of the Wilde family properties, Steeple Farm. This year Libby was reprising her version of *Cinderella*, after a couple of years allowing other companies to mount the popular annual panto. The Steeple Martin audiences were delighted to welcome her back.

Judy and Cyd were already there, lolling wearily at a table in the window, a bottle of Tempranillo between them. Despite the pub being licensed as an 'ale house', it was recognised in general that drinking establishments had to provide all forms of alcohol in the 21st century. Simon, manager of the Hop Pocket, completely agreed.

'Did it all go smoothly?' Libby asked, pulling up a chair.

'Brilliantly,' said Cyd with a smile. 'I can't thank you enough, Libby.'

'What for?' Libby raised surprised eyebrows. 'You're playing Coughdrop in my panto and you've taken Steeple Farm at an exorbitant rent for five weeks.'

'Exorbitant?' Judy scoffed. 'Have you seen rental costs in London?'

'I know, I know. And they aren't much better down here, either.'

'Compared to round our way they are,' said Cyd.

'Never mind,' said Ben, arriving with another wine glass and a pint of Ben's Best Bitter made from his own hops at his micro-brewery. 'At least you've got somewhere decent to stay until the end of the run.'

'I feel a bit guilty,' said Judy, 'thinking of all those poor people who were thrown out of their homes earlier on this year.'

'You lost your home, too,' said Libby.

'Only because I was stupid enough to remortgage it to fund my idiotic ambitions.' Judy gazed morosely into her glass.

'Stop being maudlin,' said Cyd. 'Here we are doing panto together in this lovely place and with a lovely house to live in. What more could you want?'

'True.' Judy grinned at her partner. 'A cat. That's all I want.'

'And a pony,' said Cyd thoughtfully. 'That paddock at the back is crying out for a pony.'

'That's what I thought when we were doing it up,' said Libby. 'And of course, I am going down to the marsh to have a look at a pony on Monday . . .'

'Are you?' asked three voices.

'Why?' said Ben suspiciously.

'For a photo shoot,' said Libby. 'I'm sure I told you. With your coach.'

'The pumpkin coach?' said Judy.

'Yes. Ben made it – well, it's a sort of one-sided coach – for the last time we did *Cinders*. We've got friends who live in a place called Heronsbourne Flats – it's actually a bit of salt marsh – and they know someone with a couple of ponies, so . . .'

'Why didn't I know anything about this?' asked Ben. 'That means I've got to clean up the coach earlier than I thought!'

'Sorry.' Libby looked innocent. 'I didn't think it would be a problem when Jane phoned me.'

'Jane? What's she got to do with it?' Ben frowned.

'Jane Baker's the editor of one of our local newspapers,' Libby explained. 'Well, they aren't papers any more really, are they? All online. Anyway, she called and asked if she could do a little feature on the panto. Of course I said yes.'

'So who suggested the pony?' Ben squinted at her ferociously. 'Who do I have to blame?'

'Alice,' said Libby. 'Alice is a sheep farmer on the Flats. You met her the other day with our friend Edward, Judy.'

'Oh, yes. Nice woman. Doesn't get out much, she said.'

'No – with a sheep farm and young children it's difficult,' said Libby. 'Sorry you've been a bit inundated with names, Cyd. It'll all become clear eventually.'

'Speaking of murder,' said Judy, 'we saw on your local news programme that a homeless person had been found dead in Canterbury.'

'Oh, yes, we heard about that too. So sad, isn't it?' said Ben. 'But that wasn't murder.'

'It said the police were investigating,' said Cyd.

'Well, they have to in those sorts of cases. It'll probably be labelled unexplained,' said Libby.

'Not if it's a death from hypothermia and malnutrition,' said Ben. 'And now, can we talk about something else?'

Chapter Two

On Monday morning, Libby drove down to Heronsbourne Flats and along the gravel track that led to Hobson's, the long, brick and timber building that was home to John and Sue Cantripp, who had agreed to introduce her to the prospective star of her photo shoot.

'I take it Alice couldn't get away,' said Libby, as she joined Sue on her doorstep. 'It was very nice of you to organise this, Sue.'

'No, well, you know what things are like for poor Alice,' said Sue, leading the way into the comfortable living room, where John sat in his big wingback armchair beside the fireplace. 'She can't get away too often.'

'Nice that she's got her young man now, though,' said John, getting up to give Libby a kiss. 'Friend of yours, isn't he?'

'Yes, he is,' said Libby. 'So, how are you both?'

'Oh, we're fine,' said Sue. 'We thought we'd have our coffee after you've met Cascade. And Jemima's popping over, too, as you're here. She's working in Pedlar's Row.'

'At this time of year?' Libby asked, surprised. 'I didn't think landscape gardeners worked in December!'

'Well, she is,' said John, 'so let's get a move on.'

'Did you say Cascade?' asked Libby, as they went back outside.

Sue smiled. 'I did. Recognise the name?'

'Well, yes. My favourite children's books – am I right?'

'Monica Edwards' Romney Marsh series, yes,' said Sue.

'And originally he was called Fallada, wasn't he?' said John.

'No – that was what Tamzin wanted to call him,' corrected Libby, 'but in the end she stuck with Cascade. That's lovely! And he lives on a marsh, too.'

'Not quite as big as Romney Marsh, but still.' Sue picked her way across a tussocky path.

'I don't suppose his owner lives in a vicarage?' said Libby.

Sue and John laughed. 'Not likely!'

Sue pointed. 'There. That's Cascade's home.'

Ahead was a low white building, flanked on both sides by what looked like barns.

'Please don't tell me it's called Castle Farm like the farm in the books?' said Libby.

'Stella wanted to change it,' said John, 'but the locals weren't keen.'

As they approached the house, a woman bundled up in a huge padded coat appeared from one of the barns, leading a pure white, rather plump pony.

'Hi, Stella!' called Sue. 'We've brought your visitor.'

The woman strode forward holding out her hand, beaming all over her weather-beaten face.

'Stella Black,' she said. 'And this is Cascade.'

Libby shook the hand. 'I'm thrilled to meet you both,' she said. 'I almost hoped you'd be called Tamzin.'

'Ah – you're one of us, then,' said Stella, 'Say hello, Cascade.'

Cascade obediently lifted a front leg.

'Wow!' said Libby. 'Alice said he was trained.'

'Much in demand is Cascade,' said Stella. 'Got his own agent.'

'Oh!' Libby looked doubtfully at John and Sue.

'It's all right – this is on me,' Stella assured her. 'Not much for him to do at the moment, so we're happy to have some pictures taken. Where would you want to do it? Anywhere within a reasonable distance.'

Libby was smoothing Cascade's silky neck. He turned his head and whiffled amiably into her shoulder.

'Would our theatre in Steeple Martin be all right?' she asked.

8

'Perfect.' Stella nodded. 'Now, do you want to see him perform?'

'Well, I wasn't expecting . . .' began Libby.

'I'll put him through his paces in the manège,' said Stella, and turned to her left. Libby realised that she was no longer holding the lead rein, and Cascade walked at her side perfectly happily. John, Sue and Libby followed.

In the manège, Cascade performed as if he were in the Olympic dressage event – but without a rider. When he'd finished, he went down on one front leg and nodded his head. His audience applauded loudly.

'Gosh, he's impressive!' said Libby. 'Has he always done this?'

'He was trained by a circus family, but they couldn't afford to keep him, especially as he didn't have a circus to work in. So I bought him.' Stella nodded over her shoulder. 'He's got a few friends, Rajah, Charade and Punch, and Dilly the donkey, and we've got some little pupils we're teaching to ride, although they don't usually ride him.'

'I used to ride when I was young,' said Libby wistfully. 'My parents had friends who had a stable, and I used to help out.' She grinned. 'There's always a girl or two willing to be an unpaid stable hand, isn't there?'

Stella looked her up and down. 'Punch'd be up to your weight,' she said. 'Charade's a bit of a lightweight, to tell the truth, but if you'd like to . . .?'

'I'd love to!' Libby gasped.

'But first, you'd better sort out your photographs,' said Sue. 'No time for joyriding until after the panto, surely?'

'No, maybe you're right,' Libby sighed. 'We'd better organise the shoot, I suppose.'

'Let's get Cascade back inside, then.' Stella gave a piercing whistle. Libby, John and Sue looked round, startled, and saw a small person in a large anorak appear from behind one of the barns.

'This is Alanna,' said Stella. 'One of those willing girl helpers you were talking about, Libby.'

Alanna grinned brightly and picked up Cascade's trailing lead rein. 'Nice to meet you,' she said, with just the faintest trace of an accent, and wheeled round, trotting back to the barn alongside the pony.

Libby raised an eyebrow at Stella, who nodded.

'Yes, a casualty. Whole family,' she said.

'No – migrants?' murmured Libby.

'They were, yes. Whether they'll be allowed to stay under this new legislation, God knows. But they had somewhere to live – only two bedrooms, but decent – and then they got kicked out.' Stella led the way back to the house.

'Rogue landlord?' suggested Libby.

Stella smiled. 'Of course – you were part of the protest group, weren't you?'

'I still am – if we can keep going,' said Libby.

'What are you talking about?' asked John.

Sue tutted impatiently. 'You know perfectly well. The landlords kicking people out of their rental properties.'

'Oh – yes.' John gave Libby a shamefaced smile.

'Don't worry, John,' she said. 'It's not on everybody's radar.'

'Should be, though,' said Stella, letting them into a somewhat chaotic living room. 'Lives here now.'

'Alanna?' Libby was following the thread.

'Whole family.' Stella nodded, searching through a pile of paper on a table in the corner.

'In your house?'

'Small barn.' She grinned. 'Converted it.' She looked up at Libby. 'Got the idea from your mate.'

'Hmm,' said Libby.

'Here,' said Stella, brandishing a diary. 'Have to be this week, won't it?'

'If you can manage it, please.'

'Wednesday? Early afternoon? Alanna will want to come.'

'That's great,' said Libby, beaming. 'Do you know where we are?'

'Course I do!' scoffed Stella. 'Lived here all me life. Showed Alice the ropes when she first came. Well, when she . . . er . . .'

'When her husband left?' said Libby, who knew Alice Gedding and her story well.

Stella nodded and made a note in her diary.

'Right, then,' she said. 'See you on Wednesday. Oh, sorry – would you like coffee? I always forget to offer.'

'No, we're having it at home,' said Sue, 'and Jemima's coming over. You're welcome, too, if you like.'

Stella smiled. 'No, thanks, busy, busy. You know.'

'She's great, isn't she?' said Libby, as they walked back to Hobson's. 'And Cascade's perfect.'

'I'm surprised you didn't meet her when you were here before,' said Sue. 'She does go to the pub sometimes.'

The Red Lion in Heronsbourne was another of the pubs Libby and Fran often visited in the course of their adventures, and one of those in the local pub quiz league recently set up by Tim Stevens, landlord of the Coach and Horses in Steeple Martin.

'We'll have to come over for a drink if we can before panto,' said Libby. 'Haven't seen George for ages. And I need to see Hannah Barton and her baby – Josh, wasn't it?'

'Right little tearaway he's going to be,' said John with a grin. 'She brings him over for a visit now and then.'

'I must ask her about Alanna and her family,' said Libby, thoughtfully. 'You know she works for Philip Jacobs, the barrister who represented the protest group?'

'He still does, doesn't he?' asked Sue.

'I think so,' said Libby. 'It all got a bit chaotic at the end of October.'

As they approached Hobson's, Jemima Routledge, landscape gardener, appeared, waving a white rag.

'I come in peace,' she called. 'Can't stop – I'm supposed to be in Steeple Cross by half past eleven. I'd forgotten. How are you, Libby?'

When pleasantries had been exchanged, Jemima pulled Libby aside as John and Sue went indoors.

'Did you hear about the body found in Canterbury the other day?' she said quietly.

'Yes, Joe at Cattlegreen told us.' Libby nodded.

'Did you hear who it was?'

'No. Nothing to do with us this time.'

Jemima frowned. 'It was one of the Marshams.'

'Marshams?'

'Marsham's – the brewery.' Jemima put her head on one side.

'Oh, *those* Marshams!' Libby was shocked. 'Blimey! They're still in Felling, aren't they?'

'On the creek, yes. One of the oldest family-run breweries left in the country.'

'But they're selling off their pubs! We know someone who managed one of theirs and lost her home,' said Libby.

'Exactly.' Jemima gave her a knowing look. 'Makes you think, doesn't it?'

'You're looking thoughtful,' said Sue, as Libby came into the sitting room. 'I made you tea – you prefer it, don't you?"

'Yes, thanks,' said Libby absently. 'I just heard something odd.'

'From Jemima?'

'Yes, although I don't know how she knows.' She sat down on a squashy sofa and told them what Jemima had said.

'Works over at the Dunton estate, doesn't she?' said John. 'Not far from Felling.'

'Oh, yes.' Libby nodded. 'Still odd, though.'

'Jemima knowing, or the body itself?' asked Sue.

'Oh, the body. Not the sort of person you expect to be home-less, a member of a brewing family. They must be millionaires.'

'Perhaps it was the black sheep,' suggested John.

'Mmm. Perhaps they threw him out.' Libby pulled a face. 'I'd better be going.' She swallowed the last of her tea and stood up. 'Thank you for the tea, and for taking me to Stella. Tell me what night you want to come to the panto and I'll keep tickets for you.'

'Oh, aren't you sold out already? I thought you would be!' Sue grinned at her.

'There are a few,' said Libby carelessly. 'You might have to sit on someone's lap, of course.'

She took her leave and drove slowly off the marsh, through Pedlar's Row and on to the main road to Nethergate. A short visit to Fran was called for, so she drove down to Harbour Street and found a parking place.

Fran, as she'd expected, was on duty in the shop, where Guy was at work in the back packaging mail order parcels of Christmas cards.

'They're a bit late, aren't they?' Libby hoisted herself onto a stool at the counter.

'That's up to them.' Fran shrugged. 'At least people are still buying.'

'Yes.' Libby looked round the shop, where customers were chatting and drinking coffee. 'Still doing the "warm space" initiative?'

'Yes.' Fran smiled. 'Not as much as Mavis, though. She's still packed.'

Mavis owned the Blue Anchor café on the hard at the bottom of Harbour Street.

'Bless her,' said Libby. 'Actually, that's what I came to tell you. Well, not about Mavis, obviously, but someone else who's doing something.'

'That's as clear as mud,' said Fran. 'Do you want tea?'

'No, I've just had one, thanks. Listen.'

And for the second time, Libby recounted the story of the homeless person who'd turned out to be a member of the Marsham's brewery family, then told Fran about Stella and Alanna.

Fran frowned. 'Do you mean they're linked?'

'No, no! Just that I heard about both of them this morning. And

13

it seems the whole homeless stroke rotten landlord thing is still happening.'

'Hang on a bit,' said Fran. 'It sounds as though Alanna and her family were chucked out some time ago if this Stella had her barn converted for them.'

'Oh. Yes, I suppose so.'

'And if that body is a Marsham, they're hardly likely to be a victim of a rotten landlord, are they?'

'No.' Libby sighed. 'But it's still a problem, all the same.'

'Yes, Libby. And we're still trying to protest about it and get the government to change the law. Now, go on home and start thinking panto. We'll come up for a drink on Wednesday. You're giving them the night off, aren't you?'

'Yes, miss,' said Libby, and went home.

Chapter Three

Libby rehearsed her cast, and herself as Fairy Godmother, on Monday and Tuesday nights, and during the day Ben made sure that the cut-out pumpkin coach was clean and in good repair for its starring role on Wednesday. Some of the smaller chorus members had been recruited to become footmen and coach driver, and Jane Baker herself was coming with the *Mercury*'s staff photographer.

By the time Stella's horsebox rolled up the Manor drive, everyone was quite excited. Those members of the cast who were available had all turned out, although Libby wouldn't allow most of them to appear in costume, except the footmen and the fairies Coughdrop and Snowdrop, Anything else would spoil the surprise for the audience, she averred, but she could hardly stop Cyd from coming to meet the pony.

Cascade, as placid as ever, trod sedately down the ramp and nodded his head up and down at Libby, who obediently stroked his nose. Stella grinned at her, while Alanna beamed round at the admiring crowd, as proud as if she were Cascade's true owner. At Stella's instruction, she led the pony gently towards the coach, and allowed him to have a sniff round it before giving him a treat.

'Same process as dog training,' Stella told Libby. 'But that girl's got talent. She understands horses.'

'And did you say it was likely that the family wouldn't be allowed to stay here?' Libby asked quietly.

'Don't know.' Stella shrugged, watching Alanna and the pony

circling the coach together. 'Girl over in Sussex, been in school eighteen months, family settled. Had their asylum application turned down.'

'Oh my Lord!' whispered Libby. 'How can they *do* this?'

Stella shrugged. 'Search me. They aren't bloody human, those people. And why do they want them gone, I want to know. They're useful. They add to the economy.'

Libby thought about the so-called illegal migrants used as slave labour who she had come across earlier in the year, and those she and Fran had found on a farm some years ago. Things weren't getting any better, it seemed.

Eventually Alanna was happy with Cascade's position in front of the coach and the photographer moved in to take her pictures. Jane came across to interview Libby and Stella, and on discovering Alanna's story, she asked to talk to her too.

'Don't focus on her too much,' said Libby. 'Apart from the humanitarian aspect, don't forget there are people who don't want her or her family here.'

'You think someone might harm them?' Jane narrowed her eyes.

'Yes,' said Stella. 'We've had people loitering around the farm several times. So has Alice Gedding, and she's third generation.'

'Oh dear.' Jane gazed mournfully at Alanna. 'And I was hoping to highlight the whole problem.'

'Too dangerous.' Stella shook her head, then went over to stand by Alanna.

'On another subject,' said Jane, swiping at her tablet, 'what do you know about Dickie Marsham?'

'Who?' said Libby.

'He was found dead in Canterbury.'

'Oh, him. Yes – everybody seems to want to tell me about him. I thought at first it was yet another poor homeless soul.'

'So you don't know anything else about him?' Jane peered sideways at her.

'No, Jane, I don't. I don't know something about every dead body found in the area, you know. And anyway, this wasn't murder.'

'Wasn't it?'

'I assumed it wasn't. Why, do you know something about it?' Libby turned to face her friend.

'No.' Jane looked aggrieved. 'Just seems odd that a member of the Marsham family should be found dead in a doorway.'

'No? I don't know anything about them,' admitted Libby.

'He was the CEO,' said Jane. 'Their dad had been chair.'

'*Their* dad? Did this Dickie have brothers and sisters?'

'One of each,' said Jane. 'The younger brother was the black sheep, if anyone was. The sister is rather a nonentity.'

'That's not very nice!' Libby's eyebrows went up.

'Well, she is. Married to some nice safe accountant or something.'

'And what about the little brother? What did he do that was so bad?'

Jane grinned. 'Married the wrong girl.'

At this point they were interrupted by the photographer, who came over to say she'd finished, and flicked through her shots to show them. She and Jane decided to get back and make sure everything was uploaded in order to get it online as quickly as possible, but Stella and Alanna were persuaded to stay and have a cup of tea, while Cascade was taken into the field behind the theatre by his new admirers. Alanna accepted her mug, but followed the pony into the field, unwilling to let him out of her sight.

'I think she'd sleep with him if she could,' said Stella, sitting down at the big kitchen table in the Manor after being introduced to Ben's mother Hetty.

Hetty looked down at her collie, Jeff-dog, who lay stretched out at her feet. 'Hmm,' she said. Stella and Libby exchanged knowing glances.

Ben joined them, having carefully returned the coach to its home backstage, and Libby reported that all had gone well.

'And Jane wanted to know if we knew anything about that body Joe told us about,' she added.

'Alanna knows the girl who married his brother,' said Stella, finishing her tea. 'I don't think she ever met him, though.'

Ben and Libby stared at her.

'She does?' said Libby. 'How come?'

'They both lived in the same building. Where they got kicked out from – I told you.'

'Gosh!' said Libby.

Stella gave her a somewhat surprised look at this schoolgirl comment and stood up. 'Yes. Wasn't very savoury. Bit of a shock when the girl married into the Marshams. Anyway, we'd better get off home.'

Cascade was duly persuaded back into the horsebox, and Alanna and Stella said goodbye to the pony's admirers, who promised to wave at them from the stage if they came to see the pantomime.

'So that's that,' said Libby to Ben. 'Interesting, that bit about the Marshams, wasn't it?'

Ben looked at her sharply. 'No,' he said. 'And you are not poking your nose into it.'

'Well,' said Libby, as they walked back down the Manor drive, 'I just thought, as it's Wednesday, and Ian might come to the pub tonight . . .'

'No,' said Ben more forcefully. 'It is nothing whatsoever to do with us or you. So leave it alone. Now, what's for dinner?'

Wednesday evenings at the Coach and Horses were what Harry Price, *chef patron* of the Pink Geranium restaurant in the village and civil partner of Ben's cousin Peter, called the Wednesday Night Murder Club. It had evolved slowly over the years since the Reverend Patti Pearson, vicar of St Aldeberge, began visiting her friend Anne and dining at the restaurant. They then joined Libby, Ben and any of their other friends who were free at the pub. And not infrequently discussed the latest murder case that Libby was investigating, or, as some people put it unkindly, poking her nose into.

Tonight, Libby and Ben were already at their favourite round table in the small bar when the door opened and Patti began helping Anne, amid whoops of laughter, to manoeuvre her wheelchair inside.

'So are you looking into this dead body in Canterbury?' asked Anne, who worked in the big museum and library in the city.

'No, she isn't!' said Ben, who had been thwarted by Patti in his attempt to buy their drinks.

'No, I'm not,' agreed Libby. 'Absolutely nothing to do with me this time.'

'Oh.' Anne looked disappointed. 'I thought, as it was a homeless person . . .'

'It wasn't,' said Libby bluntly.

'It wasn't?' echoed Patti and Anne together, as Patti put glasses on the table.

Ben muttered under his breath.

'No,' Libby said uncertainly. 'At least, I was told it wasn't.'

'But you don't know who it was?' asked Anne.

'Not for certain. And I don't see how I can ask.'

'That's not what you said earlier,' Ben said. 'You were all for asking Ian if he came in tonight.'

'Yes, well . . .' Libby looked uncomfortable.

'You've got enough to do with the pantomime at the moment, haven't you?' said Patti, giving Anne a 'shut up' sort of look. 'How's it going?'

'Oh, yes!' Anne brightened. 'That nice Judy Dale has moved in to Steeple Farm with her partner, hasn't she?'

'Yes, we've now got a full cast,' said Libby. 'And it seems to be going very well, thank you.'

'We even had a pony join us today,' said Ben.

'A pony?' Anne was agog, and Patti smiled indulgently.

'She's been angling for me to take her to one of these riding for the disabled places,' she told Ben and Libby.

'I bet our pony's owner could help there,' said Libby, and fell to

19

telling them all about Cascade, Stella and her own prospective riding exploits.

Half an hour later, they were joined by Edward Hall and Detective Chief Inspector Ian Connell, two more friends who lived a little way out of the village. Ian went to the bar for drinks and Edward beamed round the table.

'So, what are we talking about this week?' he asked.

'Panto,' said Ben firmly.

'And ponies,' added Libby.

'And there was I thinking you'd be dying to ask Ian about Dickie Marsham.' Edward gave Libby a wink.

'Who?' Anne sat up straight in her chair, rocking it against the table, to the imminent peril of the drinks.

'Are you stirring?' Ian asked with a formidable frown, as he planted a drink in front of his friend.

'Of course not!' said Edward, looking innocent.

'Well, I'm pretty sure Miss Marple over there will have heard about it, whatever she says.' Ian sat down and loosened his tie. He rarely appeared in the pub in anything but his work clothes.

'Is that who the body is?' Anne turned accusing eyes on Libby. 'She wouldn't tell us,' she added to Ian.

'I didn't know for sure.' Libby cleared her throat and took a sip of lager.

'Who did you hear it from?' asked Ian.

'Jemima Routledge. But Jane told me it was Dickie.'

'Ah, our favourite newshound and our gardener extraordinaire. And how did *she* know?'

'I don't know. I didn't ask. But she works on the Dunton estate, which is near Felling and the brewery. I suppose she might have heard . . .'

'Well, as it happens she was right, and it's gone out to all the news outlets, so everyone will know by now.' Ian sat back in his chair and sipped at a mug of coffee.

'You designated driver tonight?' asked Ben.

'Only fair I take a turn,' said Ian with a grin at Edward. 'My neighbour tends to act as cabbie for trips to Steeple Martin.'

'Oh, come on, Ian!' Anne was practically bouncing in her chair. 'What happened to Dickie Marsham? He's one of the brewing Marshams, isn't he?'

'As I'm sure you'll have realised from what Libby said,' said Ian.

'But I thought it was a homeless person,' Patti put in. 'Surely one of the Marshams can't be homeless?'

'No, he wasn't. We assume that was what we were meant to think.'

'But only at first? He'd have been recognised as soon as he was discovered – well, he was, wasn't he?' Anne was leaning forward, fixing Ian with intent brown eyes.

'Eventually,' said Ian. 'How's the panto going, Libby?'

Everybody, with the possible exception of Anne, accepted this as the final word on the subject, and the conversation became more general, until, just after ten o'clock, the door burst open once again, to admit Harry Price, still in his chef's whites, followed more sedately by Peter Parker.

'Right then, young Ian,' Harry said, folding his arms and frowning formidably. 'What's all this about Dickie Marsham? And why have you arrested his brother?'

Chapter Four

'Sit down, Harry,' said Peter, 'and don't make a fuss.'

Ian, looking amused, pulled up a chair beside him and waved Harry into it. 'Do as the man says, Harry.'

'What's this about, Hal?' asked Ben. 'Do you know the Marshams?'

'I knew Dickie,' said Harry, subsiding into the chair rather sulkily.

'Oh, I'm so sorry,' said Patti.

'They weren't exactly bosom friends,' said Peter from the bar.

'Well, I know you didn't like him,' said Harry, thrusting his hands into his pockets and looking belligerent.

'Come on, Hal.' Libby leant across Ian and patted Harry's leg. 'Tell us what's up.'

'It's not actually Dickie that's the problem,' said Peter, coming back to the table with two pints of Ben's Best Bitter. 'It's his brother.'

'I'm lost,' said Edward. 'I don't know who Dickie is, let alone his brother.'

'You do,' said Libby. 'You introduced the whole subject earlier on.'

Ian sighed. 'Edward knows because it's been in the media, but he doesn't know anything about the Marshams, as far as I know.'

'They're a big brewing company,' said Ben. 'One of the last family-run outfits in the country.'

'Like yours?' said Edward.

'Not at all – they're a big brewery, who own pubs.' Ben frowned. 'Although they're selling a lot of those off now.'

'So who's the brother?' asked Anne.

'Roy,' said Ben. 'Dickie is – or was – CEO, and Roy's something to do with the estates office, as far as I remember. Is that right, Ian?'

'It is,' said Ian, 'but I can't say anything more, as you well know.' He looked round the table. 'If anyone has any information to give me, that would be great, but otherwise, I think we ought to change the subject.' He smiled at Harry's sulky face. 'Sorry, Hal.'

Harry shrugged. 'Oh well. I just thought Dickie was OK. And he loved his brother.'

Ian looked interested. 'Did he? That might well be useful, Hal.'

Harry sat up straight and picked up his drink. 'Yes. Very protective, he was. I think he thought Roy was easily led.'

'How did you come to know him?' asked Patti. 'Did you buy his beer?'

'No, I've always bought through a wholesaler – we don't use enough beer. No, we met at a trade do in London and struck up a conversation because we came from the same area. Sort of kept in touch a bit afterwards.'

'When did you last hear from him?' asked Ian.

'Ooh – months ago.' Harry leant back, looking thoughtful. 'He wasn't too happy about the sale of some of the brewery's pubs.'

'Neither were the managers,' said Libby. 'We met one.'

'Who was that?' asked Edward.

'Izzy, who used to be at the Crown and Sceptre near Canterbury. She's now manager at the Puckle Inn.'

'Ah.' Edward nodded. 'Alice and I went over there a week or so back. We actually got babysitters!'

'Well, thank you, Harry,' said Ian. 'And actually, we haven't arrested him. He was merely helping with our inquiries.'

'Hmm.' Harry gave Ian a ferocious scowl. 'Same thing, isn't it?'

'Oh, come on, Hal!' said Libby, laughing. 'You ought to know better than that.'

'Yes, well . . .' Harry lifted a shoulder and turned towards Anne. 'Unsympathetic, aren't they?' he asked plaintively.

Anne patted his leg, which was all she could reach. 'Dreadfully,' she said.

Libby was looking thoughtful. 'Did you say this Roy was in charge of the estates department at Marsham's?' she asked Ben.

'Yes.' Ben frowned at her.

'Well, I'm surprised it wasn't him that got bumped off.' Libby frowned back at him. 'He'd be the one in charge of selling off the pubs, wouldn't he?'.

'Ah!' Harry turned back so sharply he nearly upset his drink. 'That's it, then! Someone didn't want Dickie looking into the sale of the pubs and murdered him!'

'Someone like his brother,' said Ben drily.

'Mmm . . .' Harry subsided again.

'It really isn't open for discussion,' said Ian with a resigned sigh. 'Although I'm sure you'll carry on whatever I say.'

'No, we won't.' Libby sent a warning look towards Harry and Anne.

'What shall we talk about, then?' asked Peter. 'Christmas shopping?'

'We never normally need to think of things to talk about,' said Edward. He looked round the table. 'Who's coming to the Christmas quiz on Sunday?'

'Where is it?' asked Patti.

'The Red Lion,' said Libby. 'George seems to be the most active in the quiz league.'

The local pub quiz league had been started by Tim at the Coach and Horses earlier in the year, and had proved popular with everyone involved.

'And it'll give you a chance to ask questions, won't it?' asked Ian.

'The Red Lion's in Heronsbourne,' said Libby. 'Nowhere near where your body came from – or where it was found.'

'Good job we don't have a member in Felling,' muttered Ben.

24

'Yes, why don't we?' asked Edward. 'You play bat and trap against a pub over there, don't you?'

'Yes, the Gate. Nice place – right next door to the Sand Gate. I'll ask,' said Ben, 'although I think we travel quite far enough as it is.'

'And quite often enough,' said Libby.

The conversation became more general, to Ian's obvious relief, only returning to the subject of the murder towards the end of the evening, when Patti asked, rather tentatively, who had discovered the body. Ian looked surprised.

'Someone out shopping,' he said. 'An elderly lady, I believe.'

'Don't you know?' asked Anne, also surprised.

'Not my case,' said Ian.

'But you know the team who'll be on it?' said Harry. 'You all work out of Canterbury these days, don't you?'

'Yes, Harry, but we don't swap notes over the water cooler,' said Ian testily. He stood up. 'I think it's time I was going, if you don't mind, Edward.'

Edward hastily swallowed the last of his pint. 'OK,' he said. 'I'll see you Sunday, Libby, Ben? Will you be around, Pete?'

'Caff's open all day Sunday at the moment,' said Peter, 'so we won't make lunch or the quiz, sorry.'

Ian and Edward left, followed soon after by Patti and Anne.

'Not the jolliest evening,' said Harry, stretching his legs out in front of him.

'Ian was stressed,' said Libby.

'We ought to avoid all things criminal,' said Peter. 'He's not supposed to talk about any of it, and we make it difficult for him.' He sent a frowning look at Harry. 'You certainly did this evening.'

'Yeah, yeah, all right,' said Harry sulkily. 'But he nearly let something out of the bag.'

'Did he? How?' Libby looked puzzled.

'Saying you would ask questions at the Red Lion.' Harry nodded wisely.

25

'How is that giving something away?' asked Ben.

Peter laughed. 'That means Harry thinks there *is* something to be found out in Heronsbourne.'

'Well,' said Harry, 'there must be.'

'Why, for goodness' sake?' said Libby.

Harry smirked. 'Roy Marsham lives there.'

Chapter Five

'*What?*' Libby gasped.

Peter gave a huff of annoyance. 'All right – and just how do you know that?'

'Dickie told me.' Harry looked indignant.

'But why did he tell you?' Ben was obviously as puzzled as the other two.

'You remember when there was all that fuss about the golf club?'

'How could we forget?' said Ben, with a grim look at Libby.

'Well, you know those houses over there?'

'What – where Colin and Gerry live?'

'No, you silly trout, the ones actually on the way to the club house.' Harry grinned at her. 'People sold up when they thought it was going to turn into a party place, remember?'

'I didn't know people sold up,' said Libby. 'I know a lot of the residents protested.'

'Yes, well, some of them sold up. And Roy and his missus bought one. His missus's idea, apparently.' He shook his head. 'Dickie didn't like her.'

'Ah – the wrong girl!' said Libby.

'What?' said Peter.

'Jane Baker told me. Dickie's little brother married the wrong girl, apparently. And,' she added thoughtfully, 'young Alanna knows her.'

'Who's Alanna?' asked Harry, now bewildered.

Libby explained.

'I don't know about that,' said Harry, 'but if she was an illegal migrant, I can see why Dickie didn't like her. Bit of a snob, he was. Typical Tory voter.'

'I don't know that she was,' said Libby. 'All I know is that she lived in the same building as young Alanna and her family, and they were all evicted.'

'Oh, for f . . . We're back to that again, are we?' Harry glowered into his drink.

'Well, local radio did think your Dickie was a homeless person,' said Ben, amused.

'He's not *my* Dickie,' Harry grumbled.

'Never mind, love,' said Peter, patting his shoulder. 'At least you've given our dear old trout something to ask questions about now. And it's time you were in bed anyway. Another busy day tomorrow.'

Ben and Libby walked home along the silent high street.

'You aren't going to interfere in this, are you?' asked Ben eventually. 'We've only just got over the last one.'

'I haven't got time,' said Libby. 'I've only got this weekend off before the first night. And I shall be doing all the techie stuff during the days, anyway. We're doing the lighting plot on Friday.'

'Peter's organised Jerry the Light to come in, it'll be fine.' said Ben.

'I know, but who've we got on follow spots? I need to sort that out on Saturday.' And Libby, all thoughts of murdered brewery executives banished from her mind, fell to worrying about the pantomime.

Out of interest, she phoned Stella on Thursday morning, after checking the *Nethergate Mercury*'s online coverage of Cascade and the pantomime. Jane had done them proud.

28

'Doesn't he look handsome?' said Libby. 'I can imagine hundreds of little girls clamouring to go and see the pony in the panto!'

Stella laughed. 'Poor things! Won't they be disappointed.'

'Oh, Jane makes it perfectly clear that he isn't actually in it,' said Libby, 'as long as the parents bother to tell the little treasures.'

'And she has mentioned us, although she has called it the Brooke Riding Stable, instead of Brooke Farm. We'll be inundated.'

'Well, all good for business, I suppose,' said Libby. 'And I was going to ask you, did you know that Alanna's friend who married the Marsham brother lives next door to the golf club?'

'Oh yes. Very gracious she is.' Stella sounded unhappy. 'She invited Alanna to the house, and the poor girl came back feeling even worse than she did when they were evicted.'

'Oh dear. I won't mention it if I see her, then,' said Libby. 'By the way, we'll be over at the Red Lion for the Christmas quiz on Sunday. Will you be there?'

'Not on the team, but I'll pop in for the mulled wine,' said Stella. 'I'll see you then.'

Libby reported both Wednesday night's conversation and this morning's to Fran, then made a determined effort to forget all about it and concentrate on all the last-minute problems that always seemed to arise in pantomimes.

On Friday, she spent most of the day running around the stage to help plot the lighting, and Friday night was the first rehearsal with the full 'orchestra', comprising keyboard, drums, guitar and a lot of technology. Some of the professional actors in the company were inclined to be a little patronising towards the others, complaining that they really didn't need this extra rehearsal time, until the musical director – a man highly respected in his field – informed them that even if they didn't, *he* did, so please just shut up. This delighted the rest of the company, who were not the greatest fans of Cooper Fallon, who was playing one of the Ugly

Sisters and was inclined to be impatient with anything that didn't put him centre stage.

Saturday was taken up with last-minute costume fittings and discovering that various props – stage properties – had been mislaid. On Sunday, Ben kept Libby away from the theatre forcibly and propelled her up to the Manor for the traditional Sunday lunch with his mother and anyone else from their wider circle who was around, and in the evening, the people carrier that Philip Jacobs had booked took the Coach and Horses quiz team to the Red Lion in Heronsbourne.

Libby was delighted to see so many friends: Fran and Guy, who were on the Coach and Horses team despite living in Nethergate; Colin and Gerry, who were now happily living in their new house in The Drive, at the other end of the golf course; Dotty and Eddy, their next-door neighbours; Lewis and Edie Osbourne-Walker from the Creekmarsh estate, and of course, the various publicans from the competing teams.

'This is nice, isn't it?' she said, as they settled down at their table. 'I haven't seen a lot of these people since the beginning of the year. Oh look! There's Hannah Barton and Gary!'

'That was when you said you didn't know if you'd be able to face coming over here again after that murder, if I remember rightly,' said Ben.

'And hasn't a lot happened since then?' put in Fran hastily, noticing the look on Libby's face. 'After that there was the missing man in Nethergate and all that trouble, then Connie Matthews' murder and the problems over the homeless people.'

'Well, that problem hasn't gone away,' said Libby, 'but I suppose there have been some good outcomes. We met Ricky, for a start.'

'And did you hear he's going to be staying with Harry and Peter over Christmas?' Edward arrived at the table with a tray of mulled wine.

'Not with his grandmother?' Libby was surprised. Linda, Ricky

30

Short's grandmother, had bought Colin and Gerry's flat in Steeple Martin when they moved out.

'No. His mum – remember Debbie? – is going to stay with Linda, and they don't think the flat's suitable for Barney.'

Barney was a liver and white springer spaniel cross, much loved not just by his owner but by most of the residents of Steeple Martin and Nethergate, especially Mavis at the Blue Anchor café.

'Oh, that's a relief!' said Libby, who had never really taken to Linda or Debbie but treated Ricky like an extra son.

'Hello, Libby!'

Libby turned round. 'Hello, Chrissie!' She smiled and held out a hand to the woman at the next table, who was a regular on the Red Lion quiz team. 'I was just saying I haven't seen everyone for ages. How are you?'

'Oh, fine – you know.' Chrissie hitched her chair from the Red Lion team table nearer to Libby's. 'Are you looking into Dickie Marsham's murder?' she whispered.

'No.' Libby shook her head firmly. 'Nothing to do with me – us.' She indicated Fran. 'We're staying well clear.'

'I've heard that's what you always say,' said Chrissie with a sly grin. 'We wondered, because the victim's brother lives down Links View.'

'Oh, is that what it's called? The houses on the way to the club house?'

'Yes, although it would suit Dotty's road better, wouldn't it? They actually look over the golf course, and the sea. Lovely view.'

'Yes, it is,' agreed Libby. 'Our friends live there now.'

'Oh yes – Colin and Gerry, they come in here sometimes, but I think their local is the Fox,' said Chrissie, peering round the crowded bar.

'It is,' said Libby. 'We're lucky, we've got a lot of good pubs round here, haven't we?'

'Good job none of them are owned by Marshams,' said a voice, and Libby turned to see Dan, another Heronsbourne local, taking his seat.

'You're not going to be able to avoid the subject,' muttered Fran. 'They're determined to talk about it.'

Silently agreeing, Libby looked round for rescue and spotted Stella.

'Hi!' she called, waving. 'Come and meet Fran!'

'Oh, you know Stella,' said Chrissie, nodding. 'Of course, her little stable girl is friendly with that Marsham woman, isn't she?'

'Oh no!' groaned Libby into her mulled wine.

Stella came over, smiling, and Libby introduced her to Fran. Before Chrissie could launch into an interrogation about Alanna and Roy Marsham's wife, they were saved by the publican, George, in the role of quiz master, calling the teams to order. Stella nodded towards Chrissie and gave Libby a wink, before going to take a seat at the bar.

The quiz proceeded in its normal fairly chaotic manner, rendered a little more riotous by the addition of the mulled wine. The Coach and Horses team suffered, as usual, from their lack of sporting knowledge, but were lucky this time as there was a literary round, where Libby, Fran and Philip came into their own. At half time, they were leading.

'Do you think Chrissie has forgotten about the Marsham murder by now?' asked Fran quietly, as they left their seats to speak to Stella.

'I doubt it,' said Libby, 'but we have to remember she was very helpful when we were trying to find out about Jackie Stapleton's death.'

'You think she might be helpful this time, then?' Fran raised her eyebrows.

'You never know!'

'Was Chrissie being a pain?' Stella asked when they reached her.

'Just interested,' said Fran. 'And we really aren't anything to do with this inquiry.'

'No one will believe that. And here comes another of your informants.' She grinned. 'Hello, Hannah!'

'Hello, Stella – Libby, Fran.' Hannah Barton smiled round at them all. 'You remember Gary, don't you?'

Greetings were exchanged and Gary tried to get George's attention for more drinks. His harassed barmaid took the order instead.

'I was just saying to the girls here, no one will believe they aren't involved in this murder inquiry, will they?' said Stella.

'Girls?' Libby laughed. 'Well, that's cheered me up, Stella!'

'No, I'm afraid she's right,' said Hannah. 'I've already been asked several times if you're looking into it.'

'Really?' Fran frowned. 'Why are people asking you?'

'Because I work for Philip Jacobs and he works for the protest group, and you're both active in that. They think I'll know everything about it.'

'Oh I see,' said Libby. 'I'm still not sure why people think there's a connection.'

'Oh, you'd be surprised,' said Hannah. 'As far as the illegally evicted tenants are concerned, what better than to have a famous barrister on your side? And he does it all for free, too.'

'I know,' said Libby with a sigh. 'He's a very good bloke. Gave us a hand in another case, too.'

'What was that?' asked Gary, handing over his partner's white wine.

'Oh – another time when the Shakespeare crowd were at the theatre,' said Libby.

'Like the last one when that woman was murdered?' asked Hannah.

'No, the time before when they were doing *Twelfth Night*,' said Libby. 'Poor things do seem to get mixed up in murders when they come to us. I just hope nothing happens next summer when they come back.'

'Midsummer?' asked Gary.

'Yes, indeed.' Libby smiled and raised her glass.

'Well, I think everything's just become a bit more difficult,' said Stella, looking over Libby's shoulder.

'What do you mean?' As Libby tried to turn round, she realised the pub had gone quiet.

'Gina and Roy Marsham have just come in.'

Chapter Six

Fran gave Libby a dig in the ribs. 'Don't look,' she muttered.

Suddenly, Ben and Guy were behind them, forming a protective wall between Fran, Libby and the rest of the company.

'If I were you,' said Stella, sliding off her stool, 'I'd move away from the bar. Go and find some of your other friends. I'll hold the fort.'

'Come on,' said Ben, 'let's go and talk to the Fox team.'

He and Guy shepherded the women through the throng to their left until they arrived next to Lewis, Edie and Dotty.

'Wassup, kids?' asked Lewis. 'You having problems?'

'Someone we didn't want to talk to,' said Fran.

'Someone to do with the latest murder,' said Guy.

'Which we are *not* getting involved with, are we?' said Ben.

'Ah.' Dotty nodded. 'I know who that is. It's the brother, isn't it?'

'The brother of what?' asked Lewis's mother, Edie.

'That body they found last weekend in Canterbury,' said Dotty. 'You said you knew something about it.'

Everyone turned to Edie, who looked surprised.

'Yeah, well, only that it was my mate Chloe who found the body,' she said.

There was a minor outcry, loudest being Lewis, who complained that he hadn't known anything about it.

'Look.' Libby turned to Ben, Guy and Fran. 'I'm going to have to ask about this. And about Gina Marsham. You must see that.'

Ben sighed. 'I suppose so.'

'But not now,' said Fran. 'George is just about to announce the second half.'

'Can I ring you, Edie?' asked Libby. 'I haven't got much time over the next couple of weeks, but I can at least ask you about it.'

'Of course, lovey,' said Edie. 'And we'll see you over Christmas, maybe.'

The Coach and Horses party began to make their way back to their table, where they were once again waylaid, this time by Hannah.

'I'll ring you in the morning, Libby,' she said softly. 'Couple of things you might want to know.'

As had become a habit, the Coach team ended up in second place, while Sid at the Poacher emerged triumphant yet again.

'You want to move over our way,' he said when Libby and Ben went to congratulate him and his team.

'I can't move away from the Hop Pocket,' said Ben, with a grin.

'I don't know – more competition!' laughed Sid. 'Too many pubs, that's the problem.'

'Not so many,' said one of his team. 'Bloody Marshams are closing 'em all.'

'Shh!' Sid looked round nervously.

'It's all right,' said someone else. 'The Poacher's freehold, like all the pubs in the league.'

'You still don't want to be saying that sort of thing when there's a Marsham about,' said Sid. 'Leave well alone.'

Libby and Ben rejoined their own party.

'We'd better say goodbye,' said Libby, 'preferably without getting into any more conversations.'

Stella, Hannah and Gary had already left, so after saying goodbye and happy Christmas to George, they waved a general goodbye to everyone else and escaped to the car park.

'I hope I wasn't rude,' said Libby, as they climbed aboard the people carrier after seeing Guy and Fran off in their taxi.

'Of course you weren't,' said Ben. 'I was proud of you, withstanding all that pressure to start nosing into another murder.'

Libby gave him a friendly poke in the ribs. 'Don't be sarky.'

'Actually,' said a slightly plummy voice over Libby's shoulder, 'I wanted to have a word about that.'

Ben and Libby turned startled faces towards Philip Jacobs' conspiratorial expression.

'I don't suppose this is the right place to have a discussion, and you're going to be a tad busy during the next few weeks, aren't you, Libby?'

'Yes, but Hannah actually said she would ring me in the morning,' said Libby. 'Is it about the same thing?'

'Very possibly,' said Philip. 'And it may well be that Ben won't mind you getting involved this time.' He gave Ben a sympathetic smile. 'All in the name of friendship,' he added, and sat back in his seat.

Ben and Libby looked at one another, puzzled.

'Well,' said Libby, 'I suppose I'll find out in the morning.'

'I hope so,' said Ben, frowning. 'We could do without this at Christmas. And what was that about Edie knowing the woman who found the body?'

'No idea,' said Libby. 'Not that I think it has anything to do with the actual murder. Just a coincidence.'

I hope, she added to herself.

On Monday morning, Libby reviewed the pantomime preparations and realised there was very little left to do. Lighting and sound were plotted, and all the scenery had been in place for well over a week, and tonight would be the technical rehearsal, commonly known as the 'tech' and universally hated by casts everywhere. Tomorrow, all the little problems that had turned up during the tech would have to be put right before the dress rehearsal in the evening, but today, oddly, there was nothing to do. She contemplated ringing Edie, but decided to wait until after she'd spoken to Hannah.

Which, as it turned out, wasn't long at all. She was just pouring boiling water into a mug for her third cup of tea when her mobile rang.

'Hannah,' she said, taking the mug into the sitting room, where she sat on the sofa in front of the unlit wood burner, installed by Ben at the beginning of the summer. 'What have you got to tell me? Philip was very mysterious on the way home last night.'

'Yes, well . . .' Hannah sounded uncomfortable. 'Not the subject for a jolly Christmas celebration.'

'That sounds serious,' said Libby.

'It is, rather. I don't know how much your friend DCI Connell tells you . . .'

'He's not allowed to say much,' said Libby. 'Except when he wants Fran and me to help. And even then, it isn't much, in case his bosses find out.'

'Yes, well – that's rather the problem.' Hannah fell silent, until Libby had to give her a prompt.

'What's up, Hannah?'

'There's going to be an investigation,' she blurted out.

'Yes, I know,' said Libby, frowning at Sidney, who was inserting himself onto her lap. 'But it isn't Ian's case.'

'No! An investigation into the *police*!'

Libby felt rather as if she was going down in a lift.

'Wha-a-a?' was all she managed.

'Oh, it's not into DCI Connell himself,' said Hannah hurriedly. 'After all, they did that after Jackie Stapleton's murder, didn't they?'

'Yes, because he'd asked for our help,' said Libby. 'So what's the trouble this time?'

'Inherent problems within the force,' said Hannah. 'There have been quite a few problems even down here, and it looks as though DCI Connell is going to be dealing with those rather than the murder of Dickie Marsham.'

'Well, that's bonkers,' said Libby sharply. 'I thought they got in the Independent Police Complaints people for that sort of thing?'

38

'Not quite,' said Hannah. 'Although why a member of the Murder Investigation Team has to do it, I can't make out. Anyway, it looks as if Ian – I mean DCI Connell – might need your services. He's got to look into most of the personnel who'll be involved in this murder case.'

'What?' Libby's mouth fell open. 'Rachel Trent? Claire Stone? He can't! They're as honest as the day is long!'

'I know, and so does he, but it's got to be done.'

'But who's going to be doing all the interviews into the Marsham murder? Although he did say it wasn't his team.'

'No, it's Inspector Maiden, and I don't know who his DCI is. It's going to be a right royal muddle.'

'How come you know all this?' Libby asked after a moment. 'It isn't in the public domain, is it?'

'No, it's all down to Philip. His network is quite alarming – and mostly underground, if you know what I mean.'

'I know.' Libby smiled to herself. 'So this investigation is, presumably, the police force – oh, no, we should say "service" now, shouldn't we? – trying to salvage their reputation. Ian won't like that.'

'He doesn't. And it's so sad, Libby. There are lovely, honest people in the force – sorry, service – like Rachel and Claire, and Rob Maiden, of course, and then there are people like that awful DI Winters.' Hannah let out a gusty sigh. 'And I'm so worried that something will get missed in this new murder investigation. Not that it's anything to do with Philip, or me, but we've worked so closely with Ian and his whole team . . .'

'I know you have.' Libby thought for a moment. 'So this is why you reckon Ian will ask Fran and me to work on the quiet?'

'It would make sense, wouldn't it?' said Hannah. 'Philip thinks so too. He was speaking to Ian today. And if Ian decides to let you two loose, Philip says we'll help all we can.'

'Wow.' Libby took a deep breath. 'All right – so what do I do next? Trouble is, my first night's on Wednesday, and we run right through until January the seventh, with only Christmas Day and Boxing Day off – although the hardliners say we should be doing Boxing Day, as that was traditional. So Fran might have to do a lot of it on her own.'

'Do you have many matinees?' asked Hannah.

'Saturdays and Sundays. It's a bloody heavy workload, especially as a lot of the cast have day jobs, too.'

'If I can get a babysitter, I'd love to come – if there are any seats left.'

'Not for the matinees, but I could squeeze you in somewhere else, I expect.' Libby crossed her fingers. She'd already said the same thing to Sue and John.

'I'll let you know if I can persuade someone to look after Josh.' Hannah heaved another sigh. 'And let me know what Ian says.'

Libby came off the phone feeling distinctly muddled and perplexed. She picked up her abandoned mug and realised the tea was stone cold. She decided to make a new one rather than heat it up in the microwave; besides, she needed thinking space before she rang either Edie or Fran.

Hannah was right, they had come across some very bad eggs in the local police force over the last couple of years. Apart from DI Winters, there had been Sergeant Peacock; although his misdeeds dated from some twenty years ago, his nephew had taken up the baton. More recently, Sergeant Powell had attempted to derail an investigation, and who knew how many more there had been?

She was just about to sit down with her fresh tea when the landline rang.

'Hello, Edie – I was just going to ring you,' she lied.

'I know you said you would, lovey, but Lewis and me are going to Ashford shopping, and we'll be out all day.'

'Oh – are you going to the shopping outlet?' asked Libby, who had never been to a shopping outlet.

'Yes, dear.' Edie gave an exited giggle. 'He's going to treat me for Christmas!'

'How lovely! You deserve it,' said Libby. 'Perhaps I ought to take Hetty there – after the panto, though.'

'She'd like that,' said Edie. 'I'll tell her all about it when I see 'er.'

'Good idea,' said Libby. 'Now, what about your friend Chloe?'

'Oh, Chloe.' Edie sighed. 'Yes, she almost fell over this 'ere body. Nasty, it was.'

'What happened?'

'She goes out for a little walk each mornin', see. You know that Goods Shed place near the station in Canterbury?'

'Oh yes – it's actually part of the station, isn't it?' Libby had been there several times.

'That's it. Well, she goes off there on Saturday and it's only just light, see. And 'er stick touches this bundle, like. Only it isn't.'

'Oh dear – how awful for her.' Libby shuddered. 'But how come *she* found it? I would have thought someone would have seen it earlier.'

'She lives in one o' those little alleyways, see. Nice little flat on the ground floor. No one goes down there much. Anyway, what's so bad about it is who she is.' Edie made a huffing sound. 'She's a Vaughan, see.'

'A Vaughan?' Libby repeated.

'Mickey Vaughan,' explained Edie. 'You know.'

'Er – no. Sorry, Edie, I don't.'

Edie tutted. 'Call yerself a Londoner. Mickey Vaughan. Didn't you come across him with all that dancing stuff?'

Libby correctly interpreted this as the investigation that had unfortunately occurred during the run of Max Tobin's ballet, *Pendle*, a few years before.

'Can't say we did,' she said. 'Sorry, Edie.'

'Right villain, 'e was.' Edie chuckled. 'No real 'arm in 'im, though. But mixed up with all sorts, and well known to the police, as they say. So o' course, they start askin' Chlo nasty questions. Weren't our nice Ian, though. Don't suppose you could put in a word?'

41

'It's not his case, sadly,' said Libby, 'but I'll have a root round. Why is Chloe living in Canterbury and not London?'

'Well, see, they banged Mickey up in the end, and 'e died after about a year. All their money went – proceeds o' crime and all that – so Chlo couldn't really afford to stay in London. An' she'd been down to stay with us, so she sorta knew the area but didn't want to live out in the sticks like us. So Lewis found this little place for 'er. She's 'appy. I see 'er every week or so.'

'Right,' said Libby after a moment. 'I'll see what I can do. You go off and have a lovely time with Lewis in Ashford.'

She finally drank her cooling tea and called Fran.

'Now,' she said, 'this is a long report, so if you're busy, it can wait until you've got time.'

'Not too bad yet. It'll pick up as the week goes on and end in a mad scrum on Saturday. So what's up?'

Libby launched into her story, beginning with Philip's gnomic utterances last night and finishing with Edie's friend Chloe. Fran didn't interrupt.

'My God!' she said at the end of the recital. 'Now what?'

'Exactly,' said Libby. 'Now what?'

Chapter Seven

'What exactly did Ian say when you saw him on Wednesday?' Fran said slowly.

'Not a lot. Warned us off talking about it, but said he knew we would anyway, and told us it wasn't his case. Said Harry's information was useful.'

'What information was that?'

'That Dickie Marsham was very fond of his brother and very protective.'

'And last night we saw that brother and his wife,' said Fran. 'At least, most people did. We were hustled away, weren't we?'

'Roy and Gina, yes. I tried to get a glimpse during the second half, but I think George had spirited them away somewhere. Round the corner of the bar?'

'Sensible of him. They didn't seem to be universally liked, did they?'

'No, although I don't think people actually know them. And I was surprised that they came to the pub. After all, it isn't a Marsham's pub, and I would have thought they were more golf club types.'

'We don't know how long they've lived there, do we?' said Fran suddenly. 'Perhaps they haven't had a chance to get to know people. Or the area.'

'Mmm . . . Anyway, they aren't they most pressing question, are they? What do we do about this suggestion of Hannah's that Ian might want to use us – again?'

'It's more Philip's suggestion, isn't it?' quibbled Fran.

'All right, all right, but what do we do about it?'

A short charged silence fell.

At last Fran said, 'The question is – do we wait for him to speak to us, or do we call him?'

'Honestly, I think I'd rather wait for him to call us,' said Libby. 'And perhaps make a few gentle enquiries while we're waiting.'

'Gentle? What does that mean?' Fran laughed. 'Frankly, I don't know where we would begin. It's all a bit big-business for us, isn't it? Not your average little local murder.'

'I suppose not. Oh well, we'll wait. At least if we aren't doing anything, Guy and Ben will be pleased.'

'And you've got your hands full anyway,' said Fran. 'Tech tonight?'

'Yes, Gawd 'elp us.' Libby sighed. 'Wish us luck.'

'Never!' said Fran. 'Break legs instead.'

Ian didn't call on Monday. The tech rehearsal dragged on, as they had a habit of doing, until after midnight. Harry sent up some of his famous 'nibbles' and Ben supplied beer and wine once the magic hour of ten o'clock had passed. Libby, Ben and Peter locked up at almost one and staggered down the drive to home and bed.

Tuesday Libby spent wrapping presents and waiting for the phone to ring. When it did, she was almost disappointed to hear her daughter's voice. Belinda and her partner, Michael, a historian who had helped the family in the past, wanted to know where they would be staying at the weekend, as her brother was also coming down for Christmas.

'Dom's staying in the flat with Ad,' said Libby, 'so you can stay here. The Manor's full up with panto people, although there probably are a couple of rooms spare. I'll ask. You'd prefer to stay there, wouldn't you?'

'It's slightly less inhibiting, Ma,' giggled Belinda. 'And your spare bed isn't exactly huge.'

'And Michael is rather large, isn't he?' Libby laughed too. 'OK. I'll speak to Hetty. When are you coming down?'

'Saturday all right? I know you'll be busy, but we can fend for ourselves. I'll bring a meal with me, then you won't have to worry between shows.' Belinda said goodbye and rang off.

The dress rehearsal went reasonably well, but as Libby said at the end, pantomime relied so heavily on interaction with the audience it was difficult to tell. She went to bed fairly happy, but woke to crippling stage fright, which meant she did absolutely nothing but fidget all day.

She and Ben arrived at the theatre just after six o'clock. There was no reason for this, other than Libby's obsessive performance anxiety, allied to her directorial worries. She checked every department, despite the fact that she knew next to nothing about the technicalities of lighting and sound, and went through all the racks of costumes, to the annoyance of the members of cast who arrived early.

Eventually, clad in the Fairy Godmother's flowing robes, with glittering tiara and wand, she was ready to open the proceedings. She stepped onto the stage into a rose spotlight and to a resounding clap of thunder, with the immortal line: 'Hello! How nice to see you all! Well, here we are at last . . .' And they were off. Judy Dale was a diminutive and spiteful Lady Aconite, the wicked stepmother, and old Richard Brandon was a suitably imposing Demon King. The two of them set the tone of the production with a waspish exchange, before the chorus launched into their opening number, and Libby heaved a sigh of relief.

It was during the interval when Bob the butcher, in his annual persona as the dame, said: 'Don't often see your mate the policeman this early in the run, Lib. Has he given up the day job?'

Libby stopped dead in the act of refreshing her make-up. 'Ian?' she said.

'Yeah. I almost picked on him as tonight's "crush".' Bob laughed. 'Decided I'd better not!'

'No, definitely better not,' agreed Libby, and crept up to the prompt corner to try and peer through a crack in the curtains.

'He's in the bar.' Ben came up behind her. 'Thoroughly enjoying himself.'

Libby frowned. 'What's he doing here?' she whispered.

'Come to see the panto,' said Ben. 'Like everybody else.'

'Tchah!' said Libby, and stalked back to the dressing room.

She was unsurprised to find Ian sitting talking to Peter when she emerged at the end of the performance. Before she could get to him, however, she was surrounded by audience members wishing to congratulate her and tell her how pleased they were to have a proper Libby Sarjeant pantomime back at the Oast Theatre. Eventually she made it to the bar, where Ben had joined Ian and Peter.

'Pleased?' said Peter, giving her a kiss.

'Yes, thank you,' she said, accepting a large red wine from Ben. 'Didn't they do well?'

'They did, and so did you,' said Ian. 'I'm glad I came.'

'I didn't know you were. You normally squeeze in at the end, if at all.'

'Ah, well. I needed to speak to you,' said Ian, and with an apologetic smile to Ben and Peter, he took Libby's elbow and propelled her over to the French doors that led to the tiny garden.

'I'm not going out there.' She glared at him. 'You can tell me here.'

'I was going to.' He let go of her. 'I was planning on calling you, but this is better said face to face. At least, to start with.' He turned away and stared into the darkness.

'OK, what is it, then?' asked Libby, after a minute of uncomfortable silence.

'I've asked for your help before, haven't I?' He turned back to face her.

'Yes, you have.' She felt a prickle of anticipation somewhere under her ribs.

'Well, I'm asking again. Only this time . . .' He paused.

'Hannah called me on Monday,' she said softly. 'She said Philip was speaking to you.'

Ian let out a breath. 'Then you know . . .?'

'About the investigation? Yes.'

'I realise this is the worst possible time to ask you to help me solve a murder,' he gave her a wry smile, 'but you'd probably ask questions anyway.'

'Probably,' said Libby, with an answering smile. 'But surely Rachel and Claire – is she on the case? – and Rob will all be working on the murder? You can trust them, can't you?'

'Yes, I can, but I shall be pulling them off the case to talk to them, and anyway . . . guess who's in overall charge again?'

'Oh no!' Libby's hand flew to her mouth. 'Big Bertha? I thought she'd gone!'

'She had – she went to headquarters. But everything's in rather a mess right now, and the powers that be needed someone to – um – *oversee* things.'

'Oh, for . . .'

'Fuck's sake, yes,' said Ian, surprising Libby into choking on a mouthful of wine.

'You never swear!' she said, when she'd recovered.

'I do now.' He grinned. 'Anyway, I wanted to ask you in person, just to make you aware of the situation. We can talk about it more on the phone when you've got time.'

'Tomorrow or Friday, and then not until next week,' said Libby. 'I suppose you'll be working over Christmas?'

'Theoretically I've got Christmas Day off. Hetty's invited me with Edward, but he's going to Alice's for the weekend. He'll be back next week.'

'Well, we might see you there, or if you get time, you know we have open house on Boxing Day, so pop in when you can.' Impulsively she kissed him on the cheek. 'I'm sorry you've been put in this position.'

47

He patted her shoulder. 'So am I. And just think how you can crow over me in the future when I tell you off for interfering!'

Ian left shortly afterwards, promising to ring Libby at some point in the next two days.

'What did he want?' asked Ben, when Libby returned to the bar.

'I'll tell you later.' She glanced at Peter. 'And I expect you'll hear over Christmas, too.'

Peter looked at Ben. 'Are you going to be all right with this?'

Ben gave him a crooked smile. 'I don't suppose I'll have a choice,' he said with a sigh.

After Libby had repeated Ian's request to Ben on their way home, he was quiet until they turned the corner into Allhallow's Lane.

'He won't like this,' he said.

'No.' Libby gave his arm a squeeze. 'Neither do I. Ian's always been such a dedicated cop, and such a decent bloke. It must hurt to have to admit there are rotten apples in the barrel.'

Ben sent her an amused look as she fumbled the key out of her pocket. 'That's remarkably poetic.'

'Oh, you know what I mean,' said Libby, tripping over Sidney. 'He's got to investigate friends. In fact, I've very surprised they – you know, the top bods – have appointed him. Hannah said the same. He's too invested in his team. I bet Big Bertha will come interfering.'

'Big Bertha?' repeated Ben. 'You didn't mention her.'

'Didn't I? Oh, yes. She's been sent to oversee the investigation.' Libby shook her head. 'I thought she'd been retired.'

'So did I. Obviously not.' Ben held up a whisky bottle. 'Nightcap?'

Thursday morning, Libby spent a happy hour or so scouring social media for mentions of *Cinderella*. As far as she could see, reviews were favourable, and many made particular mention of Judy – or

Sadie O'Day, as she was billed – while several commented that the Oast's favourite pantomime dame, Bob the butcher, threw his more famous partner, Cooper Fallon, into the shade. Libby had to admit to being delighted by this.

She had just finished getting dressed at the rather advanced time of half past eleven when her phone chirruped from the sitting room. By the time she reached the bottom of the stairs it had stopped, and the landline started ringing.

'Hello!' she panted.

'Where were you?' Ian sounded amused.

'In the bedroom.'

'Alone, I hope?'

'Yes. Ben's at work.'

'Office? Brewery?'

'Somewhere,' said Libby, making her way to the kitchen. 'Is this my briefing call?'

'I've decided I don't trust phones,' said Ian. 'Or, come to that, any of the places we usually meet.'

'Golly. That bad?' Libby stopped mid kettle-filling. 'What do you want to do, then?'

'Do you know the George and Dragon at Steeple Cross?'

She frowned. 'No. I didn't know there *was* a pub at Steeple Cross, except The Dragon on the corner of Dark Lane. Oh, hang on – yes, I do. I delivered some leaflets there for the Harriers when they did the Steeple Martin run thing.'

'It's one of these community pubs. It closed a little while ago and the residents clubbed together to buy it. It's more community space than pub – you know, second-hand books and clothes, food bank, book club—'

'I get the picture,' said Libby impatiently. 'That's where you want to meet? Won't we be overheard there even more than some-where here?'

'We aren't known there,' said Ian.

She sighed. 'OK. When?'

'Remember where it is? Go past that house you went to before and straight on. There's a church, no longer in use, sadly, and the George is opposite. Half an hour?'

'Oh, give us a bit more time than that! I've got stuff to do!'

'All right. An hour? I'll buy you lunch.'

'Blimey,' said Libby.

An hour later, Libby turned her little Fiat, fondly known as the Silver Bullet, left off the main Canterbury road from Steeple Martin towards Steeple Cross, the third of the Steeples. No one knew why they had been called the Steeples, although some schools of thought had it that the three villages' church steeples were points on an ancient ley line. Libby wasn't sure.

She found herself in the centre of what was little more than a hamlet, with the church on her right and the George and Dragon on her left. She remembered Beth telling her that there was no church in Steeple Cross so she used the village hall for services. Why had the church been closed then? She shook her head and turned down by the side of the building and parked. That was a mystery for another day.

Ian stood up as she entered the bar.

'Only ten minutes late,' he said. 'I ordered you tea as you're driving.'

'Thank you – I think,' said Libby, sitting down with a sigh. She looked around the bar, which resembled nothing more than a large private sitting room, albeit with the addition of a dart board and shelves of books announcing themselves as '50p to a good home'.

'Nice place,' she said. 'Not exactly pub-like, though.'

'None the worse for that,' said Ian, smiling his thanks at the motherly woman who delivered Libby's mug of tea.

'Of course not,' said Libby hastily. 'Perfect for a council of war.'

Ian raised his eyebrows. 'Is that how you see it?'

'Well – yes.' She shifted uncomfortably. 'It is, isn't it?'

50

'I suppose it is.' He looked down at his cup. 'It's all to do with the lack of confidence in the police force.'

'Service,' Libby corrected automatically.

'Which it really isn't at the moment.' Ian looked up and frowned. 'To be honest, I'm not very happy being part of it right now.'

'Ian!' Libby gasped in shock. 'You can't mean that!'

'Why not?' He shrugged. 'You've criticised the force in the past, haven't you? And gone on to unmask the villains, you and Fran.'

'Yes, but we always say the police get there before we do.'

'But we don't – frequently. It's often something you two turn up that closes the case.'

'Only because people talk to us and let things slip.' Libby was feeling uncomfortable again.

Ian sat back in his chair and looked at her consideringly. 'And how many times have people actually thought you were proper investigators?'

'Oh, lots!' She smiled. 'And that does help. I've suggested in the past that we should become proper PIs. But I don't think I could pass the exams.'

Ian laughed. 'I'd love to read your answers!'

'Yes, well . . .' Libby gave him a sheepish smile.

'Anyway, you've had enough experience, one way and another, to give me a hand now. Don't you think?' He put his head on one side and waited for an answer.

Chapter Eight

Libby suddenly felt inadequate.

'I don't know,' she said slowly. 'I suppose if you think so . . .'

Ian smiled – a trifle ruefully, she felt. 'I do. I wish Fran still had her occasional "moments", of course, but the psychic part of her brain seems to have gone to sleep recently, doesn't it? But nevertheless, the pair of you have enough nous between you. And you don't have to stick by as many rules as we do.' He paused and looked out of the window. 'Although sticking by the rules has been noticeably absent in some cases recently.'

'And that's what you've got to look into.' Libby nodded sympathetically. 'Although I still don't see why they've asked you to do it.'

'I know it seems odd.' Ian pushed his cup away. 'But I think, rather than a full-scale operation that would attract media attention, they – the ubiquitous "they" – want to keep it local and under the radar.'

'I can see that,' said Libby, 'but why Bertram? Of all the unsympathetic people!'

'I know. So we definitely keep your involvement as quiet as possible.'

'Until someone complains that we've been asking questions. But we'll do our best.' She sat up straight and tried to look efficient. 'So what do you want us to do first?'

Ian raised his eyebrows. 'That's rather up to you, isn't it? What had you been discussing over the last week?'

Libby thought. 'Roy and Gina Marsham,' she began, 'and Alanna, the girl who helps Stella Black at her stables.'

'Stables? Why?'

Libby explained. 'We thought it might help us understand Gina.'

Ian looked doubtful. 'Go on.'

'Well, not much more. But obviously the closure of the pubs.' She looked round at the comfortable interior of the George and Dragon. 'Was this one of them?'

He nodded. 'It was. But don't forget the victim was concerned about the closures – it was his brother who was apparently behind that policy.'

'As we discussed in the pub,' said Libby. 'I know.'

'So Roy Marsham is obviously a suspect,' said Ian. 'But he appears to have an alibi. I say appears, because we can only go on the pathologist's opinion on the time of death, which was some time on Friday evening, when Roy was, would you believe, at a very well-attended meeting of the Felling Rotary Club.'

'Oh goodness!' Libby let out an involuntary laugh. 'And where was that?'

'You'll never guess!' Ian was smiling like the Cheshire Cat.

'Oh, go on!'

'Heronsbourne Golf Club!'

'*What?*'

'I know. Unbelievable, isn't it? All he had to do was walk a couple of hundred yards from his own front door.'

'No wonder they bought a house on Links View,' said Libby. 'Why did they hold the meeting there? It isn't that close to Felling.'

'I gather most of the members are also members of the golf club.'

'And members of the Tory party too, I shouldn't wonder.' Libby scowled.

'Also, there isn't anywhere big enough in Felling.' Ian sat back and regarded his accomplice thoughtfully. 'So you see why I thought it was a good idea to ask you?'

'Because we know Heronsbourne, the locals and the golf club?' hazarded Libby. 'But to be honest, I can't see anyone from there being a likely suspect. And it's not as if the body was found there, either. It's quite a long way from Canterbury.'

'But you could find out a lot about Roy and Gina,' said Ian. 'And, of course, there's Dickie's house.'

'Is that a crime scene? We can hardly search it.' Libby looked puzzled.

'No, but you can talk to his neighbours.'

'We can?'

'Your old chum Ron Stewart and his lovely wife.'

'Oh!' Libby looked pleased. 'He lived in Bishop's Bottom?'

'He did.' Ian smiled. 'Between the Stewarts and your cousin.'

'No!' Libby was delighted. Her cousin Cassandra lived with Mike Farthing, of Farthing's Plants, just down the road from the Stewarts. Ron 'Screwball' Stewart had been a notable rock star in his day, with the band Jonah Fludde.

'Maybe you can find out a bit about Dickie Marsham's private life,' Ian went on. 'So far, we've had very little luck. He was divorced with no children, and none of his work colleagues seemed to know much about him.'

'Wasn't he a member of the Rotary Club, like his brother?' asked Libby.

'If he was, he certainly wasn't active. We wondered, or I did, anyway, if perhaps he was a regular at the Poacher in Shott. You could ask your friend Sid Best.'

Libby stared at him, realising just why he thought she and Fran might be useful. She knew an awful lot of the population of her part of Kent, as most people did, but she also kept in touch with them. Not always to their unalloyed delight.

'All right,' she said eventually, 'but you must have other avenues.

54

What about the pub staff who've lost their jobs and sometimes their homes, like Izzy over at Pucklefield?'

'Of course,' said Ian. 'Rachel and young Mark Alleyn are off interviewing some of them as we speak.'

'Oh, you've kept Mark on the strength, then?' DC Alleyn had been plain PC Alleyn during the most recent murder investigation.

'Indeed we have. We couldn't prise him loose from Rachel's coat tails.' Ian looked round for the motherly woman. 'I said I'd buy you lunch. They do a very good sausage bake, I hear.'

'Ooh! Brenda at the Fox does a good one, too. I shall have to compare.'

Sausage bakes duly ordered, Libby pulled out a battered notebook and ballpoint pen.

'I shall make notes,' she announced, 'or I'll forget something when I'm briefing Fran.'

Ian eyed the notebook. 'Why not a tablet? Then you could send your notes to her direct.'

'I know, I know. And if I had clever thumbs I could no doubt use my phone, too, but I haven't.'

He chuckled. 'Last of the techno dinosaurs, eh?'

The sausage bake was almost as good as Brenda's, Libby announced, and was followed up by another cup of tea. At a nod from Ian, she turned to the motherly woman and beamed.

'Lovely meal, thank you,' she said, 'and a really good cup of tea. Apparently the George is a sort of cooperative pub?'

Motherly woman beamed back. 'It is – and thank you. I've been very lucky.'

'Oh!' Libby was surprised. 'Did you . . . um . . . Were you . . .?'

'Yes, I was. Manager – for twelve years.' The woman leant against the neighbouring table and folded her arms. 'Thought we'd be here for life.'

'And – what? The brewery . . .?'

'Closed it and put it up for sale. Back in May, it was.' Then she smiled. 'But the locals wanted us. And they bought it.' She shook her head. 'If it hadn't been for old Sir Jonathan—'

'Sir Jonathan?' squeaked Libby. 'At Anderson Place?'

'Yes – do you know him?'

'We certainly do!' said Libby. 'Don't we, Ian?'

'We do,' said Ian. 'Did he contribute? Sorry if we're being . . . er . . .'

'Nosy!' supplied Libby, and stuck out her hand. 'Libby Sarjeant,' she said. 'Pleased to meet you.'

'Pat Bailey.' They shook hands.

'Can we buy you a drink?' asked Ian.

'No, I'm all right, thanks,' said Pat, parking her rear end more firmly on the table. 'But tell me – have you got a particular reason for . . . Well, asking questions.'

Libby sent an apologetic look towards Ian, who gave her a resigned smile.

'Yes,' he said. 'As a matter of fact, she has.'

Pat's eyes widened. 'Dickie Marsham,' she said.

Ian sighed.

'Police?' said Pat, levering herself off the table.

'No,' said Libby.

'Not exactly,' said Ian.

Pat frowned. 'What, then?'

'It's a coincidence,' said Libby, shooting Ian an evil look. 'I know Izzy over at the Puckle Inn – do you know her?'

Pat's face cleared. 'Oh yes! She's another one. Lost the Crown just outside Canterbury. We keep in touch a bit – well, most of us do.'

'That's it. She's very happy at the Puckle,' said Libby quickly, before she lost the advantage. 'And the rest of you – are there a lot of you in the same boat?'

'Five of us round here,' said Pat, settling back onto the table. 'But he's sold off a few more in other places. Not London, of course.'

56

'London? I didn't know Marsham's had pubs in London!' Libby raised an eyebrow at Ian, who simply smiled.

'One in Wandsworth – near the river, I think – and one in the City. Prestige, see?'

'Of course.' Libby nodded wisely. 'So you and the others round here keep in touch?'

'Oh yes. Izzy and I have been lucky, but the others – well, two have retired, and Stan is living with his daughter, poor sod.' Pat stared at the floor. 'Can't understand why they murdered Dickie, though. It was his brother who did the damage.'

Where do I go from here? Libby wondered, realising that Ian had deliberately let her run the inquisition.

'Well,' she said eventually, 'I'm glad you've managed to stay here. It's a lovely place. I'll have to come back.'

'Welcome,' said Pat, standing up again. 'And if I can help with' – she looked from Libby to Ian and back – 'whatever it is, let me know. You could talk to the others too, I reckon.'

'That's very kind of you,' said Libby. 'I don't want to push my nose in.'

'If you're doing anything that will show up that little bugger Roy Marsham, we'll all help,' said Pat. 'Now I'd better get back to work.'

'Did you arrange that?' asked Libby under her breath as they got up to leave. Ian smiled.

In the car park, he held her car door for her. 'See?' he said. 'I'd never have got that out of her if I'd told her I was a policeman.'

'Hmm,' said Libby. 'But did you know the George had been a Marsham's pub?'

'I did, yes.' Ian looked thoughtful. 'What I didn't know was that Sir Jonathan was behind the buyout.'

Sir Jonathan, owner of the splendid Anderson Place, which was now run as a country house hotel and wedding venue, had helped, and in turn, been helped, by Libby, Fran and Ian in the past. It was where Jane and Terry Baker had got married, Jane had held her hen night – a very sedate affair – and Peter and Harry had celebrated their civil partnership, with Libby acting as best woman.

'Fran and I will go and see him,' she said now. 'Not sure when, though. He'll be busy, too – and I've really only got tomorrow before Christmas.'

'I know. I said it was an awful time to ask for your help.'

'Never mind.' Libby patted his hand. 'I'll be free from next Wednesday.'

'Except for matinee days,' he reminded her.

'Yes, well . . . we've got a matinee only on the twenty-seventh, then matinee and evenings on the thirty-first and the first, and on the seventh, the last night. Other than that, my days are yours.' She grinned at him. 'Crime will have to wait at the panto's convenience.'

'I'm sure I'll cope. Just keep me posted.' He bent and kissed her cheek. 'Thank Ben for me.'

'What for?' Libby looked surprised.

'Lending you to me.'

'After a remark like that, you're lucky I'm still willing to help. Go on. Go back to your handcuffs.'

She ignored her phone's insistent warbling on the drive home, mulling over what she'd learnt from Ian and Pat Bailey. Back at number 17, she put the kettle on for yet more tea and lit the wood burner before checking her phone. Predictably, there were messages from Fran, Ben and, more surprisingly, her son Dominic. She called Ben and told him there would only be a scratch meal tonight as Ian had plied her with food, then spoke to Dominic and discovered he wanted to bring his girlfriend with him for Christmas. Finally she rang Fran.

'And so,' she concluded, now ensconced on the sofa with Sidney,

'I suppose we ought to go and see Sir Jonathan, and perhaps set up a meeting with the other dispossessed publicans.'

'And Ron Stewart and possibly Sid at the Poacher,' added Fran.

'Oh yes, I'd almost forgotten them. And Cassandra and Mike. Just in case.'

'And all while you're doing panto!' said Fran.

Chapter Nine

The second night of *Cinderella* was slightly calmer than the previous performance, but, as the cast all told each other, Thursdays were often like that.

On Friday morning, as they had decided yesterday afternoon, Fran phoned Sir Jonathan and asked if they could pop in to say happy Christmas.

'Of course he said yes,' she reported. 'So I'll pick you up at about eleven – all right? And he made noises about lunch, so don't have too much breakfast.'

Once again, Ben was warned that he might not be adequately fed that evening, and Libby washed her hair to get the green make-up out of her hairline and made herself look vaguely respectable, as befitted the guest of a hereditary baron.

They duly arrived at Anderson Place just before half past eleven, and were met in the spacious and stately hall by Melanie, formerly events manager and now, apparently, general manager.

'You can go up,' she said. 'I'll send coffee in a minute. And do you want to have lunch up there or in the restaurant?'

'Oh . . . er . . .' said Libby.

'Whatever Sir Jonathan wants,' said Fran. 'We'll see you before we go, shall we?'

They rode up to the second floor in the gilt cage lift, where Sir Jonathan was waiting, a delighted smile on his face.

'Well, this is a lovely surprise,' he said, kissing both their cheeks.

'I half expected to see you back in October when Sir Jasper was staying with me. You know – when he went to see your Shake-speare production. You should have come over then.'

'Sorry, Sir Jonathan,' said Libby. 'I was a bit busy. And Fran always is, these days.'

'Yes, I gather your lovely gallery is doing extremely well, Fran.' Sir Jonathan ushered them into his sitting room.

'Surprisingly, and against all the odds, yes, it is,' said Fran. 'I think it's because the shop is able to be open all the time now, instead of being closed when Guy's painting.'

'And you're in the middle of pantomime, Libby.' Sir Jonathan turned to her with a smile. 'I'm coming to see it next week, I think. I shall have to ask Mel.'

'Oh, that's nice!' said Libby. 'You don't often come.'

A tap on the door was followed by a liveried young man with a tray of coffee. When he'd departed, Sir Jonathan crossed his legs and regarded them both benevolently.

'So what's it about, then?' he asked.

Libby groaned. 'Honestly, we don't only visit our friends just because we want something.'

'But we would like to ask you a question, Sir Jonathan, if you don't mind,' said Fran.

He laughed. 'I have only one condition. That you both drop the "Sir"! How many times do I have to ask?'

Fran poured coffee for them all, then Libby cleared her throat.

'Yesterday Ian and I had lunch at the George and Dragon in Steeple Cross,' she said.

'Ah.' Jonathan nodded. 'And you talked to Pat Bailey.'

'Yes.'

'Well, it's no secret. Steeple Cross is our closest village, and once it looked as though they were going to lose their only remaining community facility . . . Their church is closed, did you know?'

The women nodded.

'Well, a couple of the locals and I got together and decided the

61

pub ought to be saved. I just started them off with a donation. And we held some fundraisers here.'

'But Pat said they were only closed back in May. Didn't it take ages to set up?' asked Libby.

Jonathan's colour deepened rather surprisingly. 'Er . . . no.'

Fran squinted at him. 'You bought the pub,' she said.

'Only a loan,' said Jonathan hastily. 'It would have taken months otherwise, you're right.'

'I bet Roy Marsham couldn't believe his luck,' muttered Libby.

'No.' Jonathan frowned. 'Rather a weak fellow, I thought him. Not the sort to be ruthlessly reorganising his business. And I'm not at all sure he'd actually got full approval from his board.'

'How could he do it, then?' asked Libby. 'It doesn't make sense.'

'Only too easily, my dear Libby. After the pandemic, many businesses, particularly those in the hospitality sector, had lost so much they couldn't recover. I'm sure young Roy manipulated his figures.'

'Is he that clever?' asked Fran. 'I rather got the impression he wasn't.'

'I'd agree with that.' Jonathan leant back and looked at the ceiling. 'If it wasn't for the fact that she didn't really seem the type, I'd be saying *cherchez la femme*.'

Fran and Libby looked at each other.

'You met Gina, then?' asked Libby.

'No, I didn't. I saw her, though. They came here for a function of some sort and she was pointed out to me. Have you met her?'

'No.' Fran put down her coffee cup. 'We avoided her when they arrived at a event we attended.'

'Don't be so pompous, Fran!' Libby laughed at her friend's offended expression. 'We were at a pub quiz, Jonathan, and they arrived. Down in Heronsbourne, where they live.'

'Ah yes. Near the golf club, I believe.'

'That's right.'

'So.' Jonathan sat forward and leant his elbows on his knees.

'You're investigating the brother's death, then? With DCI Connell's approval?'

'Actually,' said Fran, 'yes. Strictly between us, he's asked for our help. He thinks we can get more information from people than the police can, particularly at the moment.'

'Yes – the public are losing faith in the police, are they not.' Jonathan nodded sadly. 'So he's probably right.'

'The trouble is,' said Libby, leaning in confidentially, 'we know nothing about Dickie Marsham's private life. If it had been Roy, we would have had all the homeless publicans to choose from as suspects, but Dickie himself was apparently against the sales.'

Jonathan frowned. 'I don't know the details, but wasn't the body left in Canterbury? And mistaken for a homeless person?'

'Yes. A friend of ours knows the woman who found him,' said Libby.

'Horrible.' Jonathan shook his white head. 'But if that's the case, it must have been planned, don't you think? I would have thought if it had been related to the closure of the pubs it would have been someone lashing out spontaneously.'

'You're right,' said Fran. 'That's why we've got to look further afield.'

'I wish you well with it,' said Jonathan. 'And let me know how you get on, or if you need any help. I feel I have a vested interest.'

'I'm not surprised that he bought the pub,' said Libby, when they left, full of Anderson Place's best salmon ceviche. 'I bet he contributes to every charity under the sun.'

'And there were three food bank depository stations in there – did you notice?' added Fran.

'I did.' Libby climbed into the little Smart car. 'When are you going to upgrade this?'

Fran looked amused. 'Why? It's only me and you who use it.'

Libby sighed. 'Because I'm getting old and decrepit. Where are we going now?'

'Home!' Fran was surprised. 'You're working tonight.'

'It isn't tonight yet,' said Libby. 'I wondered if we could drop in on Pat Bailey and ask about the publican she mentioned – Stan.'

'No,' said Fran firmly. 'Definitely not. Poor bloke's got enough to contend with.'

'Oh.' Libby stared out of the window for a moment. 'Well, how about a detour to Bishop's Bottom? We could turn off the main road just up here.'

'We need a whole day to do Bishop's Bottom, Lib, and it's the day before Christmas Eve, don't forget. Everybody will be busy. We're going home.' Fran pressed her foot down in a determined manner and ignored her friend's disappointed grunt.

At home, Libby reported what they'd learnt from Sir Jonathan to Ian's voicemail, then lit the wood burner and settled down with her notebook. When she woke up, Ben was standing over her with a grin on his face.

'Good lunch?' he asked.

She grinned back and went into the kitchen to make tea and sandwiches before turning herself into a fairy for the evening.

Tonight's audience were fairly riotous, and took their participation seriously, to the detriment of the running time, meaning that an exhausted cast and crew finally brought down the curtain at almost twenty to eleven instead of quarter past ten.

To Libby's surprise, she was met in the bar by the entire Bishop's Bottom contingent: her cousin Cassandra, her partner Mike, Ron Stewart and his wife Maria.

'We thought we might as well come together,' said Cass, while Ron and Mike were buying drinks, 'so we got a cab.'

'It was brilliant, Libby,' said Maria. 'I'm so glad you've come back.'

'I didn't actually go anywhere,' said Libby. 'I was just having a break. And *Puss in Boots* last year was good, wasn't it?'

'Of course it was,' said Cass, 'but it didn't have the Libby touch, despite having some of your regulars in it.'

'Well, actually, it was my script,' said Libby. 'When Lady Amanda put it on at Nethergate, it was such a success that she wanted to do it again here, and I wanted a rest!'

'Oh, I'd forgotten that!' said Maria. 'That was when the pantomime cat was murdered, wasn't it?'

'Always surprised me that she wanted to do it again,' said Ron, coming up behind them. 'I thought it would be the same audience.'

'Panto audiences never mind seeing the same panto – much like fans of rock bands,' said Libby.

'Cheeky,' said Ron.

'Actually,' she continued, 'Fran and I want to come over and see you all next week, if it would be convenient. And probably Sid as well.'

'Oh-oh,' said Mike. 'I sense an investigation.'

'Dickie Marsham, then,' said Maria. 'Right?'

'Yes,' said Libby. 'Sorry.'

'Should have known,' said Ron. 'But there's not much we can tell you.'

'Why don't we all meet at the Poacher for lunch on Wednesday?' suggested Mike. 'You'll only be performing in the evening, won't you, Libby? And everyone else's festivities should be over by then. That way you can put us all through the wringer together.'

Libby laughed. 'I'll bring the thumbscrews.'

On Saturday, Libby didn't see her visiting children before she left for the matinee, and only briefly between shows. Dominic and his new(ish) girlfriend, Stephanie, went straight to Adam's flat, while Belinda and Michael served Libby and Ben a slightly travel-worn lasagne before they had to return to their theatrical duties.

The matinee was, as usual, full of shouts, cries, squeals and pleas to 'Pause it, Mummy!' The evening show was a model of decorum by contrast, and finished with an uproarious rendition from audience, cast and crew alike of 'We Wish You a Merry Christmas!'

After which, there was a mad dash for the church, as Libby had promised Owen, to take part in the midnight service.

And then it was Christmas Day. There were presents round the huge Manor Christmas tree, the traditional Christmas dinner, which Hetty never managed to get on the table until at least three o'clock, a cheerful and somewhat drunken washing-up by everyone except Hetty, her brother Lenny and her best friend Flo, and in the evening, games and turkey sandwiches. Stephanie, the only newcomer, spent most of the day in a state of confusion, but in the evening confided to Libby that she'd never had a proper family Christmas like this one, and it was wonderful!

Boxing Day was open house at number 17 Allhallow's Lane. Libby was delighted when, at just after five in the afternoon, Ian arrived with food and drink and announced that Hetty had found him a corner to stay overnight.

'And I'm not answering my phone under any circumstances,' he said, subsiding onto a stair with Sidney, all other seats being occupied.

'Has it been a bad day?' asked Libby.

'A bad couple of days,' said Ian. 'And I might as well tell you, or I'll never get any peace.'

'You don't have to,' said Libby. 'It'll keep.'

Ian shook his head. 'No, you deserve to know, as my unofficial assistant. There was an attack on Roy Marsham's house on Christmas Day.'

Chapter Ten

'What?' Libby was stunned. 'An attack? How? Was he hurt?'

Ian gave her a tired smile. 'It was actually about one in the morning, and someone tried to set fire to the house. And yes, he did suffer minor burns. Luckily, he and his wife were just coming home from the golf club and saw the flames behind the front door.'

'Petrol through the letter box, was it?'

He nodded. 'And as I spent most of yesterday dealing with it, and a lot of today, I would now like to forget about the Marshams and all their doings for at least a few hours.'

Libby left him on the stairs with a large whisky and went to find Fran, who was in the conservatory with Guy, Ben, Belinda and Michael.

'Come and help me top up the table,' she said brightly, grabbing Fran's arm.

'We'll do it,' said Belinda.

'No, thank you, darling, it's fine,' said her mother firmly. 'You stay and . . . erm . . . enjoy yourselves.'

She was followed by suspicious looks from the men, as she dragged Fran into the kitchen.

'So what do you think?' she asked, when she'd finished whispering her news in Fran's ear as she sliced more turkey.

'I think it's awful,' said Fran, 'but at least nobody died, and Ian's off duty for at least tonight. So we leave it alone too until we go to the Poacher on Wednesday. Ian will update us as and when necessary.'

And with that, Libby had to be content.

In the evening, the entire party decamped to the Hop Pocket, where John Cole was pressed into service on the ancient piano, once resident in the church hall until it was liberated by John's wife, vicar Beth. Various members of the Sarjeant/Wilde party and other village locals joined in with their party pieces, including several old music hall songs led by Libby, Ben and, surprisingly, Hetty and Flo.

Tired and happy, Libby and Ben fell into bed well after midnight. Libby woke somewhere after eight and staggered downstairs to face the wreckage. Luckily, she had many willing helpers, so by the time she left to become a fairy again, Sidney was able to creep back into the sitting room and regain his rightful place on the sofa.

At last, Wednesday, and life was beginning to return to normal. Although, as Libby said to Ben just before he left for the brewery, lunch with friends at the Poacher and pantomime in the evening wasn't exactly normal.

'It is for you,' Ben said, putting the hood up on his waterproof jacket. The rain had barely let up over the whole holiday and showed no sign of doing so now.

Libby waved him off and sent a text message to Ian's private mobile. He called almost straight away.

'I guessed you'd be back on the case,' he said, still sounding tired.

'I told you we were having lunch at the Poacher today. You did suggest we talk to my cousin and the Stewarts.'

'I know. But I'd prefer it if you didn't mention the attack on Roy Marsham. We've managed to keep it out of the media, although there has been a little flurry of interest.'

'On the socials?' asked Libby.

68

Ian laughed. 'Social media, yes. There's always someone who knows something – even if they don't.'

'Was it just speculation?'

'Yes. Someone had seen the fire engine – only one, luckily – and commented wittily that Santa was coming by fire truck these days.'

'Predictable,' said Libby. 'Did they know whose house it was?'

'Of course.'

'Oh, well, everyone will know soon, then. Is there anything particular you want to ask the Bishop's Bottom lot?'

'Only what they know about Dickie Marsham. How long he'd been there, did he have a partner – that sort of thing.'

'He was divorced, wasn't he? And you must know if he had a partner – you searched his house, didn't you?'

'Not personally, no, Libby, but yes, it has been searched. No sign of a resident female – or male, come to that – but he could have had a girlfriend.'

'Wouldn't she – or he – have come forward by now?'

'Maybe not. If it wasn't . . . how shall I put this? Official?'

'Oh, I see what you mean. Someone else's wife, maybe.'

'Well, you never know.' Ian was brisk. 'I'll hear from you later – if you've got time before your performance.'

Fran's car was already in the car park at the Poacher when Libby arrived, and inside, the whole party had assembled at a table in the window.

'Well, if it isn't Inspector Sarjeant!' said Sid Best from behind the bar. 'What can I get you?'

'Tonic, please, Sid – I'm driving, as usual!' Libby went to join the others.

When they'd all exchanged Christmas news and placed their orders with Sid, Ron opened the proceedings.

'Dickie Marsham,' he said. 'Lived just off the road between us. Halfway, would you say?' He looked at Mike.

'About that,' agreed Mike. 'Nice little house – quite ordinary.'

'Not a big one like his brother's, then?' said Fran.

'He did have,' said Mike. 'Before Cass came here. Over the other side of Felling, but his wife got that.'

'Was she anything to do with the brewery?' asked Libby.

'Don't think so,' said Mike, 'but I don't know much about it. I only knew Dickie because he was a neighbour and I helped him with his garden.' He made a face. 'Not much of a gardener, though. Just wanted grass and a couple of shrubs.'

'He came in here,' said Ron. 'Even thought about joining the ukulele club for a bit, didn't he?'

Maria laughed. 'Yes, he did, but only because that girl was a member. What was her name?'

'Can't remember,' said Ron, 'and she didn't stay, anyway.'

'So I wouldn't have met her?' asked Libby.

'Oh no,' said Mike. 'She just flitted in for a while and flitted out again. She wasn't a permanent resident.'

'So what else do you know about him?' asked Fran.

'Not a lot.' Ron lifted his voice. 'You knew him, though, didn't you, Sid?'

'Yes.' Sid came out from behind the bar. 'Nice enough bloke. Used to joke about buying this place for his brewery. I think he enjoyed being away from the business, so to speak. Played darts sometimes.' He turned to Libby. 'Knew your friends the Farrows.'

'Oh, yes, Sandra and Alan – she used to live in Steeple Martin,' said Libby. 'She plays darts, doesn't she?'

'If you want to find out about Dickie, you ought to talk to them.' said Mike. 'I think he was quite close to Alan.'

'Thank you,' said Libby, 'I shall. I'd like to see Sandra again.'

'Even if it is to talk about murder,' said Cassandra, giving her cousin a dig in the ribs.

'Did he ever bring friends in here?' Fran asked Sid. 'Bring anyone to dinner?'

'We're not the sort of place he'd go for dinner,' said Sid. 'Strictly pub and bar food, us. And no, he never brought anyone in here. Used to talk to all the regulars, though. As I said – nice enough bloke.'

No one seemed to have much more to say about Dickie Marsham, but as the little lunch party was breaking up, Maria caught Libby's arm.

'I didn't want to say too much in front of everybody,' she said, 'but didn't I see something about the other Marsham brother's house burning down?'

'Not exactly. Someone threw a petrol bomb, but luckily there wasn't much damage.' *I hope*, she thought.

'Oh, I see. Usual social media exaggeration, then.' Maria raised an enquiring eyebrow.

'I imagine so,' said Libby.

'Well, I think you ought to go and see Dickie's sister,' Maria went on, pulling on her coat. 'She'd know more about him, wouldn't she?'

Libby stared open-mouthed.

'Sister?' said Fran, who'd caught Maria's suggestion.

'Yes!' Maria looked surprised. 'Ruth. Didn't you know? She's married to our accountant.'

Libby pulled herself together. 'I knew there was a sister, yes. It was . . . ah . . . mentioned.'

Maria gave her a rueful smile. 'She doesn't figure highly in the Marsham story. But she's the reason we were on speaking terms with Dickie. She was visiting him and we met when I was passing on my way to see your cousin one day. After that, she used to pop in on us if she was visiting him – which wasn't very often, I have to say.'

Fran was frowning. 'Would it be very intrusive if we spoke to her?'

'I could ring and ask,' offered Maria. 'I ought to ring anyway – you know, to say how sorry I am.'

'For her loss?' Libby shuddered. 'Awful phrase, but appropriate, I suppose.'

'Lib, you're in danger of offending again,' said Fran. 'I know you don't like all these phrases, but they are in common use and people find them comforting.'

Maria was watching with amusement.

'I'll just say I'm sorry he was murdered,' she said. 'And I am. I quite liked him – what I saw of him. He didn't seem to fit into a big business background.'

'No. Even our Harry liked him,' said Libby. 'They met at some do in London, apparently.'

'Well, there you are,' said Ron, coming to retrieve his wife. 'We must all try and find out who killed him.'

Libby and Fran waited until the others had left, then went to say goodbye to Sid.

'You know,' he said, coming out from behind the bar to see them to the door, 'you're the perfect people to investigate Dickie's murder.'

'Oh?' said Fran. 'Why?'

'Because you know so many pubs and publicans!'

'Libby does. I'd never been in so many until I met her.' Fran gave her friend a wicked grin.

Libby sniffed. 'Excellent source of local news and views.'

'Gossip,' amended Fran.

'Yes, all right, but think how many times a local pub has provided us with essential information. George at the Red Lion . . .'

'Frank and Brenda at the Fox,' added Fran.

'And Sid at the Poacher!' finished Libby, digging Sid in the ribs.

'Well, there you are!' said Sid. 'And you've even got a pub of your own now.'

'Nothing to do with me,' said Libby. 'And Ben's not supposed to be doing anything but holding a watching brief. Simon's an excellent manager.'

'Tell you what,' said Sid, thoughtfully, 'apart from going to talk to Sandra Farrow – and did I hear Maria mention Dickie's sister?'

'Ruth, yes,' said Libby.

'Well, there's always the Bell and Butcher. That's a Marsham's pub – and the landlady's a bit of a pal of mine. She might give you the inside track.'

'The Bell and Butcher?' said Fran. 'Where's that? Can't say I know it.'

'Oh – hang on! I do,' said Libby. 'It's in Steeple Mount, isn't it, Sid?'

'That's it. Thought you must know it – they always have the mummers and the Morris stuff there.' Sid smiled. 'Tell Jenny I said to talk to her.'

'Well!' said Libby to Fran, once they were alone in the car park. 'That was all very useful, wasn't it?'

'It was,' said Fran slowly. 'And you can see exactly why Ian wanted us to do this, can't you? The police would never have questioned Maria or Sid – or not until everything else had failed, anyway.'

'And it wasn't even questioning. It was all offered – Sandra, Ruth, Jenny . . . I say! Do you think there's something going on with Sid and Jenny?' Libby's face was alight with interest.

'Oh Libby, really!' Fran laughed. 'No, I don't! Though come to think of it, we've never seen Sid's wife, have we? Do we even know if he's married?'

'I don't know. I do remember him saying things like "I'll ask the missus", though, so he probably is.' Libby frowned. 'And another thing: that nice Pat Bailey at the George and Dragon – blimey, we do know a lot of pubs, don't we? – when Ian and I met her she said "we thought we were here for life" or something like that. I wonder if that meant she had a husband? She never said, and Sir Jonathan didn't mention one either.'

'Well, that's something else to find out, isn't it?' said Fran. 'But not today. You've got to go home and rest up for tonight. I'll allow you to phone Sandra when you get back, but that's all.' She gave Libby an affectionate hug. 'Go on, off you go.'

Chapter Eleven

Libby did call Sandra when she got home, but had to leave a message, and as she didn't have a mobile number for either of the Farrows, she had to be content with that. She left Ian a voicemail with the results of their lunch party, and tried to find some reference online for Ruth Marsham. However, not knowing the name of her accountant husband, this was not exactly successful. The oddly named Bell and Butcher in Steeple Mount, however, had a very professional website, although no details of landlady Jenny. There was a rather nice-looking menu on offer, though, and Libby decided to treat Ben to lunch there over the next week or so.

While she was happily searching for items of interest, she tried the ill-fated Crown and Sceptre, Izzy-from-the-Puckle's old home. She eventually found a reference to it having been sold back in May.

'It all seems to have occurred around that time,' she told Sidney, as she went into the kitchen to make tea and find something to cook for an early dinner. The snack lunch at the Poacher would not sustain a Fairy Godmother in full flow this evening. Sidney jumped up by the bread bin and staked his own claim to food.

'I wonder what happened in May?' she wondered out loud as she threw mince into a casserole to make a bolognese. 'Or perhaps before May, if all the sales were that month. I wonder if they managed to sell all the pubs? I ought to have asked Pat.'

She put this to Ben over dinner.

'I wouldn't poke too far into it,' he said. 'Didn't she say something about someone who had suffered from the whole business?'

'Yes – Steve, was it? No, Stan. And they've all suffered.'

'Yes, but you don't want to open old wounds, do you?'

'Sometimes it's the only way,' muttered Libby into her spaghetti.

'Come on, Lib, you're not that hard.' Ben looked worried.

'No.' She glanced up. 'I get very upset sometimes. The victims of crime aren't only the obvious ones. The fallout is tremendous. Well, we know that personally, don't we?'

'We do.' Ben pushed his plate away and put a hand over one of Libby's. 'Don't go crusading too evangelically.'

'I won't.' She smiled sadly and turned her hand over to squeeze his. 'Come on – we'd better get organised.'

When they arrived home after the performance later that evening, Libby found the little red light winking on her landline.

'Hello, Libby! It's Sandra. Got your message. I'll be in tomorrow, if you want to give me a ring – or come over if you like? Cheerio!'

'I suppose you'll want to go over there,' said Ben, pouring two large whiskies. 'Is Guy going to mind Fran going out yet again?'

'Today was the first time since Christmas,' said Libby. 'And I don't suppose they're very busy.'

'Did Fran see her children over Christmas?'

'Lucy and the kids came down on Christmas Eve and went back Boxing Day morning before Fran and Guy came here.' Libby settled back on the sofa with a sigh. 'Chrissie and Brucie Baby are now ensconced up north and couldn't spare the time, apparently.'

'You're very lucky, you know.' Ben came to sit beside her. 'You get on well with all your kids – and see them regularly.'

'I know.' Libby kissed his cheek. 'I'm sorry you don't see yours as much.'

He shook his head. 'I see them sometimes. We just don't seem to get on.'

'I suppose if we lived nearer . . .'

'We are not moving up north like Chrissie and Brucie Baby!' Ben laughed. 'Give over.'

On Thursday morning, Libby called Fran and asked if she would like to visit Sandra Farrow.

'No, I'll stay and give Guy a hand,' Fran said. 'I don't really know her, do I? When we track down Dickie's sister, we can both visit her.'

'I've suggested to Ben that we go to lunch at the Bell and Butcher. Would you like to come and see what we can get out of this Jenny?'

'Did Ben say yes?'

'Well . . .'

'I'll come if it's just us. I'm not going to play gooseberry with the two of you.'

'OK.' Libby heaved a sigh of resignation. 'I'll go and see Sandra later on my own.'

So on the stroke of midday, Libby drove into Itching, just short of Shott, and into Perseverance Row. Sandra, warned of her visit, was standing at the gate of her beautifully neat cottage, and led the way through the impeccably groomed front garden, both a match for the lady herself, with her silver hair drawn back in a French pleat and immaculate make-up. It still surprised Libby that this perfect example of an English country gentlewoman should be captain of a ladies' darts team and an erstwhile member of a ukulele group.

'So you want to know about Dickie Marsham?' said Sandra, when coffee had been provided and they were seated in her kitchen, as immaculate as everything else about Sandra Farrow.

'Yes, I'm sorry.'

'Why sorry?' Sandra raised her eyebrows. 'Only too happy to help, if it means his murderer is caught.'

'Thank you.' Libby smiled. 'Hetty said to send her love, by the

77

way.' Hetty hadn't actually been applied to, but Libby knew she would have done so.

'Oh, lovely! Send her mine,' said Sandra. 'And how's Ben? And Fran?'

When the essentials had been dealt with, Libby put down her coffee cup and took a breath.

'Now. Dickie Marsham. Sid at the Poacher said you knew him. He was close to Alan?'

'Yes, indeed.' Sandra nodded. 'He didn't seem to have many close friends, too wrapped up in the business, I suppose, and he'd left his previous social circle behind in Felling when he and his wife split up. But he enjoyed coming to the pub, and he played darts – which is how we came to know him. He was very good.'

'So what else do you know about him? The police are looking into the business side of things, but Fran and I are doing his private life. We seem to learn more than the police do in a lot of cases.'

'I know you do.' Sandra gave a gentle smile. 'Well, what can I say? He was quite quiet – he and his sister were both quiet and retiring.'

'Oh, you know Ruth?' Libby was surprised.

'Not well, but he introduced us.'

'Maria Stewart said she would ask her if she'd speak to us. Do you think she would?'

'If she's not too distressed,' said Sandra. 'I imagine she'd be as keen to find the murderer as anyone.'

'What about the brother – Roy. Did you ever meet him?'

Sandra pulled a face. 'No. There was no love lost there.'

'I heard that Dickie was very protective of his brother.'

She nodded. 'He was. Roy was always rather easily led, Dickie said, so he looked after him. Until he married his wife.' Her face went into lemon-sucking mode.

'Oh, yes. Someone said Roy married the wrong girl.'

'Indeed.' Sandra lifted her chin. 'Now, I'm not a snob . . .' *Oh yes you are*, thought Libby, 'but really! That girl. She persuaded Roy into all sorts of things that were totally unsuitable.'

'Like what?' Libby sat forward. 'What was he doing?'

'Gambling, for a start, Dickie said. He was really worried about him.'

Light bulbs were exploding all over Libby's imagination now. Gambling!

'My goodness!' she said out loud. 'That hasn't come up before.'

'Well, it isn't Roy who's been murdered, is it?' said Sandra sharply. 'Dickie was hardly going to be killed for his brother's gambling debts!'

'He has *debts*?' Libby gasped.

'Well, I'm assuming so,' said Sandra, looking slightly embarrassed. 'Gamblers usually do, don't they?'

'Perhaps. But as you say, that's hardly likely to have anything to do with Dickie's murder.' Libby sat back and looked at her assessingly. 'So what theories have you got?'

'Theories? Me?' Sandra looked startled. 'Oh, I haven't . . .' She stopped and stared down at her cup. 'Well, I always wondered about his ex-wife. And the other girl, of course.'

Huh? 'Explain, please,' said Libby.

'Well, his wife . . . He always gave the impression that she was . . . um . . . *greedy*, if you know what I mean.'

'Grasping?' translated Libby. 'She got the house, didn't she?'

'She did, but she was always asking for . . . well, for more. A bill to be paid, or a new television, that sort of thing.'

'Good heavens!' Libby shook her head. 'Did he give in?'

'I think he used to, although more recently he seemed to have stopped.'

'And the other girl? Who was she?'

'Oh, that was the girl Roy was supposed to marry. Dickie had a soft spot for her. She was very cut up about Roy.'

'Ah!' Libby nodded. 'And she blamed Dickie?'

'I think so,' said Sandra hesitantly. 'I don't know for certain, mind. Dickie used to talk to Alan about it. I don't think he had anyone else, not since his father died.' She thought for a moment.

'Actually, there was an old friend. A school friend, I think. But he'd moved away. Dickie used to go and stay with him now and then – when he could manage it.'

'It sounds as though he was terribly lonely,' said Libby. 'Thank goodness he found you all at the Poacher.'

'Yes.' Sandra looked down at the table. 'I felt sorry for him.'

Libby allowed the silence to stretch for a long moment. Then: 'Did he ever tell you the name of the girl? The one who should have married Roy?'

'Not that I remember. He may have told Alan. I'll ask him. He's out this morning – at the allotment, would you believe it!' Sandra's face lightened. 'They've turned the garden behind the old chapel – you know, the one you pass on the way down the hill? – into allotments for the village. Alan loves it! I think they just sit around drinking tea in each other's little sheds.'

Libby laughed. 'Sounds wonderful! Ben just goes off to his brewery.'

'Oh, of course! Alan would love to see that.'

'I'll tell Ben, and you can both come over and have a look.'

'After panto, of course!' Sandra sent her an arch smile. 'We're coming next week. Taking Una.'

'Oh, that's nice.' Libby smiled. Una was Sandra's old next-door neighbour in Steeple Martin.

Soon after this, Libby took her leave. Sandra had provided even more information, and some of it really important, she felt. She needed to talk to Fran about it, and report to Ian.

To her surprise, Ian answered his personal mobile.

'I'm in the car,' he said, 'and yes, I have pulled over. But I need to know what you've got to tell me – you've turned up some pretty useful information already.'

'Thank you,' said Libby, slightly confused. 'Well, I have got a bit more – from Sandra Farrow over in Itching.'

'Do I know her?' asked Ian.

'I can't remember. Used to live here, but married and moved. Plays darts, and she was in that ukulele group.'

'OK. Go on then. What did she say?'

Libby reported.

'So there are a quite a few leads there, aren't there?' she said when she'd finished. 'Or do you know about them all already?'

'No, we don't. Oh, we know about the wife, obviously, but not that she kept asking for more money. And we certainly didn't know about Roy Marsham's gambling, or his ex. No reason why we should, really, is there? It wasn't Roy who was murdered.'

'But Dickie might have gone after the people Roy owed money to,' said Libby. 'And Roy's ex might have blamed Dickie for their break-up.'

'Except that by all accounts, Dickie was furious about Roy marrying Gina.' Ian was quiet for a moment. 'Well, thank you, assistant. I think you've earned a bonus already.'

'Ooh, goody!' said Libby. 'How much?'

After heating some soup for lunch, she called Fran and told her about the meeting with Sandra.

'So do you think we ought to sit down for a planning session?' she asked.

'I'm worried that you're spreading yourself too thinly,' said Fran.

'The only thing that's suffering so far is the housework,' said Libby. 'And that's hardly unusual. Would Guy let you out tomorrow? Or should I come to you?'

'I'll come to you,' said Fran. 'Now go, and for goodness' sake – relax!'

Chapter Twelve

The planning session somehow found itself relocated to the Pink Geranium, where Harry installed them at the table in the window and provided an elderly cafetière and mugs.

'I take it you don't mind not having the issue of the rabid monster in the corner,' he said, sending a fulminating glare at the coffee machine.

Fran was amused. 'Still not getting on with it?'

'No. This is a restaurant, not a coffee shop. People have coffee at the end of the meal, or as genteel coffee and cakes like proper ladies. They don't want flat blacks or amigos, or whatever they are.' Harry sniffed.

'You know perfectly well what they are,' said Libby. 'And you're young – the young always want Americanos or flat whites.'

'Rubbish. I'm not young. I'm positively middle aged.' Harry tossed his head and left with a flounce.

Libby watched him affectionately. 'He does love putting on an act, doesn't he?'

'It's part of his charm,' said Fran. 'And he can be perfectly normal when he wants.'

'And quite helpful,' agreed Libby. 'Now. What do we know so far?'

'And what exactly are we trying to find out?' added Fran.

Libby pushed the plunger down on the cafetière and began to pour.

'Possible motives for Dickie Marsham's murder in his private life,' she said. 'While Ian's team, under Rob Maiden, I think, look into the business motives. And Ian investigates said team.'

Fran pulled a face. 'It's so unpleasant.'

'Yes, it is, but I'm pretty sure he's not going to find anything nasty in the woodshed now.' Libby sipped her black coffee and winced. 'Why do I have this?'

'I don't know. You've always preferred tea.' Fran shook her head. 'And we all know you do, so who are you trying to impress?'

Libby grinned and added milk and sugar. 'No idea.'

'Right. Back to Dickie Marsham, then,' said Fran. 'And do we know why he's called Dickie? Seems a singularly inappropriate name for a high-powered businessman.'

'Childhood nickname?' suggested Libby. 'Presumably he's Richard. Wonder what it says on the firm's website.'

'Don't suppose it matters,' said Fran. 'Sorry, it was a digression.'

'OK – what have we learnt so far, then?' Libby dragged her notebook out of her bag.

'I still can't get used to you without your cape and basket,' said Fran. 'They were your trademarks.'

'Cape wasn't warm enough in winter, and I couldn't find a decent replacement for the old one anyway,' said Libby, 'and the basket more or less fell apart. Seemed more sensible to use this.' She patted her capacious black bag. 'Anyway, stop digressing.'

'Sorry. Go on.'

'Right. We've found out that he had a sister, Ruth, who both Maria and Sandra Farrow know, or have met, at any rate.'

'And an ex-wife who was the grasping sort.'

'And a girl who was engaged to his brother – or expected to marry him, anyway.'

'And who blamed Dickie for the break-up.' Fran sat back. 'So are we leaving it to the police to follow them all up?'

'The slighted ex-fiancée, or whatever she was, I think we have to leave to the police,' said Libby. 'I don't know how we'd find her.'

'Unless the sister knows.'

They fell silent. Eventually Libby said: 'What about young Alanna? Do you think I could talk to her?'

'Alanna? Oh – Stella Black's stable girl.' Fran topped up her coffee cup. 'Not sure Stella would like that. Or Alanna's parents. come to that. She's only – what? Sixteen?'

'No idea,' said Libby. 'And she isn't exactly a stable girl. She might even still be at school. I just thought, as she knew Gina . . .'

'Oh, yes. It would be nice to know a bit about Gina's background.'

'Especially as Sandra obviously thought she was no better than she should be!' Libby chuckled. 'Lovely expression, that.'

'What exactly did she say? Sandra, I mean?'

'Actually, she just said that Gina persuaded Roy to do all sorts of things he shouldn't – and of course, she mentioned the gambling.'

'Yes, but that's Roy . . .'

'Not Dickie, yes, I know. But I think Ian might look into it. Oh – and the old school friend, or whatever he was. No one else has mentioned him.'

'Again, the sister might know,' said Fran. 'I think she ought to be our next interviewee, if we can manage it.'

'Yes. Although there's Edie's friend. You know – the one who found the body.'

'But she's got nothing to do with it, surely?' said Fran.

'Only that she's the widow of a notorious London criminal,' said Libby.

'You said there was no harm in him!'

'Well, yes, but he was known to the police, so there had to be *some* harm in him.'

'As long as you don't go ferreting about in the London under-world again, like all that stuff when you had the ballet here,' said Fran.

'All hellfire clubs and mad monks?' Libby laughed. 'Can't see it, can you?'

'No, I can't. But then I couldn't see it being connected to a blameless troupe of dancers, either.' Fran looked round for Harry. 'Are we eating?'

'I suppose we ought to,' said Libby. 'Do you realise how many times I've eaten out over the last week or so? Poor Ben's been suffering.'

'I bet he's been secretly eating lunch with Hetty,' said Fran. 'Oh, yes, Harry – could we have some soup, please?'

'Soup and bread?' Harry raised an eyebrow. 'Cheese?'

'Go on, then,' said Libby. 'Thanks, Hal.'

Harry went off to the kitchen, and the latest in his floating population of student helpers – or 'apprentices', as he called them – brought over cutlery and napkins.

'I'm not sure what else we can do, you know.' Libby leant back in her chair and closed her notebook. 'We've turned up quite a bit of info for Ian, and unless this Ruth agrees to talk to us, which is, as you said, our best option, I think we've shot our bolt.'

'I think you're right,' Fran agreed. 'I can't say I'm sorry.'

Libby wasn't sorry, either, as on both Saturday and Sunday there were *Cinderella* matinees and evening performances. The non-professionals in the cast were showing signs of flagging, and Libby was glad that she'd decided to allocate Monday and Tuesday as rest days.

The Sunday evening performance had been followed by a party at the theatre to see in the new year, which meant a good portion of Monday was spent clearing up before the professional cleaners came in on Tuesday. After all, Libby said, it was hardly fair to make them clear up bottles, glasses, plates and the remnants of food.

It was when she and Ben got back to Allhallow's Lane that Libby discovered she'd left her phone on the kitchen table.

'Oh, bugger,' she said tiredly. 'I've got messages.'

'That's what the phone's for,' said Ben. 'Do we want tea? Or are we going to eat?'

'There's bread in the bin,' said Libby. 'I thought we were eating with Tim this evening?'

'We are, but I can't last until them. I'll make some sandwiches and tea. You see to your messages.'

Three of these were from Libby's children wishing her a happy New Year, and the fourth was from Fran doing the same. The fifth, however, was from Ian, which she decided to answer as soon as she'd read the sixth. And then changed her mind.

'Maria!' she said when the call was answered. 'Happy New Year! Sorry, I was clearing up after our party at the theatre.'

'You must be exhausted!' said Maria. 'Are you on tonight?'

'No, thank goodness. Nor tomorrow. Back on Wednesday. What can I do for you?'

'It's what I can do for you,' said Maria. 'I've got an invitation for you.'

'You have?' Libby was surprised. 'Who from?'

'Ruth Baxter – our Dickie's sister!'

'Good Lord! So you got hold of her?'

'Actually she got hold of me,' said Maria. 'She called to apologise for cancelling their annual New Year party – because of her brother, of course.'

'Oh. And she said she'd see me? Sounds unlikely.'

'She'd heard of you, apparently. And when I suggested a meeting, she agreed straight away. She said could she meet you at our house, though, if you don't mind. I gather she's a bit fed up with the media.'

'Oh goodness! Have they been doorstepping her?'

'Quite a bit,' said Maria. 'There's no one at Dickie's house, after all, and his ex-wife slipped off to the Caribbean for Christmas, despite the police asking her to stay put. So there's no one else – except brother Roy, of course.'

'I would have thought he'd be the journalists' favourite. He was taken in for questioning right at the start, wasn't he?'

'Yes, but they let him go. And as far as I can see there's been no progress since then. Officially, anyway.'

'No,' said Libby slowly. 'And I haven't heard a word from Ian since last week either.'

'Who? Oh – Inspector Connell. Well, do you want to see Ruth?'

'Yes, please, if you don't mind. Would it be possible tomorrow? Then I haven't got to rush back for a performance.'

'Of course. I'll check with her and ring you back. Preference for time?'

'Whatever suits her – and you. Thanks so much, Maria.'

Ben put a mug of tea in front of her and raised an enquiring eyebrow. Libby explained.

'And now I'd better return Ian's call,' she said.

'Libby! Where have you been?' Ian answered almost before the first ring.

'And a happy New Year to you too!' Libby was affronted. 'As it happens, we were cleaning up at the theatre. What do you want?'

'Sorry, sorry.' He sighed. 'I'm already having a bad week.'

'Well, if it'll cheer you up, I'm meeting Dickie Marsham's sister tomorrow at Maria Stewart's house.'

'Oh? That's a piece of good news, thank you. Do you think she'll come up with anything?'

'I think she just wants to find out if you've made any progress,' said Libby. 'The meeting was her suggestion.' Well, almost, she said to herself. 'Did you have something to tell me?'

'Ask you, more like.' Ian paused. 'I wondered if you could possibly find out the contact details for those publicans Pat Bailey told us about?'

'I can try.' Libby was surprised. 'But they'd be more against Roy than Dickie.'

'We're trying to find out who tried to fire Roy's house.' Ian sounded more tired than ever.

'Oh! Yes, of course. I'd forgotten that. How awful.' She went quiet.

'Never mind, Lib. But if you can, I'd be grateful. I could do it myself, officially, but I'm up to my ears.'

'How's the investigation going?' Libby asked. 'The police one, I mean, not the Marsham one.'

'Don't ask. It's quite ridiculous, frankly – especially the supervision, if you know what I mean. That keeps getting in the way of Rob's investigation into the Marsham murder.'

Libby correctly interpreted this as meaning that Superintendent Bertram was interfering. 'I don't suppose you can get off this evening, can you? Ben and I are eating at the Coach – you could join us.'

There was a pause. Then: 'Do you know, I might just do that! Thank you, Libby. I could do with the company. Edward's been staying with Alice since Christmas, so I've been on my own.'

'So you've been spending even more time at work,' said Libby. 'Right. See you at seven thirty at the Coach, then. Don't be late.'

Chapter Thirteen

When Libby and Ben arrived at the Coach and Horses, Ian was already sitting at the bar chatting to Tim.

'I've laid up the little table by the fireplace,' said Tim. 'Thought you'd prefer that, as there's only three of you – and you don't want to go in the dining room, do you?'

Since Tim had been promoting the Coach as a boutique hotel and venue, the room on the other side of the hallway – now a proper reception area – had become a formal dining room,

'No, that's lovely, thanks, Tim,' said Libby.

'What would you like to drink?' asked Ian. 'My shout this evening, as you've been kind enough to offer me . . . er . . . sanctuary?'

'A respite,' said Libby. 'Although sanctuary will do. And red wine, please.'

Food ordered, they took their seats at the small table.

'So – anything you can tell us?' asked Ben. 'Your assistant here is dying to know.'

Ian smiled. 'I can't tell you an awful lot, and you've provided us with some of the most useful information already. Rob and Rachel know what you're doing, but under the circumstances, they don't feel they can speak to you themselves.'

'No, I see that,' said Libby. 'Big Bertha would be down on them like a ton of bricks. But it must make it awfully difficult for you.' She eyed him sympathetically. 'Trying to help their investigation while investigating *them* at the same time.'

'Or appearing to,' said Ian. 'Luckily, or unluckily, perhaps, we have uncovered pockets of the usual problems.'

'Misogyny?' suggested Ben.

'Homophobia? Racism?' added Libby.

'Sadly, yes. And hopefully, what I've found so far will keep Bertram occupied and leave me free to help Rob. And Acting Detective Inspector Trent, of course.' Ian smiled at Libby. 'Who always appreciates your help.'

'I was remembering,' said Libby thoughtfully, 'when we helped out with that Notbourne Court business.'

'Oh, the running club thing?' said Ben. 'Adam and Sophie got caught up in it as well.'

'Yes, that's it. Mike and Cass were helpful then, too, weren't they?'

'They were. And Mike Farthing had no reason to be particularly friendly towards the police, did he?'

'Oh, that was all cleared up,' said Libby. 'I'm sure he understood.'

'It's such a shame when innocent people get caught up in this sort of investigation,' said Ian. 'So many people get hurt.'

'And unfortunately, mud often sticks. There are still some hidebound people who believe in "no smoke without fire".'

'Surely no one still thinks Mike was mixed up in the ukulele case?' Ben was surprised.

'Cass says there are some. The business lost some regular clients – old people, mainly.'

'Like us?' Ben gave her a grin.

'Let's give it all a rest, at least until we've finished eating,' said Ian. 'Oh – and I've booked a taxi, so I can drink as much as I like.'

'That'll be the day,' said Ben. 'I've never seen you even slightly the worse for wear in all the years we've known you.'

Ian grinned. 'Well, I'll give it a try.' He lifted his glass. 'Cheers.'

They'd finished their meal and started on a fresh bottle of red wine before Ian returned to the subject of the Marsham murder.

'So what made you start remembering your former triumphs

like the running club murder?' he asked. 'Does it have some relevance to our current little problem?'

'Not really.' Libby sat back and looked up at the ceiling. 'It was just going over to Bishop's Bottom and Shott, really. And the fact that our friends over there were helpful. After all, I'm going to the Stewarts' house to meet Ruth Baxter tomorrow, aren't I?'

'You are.' Ian nodded. 'And you can ask her about all these other people you've heard about. She'll probably know.'

'Yes, that's what I plan to do. Although Fran and I thought you – the police – would be the best people to find Roy's ex-girlfriend. I wouldn't have thought Ruth would know much about her.'

'But you said Dickie had a soft spot for her?' Ben put in.

'True. But he also apparently had a soft spot for a girl who used to go into the Poacher. Perhaps he was a bit susceptible.'

'You didn't mention her,' said Ian.

'No – she flitted in and flitted out, they said.' Libby swirled the wine in her glass. 'Shame. She might have been a source of information – or even a motive.'

'A motive?' said Ian and Ben together.

'If she had a boyfriend – or a husband, perhaps – who objected to Dickie taking an interest.'

'How long ago was this?' asked Ian.

'Hmm, around the time of the ukulele stuff, so probably not relevant.' Libby heaved an impatient sigh. 'Oh, it's so annoying.'

'If it wasn't complicated, you wouldn't be interested,' commented Ben.

'How true!' Ian smiled across at his 'assistant'. 'And on occasion, I have to admit to being grateful for her "satiable curiosity".'

'I think I've been compared to the Elephant's Child before,' said Libby sending a lowering glare across the table.

'So what else will you ask about?' Ben said, topping up his glass.

'Dickie's ex-wife, who went off to the Caribbean, apparently, just before Christmas; his old school friend; his relationship with Roy, and Roy's gambling. Oh, and Roy's wife, I suppose.'

'And anything else she cares to tell us,' said Ian. 'Although it strikes me that Dickie Marsham lived mainly for his work.'

'I said that to Sandra,' agreed Libby. 'He must have been lonely. It was a good job he found some kindred spirits at the Poacher.'

'I would also like to know why he went to live in Bishop's Bottom,' mused Ian. 'I know it isn't far from Felling, but it's very off the beaten track.'

'Well, Roy went to live in Heronsbourne,' said Libby. 'That isn't city central, either.'

'But it's closer to Felling,' said Ben.

'Perhaps he just wanted to be right away from work and family,' suggested Libby. 'But not too far.'

'Well, see if Ruth knows, anyway,' said Ian. 'And anything at all that she can tell us about Roy and Gina, of course.'

'Of course,' said Libby. 'And when Ben and I go to the Bell and Butcher, what do we ask there?'

'The where?' Ian raised his eyebrows.

'It's a Marsham's pub that Sid at the Poacher told us about. One of the few Roy hasn't sold.'

'You don't mean to tell me there's a local pub you don't know?' Ian grinned at them both.

'Actually, we have been there,' said Ben. 'Or at least I have. I waited in there for you, Lib, when you went to see that baker when there was all that trouble with the Morris Men.'

'Oh Lord, yes.' Libby frowned. 'Richard Diggory. I remember now.'

'Well,' said Ian, 'if you can get into conversation with the manager—'

'Oh, we can,' said Libby. 'Sid said to say he sent us.'

'In that case, anything he can tell us about the brewery would be helpful.'

'He's a she. Jenny, I think Sid said.' Libby finished her wine. 'But it probably won't be this week. Panto doesn't finish until Saturday.'

'A fairy's work is never done,' said Ian. 'And so, as my taxi will be here in a minute, I'll let you go to your fairy bower. Let me know what happens tomorrow.'

On Tuesday morning, Maria having confirmed the meeting with Ruth Baxter, Libby made herself look respectable and bade Sidney be good. Before she set off, she left a message on the George and Dragon's voicemail, asking Pat Bailey if it would be possible to ask her a few questions.

'I just mustn't muddle up the questions,' she said to Sidney as she let herself out of the cottage.

The rain had stopped, but the sky was still a uniform grey. She drove to Bishop's Bottom, passing Shott and the Poacher, and waved to a surprised Mike Farthing, who was waiting to pull out of his driveway. Then she remembered that Dickie Marsham's house was also on this road, between Mike and Cassandra's and the Stewarts'. However, she noticed nothing other than the lane she and Fran had once explored, that led eventually to the edge of the Notbourne estate.

Ron Stewart let her in, and promptly disappeared to his attic studio.

'Don't want to inhibit the poor woman,' he said, with a mock salute.

Maria met her in the hall. 'She was early,' she whispered. 'Very nervous.'

'Of me?' Libby, wide-eyed, whispered back.

'The situation,' said Maria, and led her into the kitchen.

'Ruth, this is Libby Sarjeant,' she said. 'Libby – Ruth Baxter.'

Libby held out her hand to the small woman perched on a stool by Maria's island unit.

'Hello, Ruth, I'm very pleased to meet you.'

Ruth Baxter slid awkwardly off the stool and took Libby's hand in a brief, limp grip.

'Hello,' she said, and cleared her throat.

93

'Sit down, Lib,' said Maria brightly. 'Tea? Coffee?'

'Tea, please, Maria.' Libby climbed onto another stool and shrugged off her jacket. Maria took it and switched on her kettle.

'I was very sorry to hear of Dickie's death,' said Libby, looking as sympathetic as she could manage.

'Richard, yes. Did you know him?' Ruth's expression brightened.

'No, but we have several mutual friends. Do you know Sandra and Alan Farrow?'

'Oh, yes. Richard introduced us. I liked Sandra.'

Yes, you would, thought Libby, eyeing Ruth's smooth fair bob and expensively nondescript cardigan and trousers.

'And of course, Maria and Ron – and I believe you know my cousin and her partner? Mike Farthing?'

Ruth brightened even further. 'Mike has helped us with our garden – and he helped Richard, too, didn't he?' She gave a rather weak laugh. 'Not much of a gardener, my brother.'

'No.' *Now where do I go?* wondered Libby.

'Maria says you help the police with their cases.' Ruth leant forward and fixed earnest blue eyes on her. 'Do you know anything about Richard's death?'

'Very little, I'm afraid.' Libby smiled her thanks as Maria placed a large mug in front of her. 'But they were hoping you might be able to tell me something about his private life. They only really know about his business dealings.'

'But it must have been something to do with the business, surely?' Ruth's voice turned querulous. 'Nobody we know would . . .' She tailed off and looked down at her coffee cup.

'No, of course,' said Libby. 'But it helps to get a rounded picture. His wife, for instance? She's not been in the country since he was found, I gather?'

'Ex-wife,' said Ruth. 'Why aren't they looking for her? She's a bitch!'

'They're hoping she'll come back from the Caribbean,' said

Libby, crossing her fingers. 'But has there been no one else, since the divorce?'

'We-ell . . .' Ruth looked down again. 'There's Trisha, of course.'

'Trisha?' prompted Libby, after a pause.

'Roy's ex.' Ruth glanced up. 'You know about that, I suppose?'

'Um . . .' Libby darted a glance at Maria for support.

Maria smiled and sipped her coffee. 'Well, yes. Before he married . . . er . . . Gina, isn't it?'

'He was engaged to Trisha.' Ruth sat up straight. 'He let her down – almost at the altar!'

'Not quite at the altar, Ruth,' said Maria gently.

'Well, no. Not exactly. But it was only six months away.'

'And where did Dickie . . . Richard come into it?' asked Libby.

'Oh, he thought she'd turn to him.' Ruth sounded scornful. 'But she more or less blamed him for the whole situation.'

'Surely it wasn't anything to do with him?'

'No, but . . .' Ruth fell silent again.

'She thought Dickie could have put things right,' said Maria.

'How?' Libby looked from Maria to Ruth and back again, frowning.

'She said Richard should have stopped Roy.' Ruth threw her head back. 'When he sold that building.'

'What building?' Libby was now on high alert.

'The building in Nethergate. Where Gina lived. She was going to be evicted by the new owners.' Ruth looked vicious. 'And Roy' – she took a deep breath – '*rescued* her!'

Chapter Fourteen

'Rescued her?' Libby was stunned. 'But . . .'

'Oh, I know.' Ruth drank the remains of her coffee in one gulp. 'Roy sold the building – he was in charge of the estates department at Marsham's.'

'Yes, I know.'

'I don't know why they owned it – it wasn't a pub. He said it was a surplus building, or something.'

'Surplus to requirements,' said Libby.

'Something like that. So he sold it to some company.'

She could guess what happened next. 'And I suppose they were going to turn it into holiday lets?'

Ruth nodded. 'That's right. All the tenants had to go. It made good business sense, actually. So Gina' – she positively spat the word – 'goes to Roy to persuade him to help. Of course, the idiot fell for it, didn't he?'

'I see.' Libby nodded. 'But how did she manage to get in touch with him? He wouldn't have been going to the building himself, would he?'

Ruth shrugged.

'And Trisha thought Dickie should have – what? Stopped Roy helping Gina?' Libby went on.

'Well, yes, but she said Dickie should have stopped the sale in the first place.'

'Ah. Could he have done that?'

'I don't know. The board were supposed to approve sales, so that had already been done.' Ruth subsided, drooping on her stool.

'Trisha wouldn't have killed Dickie, though, surely?' said Maria. 'And this was a year or so ago, wasn't it?'

'Two years, just over.' Ruth sighed. 'Roy's the youngest of us, you see. Richard was the eldest, then me. Roy was always getting into scrapes when he was younger, and Richard would rescue him. We thought he'd settled down now he had responsibility in the business. Stopped all the gallivanting around.'

'And of course,' said Libby, 'he's been selling off more of the assets recently, hasn't he? Some of the pubs.'

'Yes.' Ruth looked down and cleared her throat again.

Libby looked at Maria and raised an eyebrow. Maria shook her head.

'But it isn't Roy who's been murdered,' said Libby. She paused. 'What about Dickie's old school friends? Would they know more about him?'

'There's only one.' Ruth looked up, her face going a rather sickly pink. 'Anthony Leigh. Dickie didn't see much of him, though. He moved away.'

'Oh, that's a shame,' said Libby.

'Yes, but he used to go and stay with him. Anthony lives in Spain, you see. And he comes back here to visit; he has a lot of friends in the area.'

Libby swallowed hard and tried to stop her imagination taking flight.

'In Felling?' she asked.

'Oh yes. And St Aldeberge. Do you know it? It's a little village just down on the coast.'

'Yes, we know it,' said Maria and Libby together. Ruth looked surprised.

'We know the vicar,' explained Libby.

97

'Oh, right,' said Ruth, and subsided again.

'So is there anyone else you can think of who might have wished Richard harm?' asked Libby, after another silent pause.

'No.' Ruth shook her head. 'He was such a nice person – wasn't he, Maria?'

Maria nodded. 'Yes, he was.'

'And he never hurt anyone. Always tried to help. Even Veronica – his wife, you know – he was always helping her out. Money, mostly. And he let her keep the house. And the break-up wasn't his fault.' A hard expression flitted across Ruth's face.

'No?'

'No. She just wanted to get rid of him. He worked so hard, you see . . .' Ruth looked forlorn, and Libby wondered if her own marriage suffered along the same lines.

'Well,' said Libby, after a moment, 'if I hear anything at all about the investigation, I'll let you know. And if I, or the police, need to know anything else, may I ask?'

'Oh yes.' Ruth sat up straight. 'I'll give you my number.' She felt down by her side and fished out a wallet, from which she extracted a business card. She blushed as she handed it over, and Libby read: *Ruth Baxter FCA*.

'You're an accountant too!' Libby said. 'Wow.'

'I started out with Marsham's – well, I would, wouldn't I?' Ruth tittered.

Maria and Libby laughed politely.

Ruth slid off her stool again. 'I must get going,' she said. 'We've got a meeting this afternoon, and I need to get stuff organised.' She held out a hand to Libby as Maria retrieved an expensive-looking leather coat from behind the door. 'Thank you for talking to me, Libby.' She took her coat and kissed Maria's cheek. Maria looked surprised. 'And thank you, Maria, for introducing us,' she said.

They both went to the door to see her off in her large white SUV.

'That was interesting,' said Libby as they returned to the

kitchen. 'I'm not sure if I remembered to ask everything Ian wanted me to, but I was a bit floored by the mention of the old school friend.'

Maria frowned. 'Why?'

'Well,' said Libby, settling back on her stool, 'I knew there was one, Sandra told me, but when I heard he lives in Spain . . .'

'Is that helpful?' Maria was still frowning.

'It's just . . . Oh, it's me making bricks out of straw again.' Libby peered gloomily into her mug. Maria took it away from her.

'More tea?'

'Yes, please.' She stared at Ruth's abandoned coffee cup.

'So what were you making bricks about?' Maria poured water into Libby's mug.

'That business we got involved in over in St Aldeberge. And on the Dunton estate.'

'Yes?'

'Well, that all began with expats from Spain. Our friends Colin and Gerry – you've met them. They came back here to live.'

'So?' Maria was still looking puzzled.

'Well, there were a few . . . um . . . criminals.' Libby glared down at her fresh tea.

'Oh, I see.' Maria smiled. 'But not everyone who lives in Spain is a criminal – your friends aren't!'

'I know. It's just my stupid imagination.'

They sat in silence for a few moments.

'I know what I was going to ask,' said Libby. 'Where is Dickie's house? I was looking for it on the way here.'

'You can't see it from the road,' said Maria. 'There's a little lane – rather overgrown, but Dickie said it stopped unwanted visitors.'

'The lane that leads to the Notbourne estate?'

'That's it!' Maria was surprised. 'Oh – of course. All that business with the runners.'

'Yes. Fran and I tried to explore up there. It turns back on itself to join the Canterbury road, doesn't it?' Libby smiled. 'Good. I'm glad I settled that.'

After another ten minutes, she got up, retrieved her coat and said goodbye, shouting up the stairs to Ron.

'Thanks for that, Maria,' she said. 'One day I'll do the same for you.'

'Oh, I do hope not,' said Maria, laughing.

Deciding against driving down to Nethergate to report to Fran, Libby returned home, found a tin of soup for lunch, lit the wood burner and settled down to make her reports. Pat Bailey had left a message saying, rather cautiously, that she would do what she could to help, but Libby thought she probably needed a clear day for that part of the investigation.

She reported first to Fran, who was, surprisingly, not at the shop.

'Interesting,' she said. 'Especially the Spanish angle.'

'That's what I thought, but it can't be – can it? Too much of a coincidence.'

'Worth asking Colin and Gerry if they know him, though?'

'Maybe,' said Libby doubtfully. 'But I was most interested in the sale of the building in Nethergate. That was the sale that resulted in young Alanna's family being thrown out, too. Do you think we should talk to her after all?'

'See what Ian says,' said Fran. 'But Stella won't like it.'

'I can't help feeling that all this selling-off of the assets is significant, though,' said Libby. 'Even if that was Roy, not Dickie.'

'But didn't Ruth say the sale would have been approved by the board?'

'Yes, she did.' Libby looked thoughtful.

'And now, of course, there's the angle of the discarded girlfriend. That links the brothers, doesn't it?' Fran sounded thoughtful. 'Go on, tell Ian. And I'll have a think about it.'

Ian wasn't overly enthusiastic about Ruth's revelations.

'The friend in Spain is unlikely to know much,' he said, 'and the ex-fiancée is more likely to go for Roy than Dickie. In fact, most of the possible motives relate to Roy. Even the gambling, if that's true. Did Ruth mention that?'

'No.' Libby was disappointed. 'Oh well, I hope I have more luck with Pat Bailey. She's said I can ask her questions, although she didn't sound too happy about it.'

'Go and use your famous charm,' said Ian.

The rest of Tuesday was spent making a half-hearted attempt at catching up on housework – washing, changing beds and ignoring the ironing. She put a throw-it-all-in casserole into the slow cooker, then sat down to relax. Her brain, however, kept plugging away at the problem of the Marsham brothers. Dickie seemed an unlikely candidate for a murder victim, whereas Roy had stacked up a whole raft of possible enemies. After a while, she called Pat Bailey and made an appointment for the following morning.

'I'll try not to impinge on your lunchtime trade,' she said. 'Would eleven be all right? Or earlier?'

'You won't be here long, will you?' Pat sounded nervous. 'Eleven should be fine.'

'Right.' Libby thought for a moment. 'Pat, if you're not happy about this, just say. I'm not the police – you don't have to answer my questions. I'm just doing it to help them out and because I want to find out who killed Dickie Marsham.'

'Yes, I know.' Pat's voice softened. 'But I don't see what my friends have to do with that. Their argument would be with Roy.'

'That's the problem,' said Libby. 'Everywhere we go with this, Roy comes out on top as the villain.'

'Oh, I wouldn't go that far,' said Pat, hastily backtracking. 'I expect there were good reasons for what he did. After all, no one's had any money to spend over the last few years, have they? People

101

don't go to the pub like they used to.' *They do here*, thought Libby guiltily.

'No, you're right,' she said aloud. 'The whole entertainment and hospitality industry has suffered badly. I know musicians and actors who've been reduced to penury.' Well, that was true, she thought. 'So I expect Roy was only doing what other breweries had to do.'

Having agreed on eleven o'clock, Libby sent Fran a text asking if she wanted to join them. Fran rang back.

'You never send me texts,' she said.

'I didn't want to disturb you. OK, OK, I won't do it again. So – do you want to come?'

'Will she mind?'

'I'm sure she won't.' Libby related her conversation with Pat.

'All right, I'll pick you up on the way through,' said Fran. 'About half past ten. And I was thinking.'

'Yes?' said Libby, after a long pause.

'I know I said Stella Black wouldn't like us talking to Alanna, but now we've heard what Ruth had to say, I can't help thinking that a conversation with her – and possibly her parents – would be helpful.'

'Yes, though only regarding Roy, really,' said Libby. 'I would love to know more about him and his doings, but does it help? I know that's why we're going to see Pat tomorrow, but . . .'

'It's an insight into the workings of the company,' said Fran. 'Didn't you say Ruth was sure the murder had something to do with that?'

'Yes.' Libby frowned at the fire. 'And of course, there's the attempt at firing Roy's house.' She suddenly sat bolt upright as a thought struck her. 'Could it be a case of mistaken identity?'

Chapter Fifteen

'Wow!' Fran laughed. 'That's a bit of a leap!'

'But possible?' said Libby enthusiastically. 'Go on, admit it. It's possible.'

'Yes, I suppose it is.'

'Shall I tell Ian?'

'Good Lord, no!' said Fran. 'They've probably thought of it already, anyway.'

'Oh, yes.' Libby sat back again with a sigh. 'I suppose they have. I wonder if they've made any headway on the arson attempt.'

'Hasn't Ian said anything about that?'

'No, except that he's working on it. I'm not sure how much is in the public domain. I mean, do we mention it to Pat?'

'Definitely not. If she does, all well and good – except that we don't know anything apart from that it happened, do we? No details at all.'

'No.' Libby frowned at Sidney. 'It happened late on Christmas Eve – or Christmas morning, to be precise – and Roy and Gina saw the flames behind the front door. But Ian said Roy had minor burns, and there was little damage, so it must have only just happened, and they caught it before it spread. It all sounds rather odd, doesn't it?'

'It does.' Fran went quiet for a moment. 'You don't suppose . . .'

'Just what I was thinking.' Libby hesitated. 'Is it possible?'

'It would be very tricky,' said Fran. 'And it seems an excessively dangerous way to divert suspicion from yourself.'

'How would you do it?' Libby paused for thought. 'Pour petrol through the letter box, throw in a match, then immediately open the door and stamp it out. Hmm.'

'It's just possible – but unlikely, surely?'

'Oh, well. They'll get to the bottom of it. Meanwhile, I'll see you tomorrow, and shall I try and fix something up with Stella for next week? She's promised me a ride, so I could take her up on that.'

'All right, see what you can do. At least the panto will be over.'

On Wednesday morning Libby felt considerably restored after a restful afternoon and evening.

'So I rang Stella this morning,' she said, when Fran picked her up, 'and I'm going over for a ride on Tuesday. You can come too, if you like.'

'You know I don't ride,' said Fran. 'And you'll find it a bit painful after all this time, won't you?'

'Oh, I expect so. But it'll go some way to keeping me fit if I start doing it regularly. I wonder if she'll let me ride Cascade?'

'I doubt it!' Fran sounded amused. 'I should imagine that's Alanna's prerogative. By the way, will she be there? Not at school?'

'No, I asked. She's left – she was sixteen sometime last spring, and Stella employs her officially. Sensible, really, as Stella was telling me that effectively she has a smallholding. A few cattle – milkers only, she said – chickens for eggs, and some veg. Just sells to the locals.'

'Interesting,' said Fran. 'I seem to remember Jemima telling you she had a veg box delivered via George. That wouldn't be from Stella, would it?'

'I shouldn't think she grows enough,' said Libby. 'Anyway, I'm going over on Monday. Oh and Stella and Alanna are coming to the panto with John and Sue. Not that I'll get a chance to talk to them then.'

'How did you squeeze them in? I thought you were sold out?'

'Cancellation.' Libby's mouth turned down. 'Family who were coming won a holiday, would you believe!'

'Lucky all round, then!' said Fran.

Pat Bailey came out from behind the bar as soon as they stepped through the door of the George and Dragon. Libby introduced Fran.

'I know who you are now,' said Pat, as she led them to a table in a corner. 'I spoke to Izzy.'

'Izzy at the Puckle,' Libby clarified for Fran. 'How is she?'

'Oh, fine. Sang your praises.' Pat gave them both a quizzical look. 'So did Sir Jonathan.'

Libby felt the colour creeping up her neck, but Fran was unfazed.

'Yes, we get a lot of help from people,' she said, turning the tables neatly. 'Sir Jonathan's been very kind.'

'Oh.' Pat's eyes grew wide and Libby, sensing that she was about to start asking questions, jumped in with her own.

'So you're all right with us asking you a couple of questions, then, Pat?'

'Yes – I suppose so.' Pat looked from one to the other. 'You want to know who the other landlords are, don't you? The ones who lost their pubs.'

'If they wouldn't mind,' said Fran.

'Yes, well.' Pat stood up. 'Would you like a drink? I remember Libby liked tea.'

'Two teas, then, please,' said Fran. 'It's very kind of you, Pat.'

Mumbling what could have been 'Quite all right' under her breath, Pat scurried off behind the bar and into what was presumably the kitchen.

'At least she knows what she's in for,' said Libby. 'Good job she spoke to Izzy and Jonathan.'

'And good job they both like us,' said Fran, with a grin. 'This is a very nice pub, isn't it? Bit like what Mavis has done in the Blue Anchor.'

'Just a shame these sort of places have to exist, though,' said Libby. 'Who'd have thought that at the beginning of the twenty-first century there would be such widespread poverty that we'd need places for people to keep warm and get access to cheap food?'

'Or free food.' Fran shook her head. 'And that renting property would have become the norm again after so many years of every-one owning their own homes?'

Libby nodded, and they both sat staring solemnly at Pat's imita-tion coal fire.

Pat came back with a tray and sat down. 'Milk in the jug,' she said, 'and sugar or sweeteners if you want them.'

They thanked her, helped themselves, then looked at each other.

Libby laughed. 'I'll start then, shall I?'

'Well, I know you'll want Stan's number, so I'll ask him if he minds me giving it to you. I told you he's living with his daughter, didn't I?'

'You did. Is she local?'

'Over the other side of Canterbury.'

'And what about the pub?' asked Fran. 'Where was that?'

'Over on the way to the A2. Near Harbledown.'

'Not . . .' Libby looked at Fran. 'Not Shittenden, by any chance?'

'That's it! Do you know it?' Pat looked delighted.

'The pub wasn't the Fox and Hounds, was it?' Libby almost held her breath.

'That's the one! You *do* know it!'

'Yes.' She smiled rather half-heartedly. 'I've been there. I was told it wouldn't be there much longer when I went in last year.'

'May, it would have been – or June,' Pat said, nodding. 'Lots of changes round there.'

'Yes,' said Libby, not wanting to go into it. 'Pretty pub. Beauti-ful hanging baskets, I remember.'

'Yes.' Pat smiled reminiscently. 'Very fond of his baskets, was Stan. His wife started them, of course, but when she got the cancer, he learnt how to do them.' She shook her head. 'And then they took it all away from him.'

Libby felt the treacherous closing of her throat and hastily coughed. Fran took over.

'That's awful,' she said. 'Poor Stan.'

'I think it hit him harder than any of us.' Pat sighed. 'And he didn't have a Sir Jonathan to bail him out.'

'Some oast houses over there have been converted into homes, haven't they?' said Libby, having gained control of her voice. 'A property developer went in and built up the whole area. Was it him who bought the pub?'

'Oh no.' Pat shook her head again. 'It was just closed and put on the market. I don't think the developer wanted the competition. He had a sort of community centre in one of the oast houses, you see.'

'So who did buy it?'

'Why, no one!' Pat looked surprised. 'I think it's going to be knocked down.'

'*What?*' exclaimed Fran and Libby together, appalled.

'But it must be a listed building!' said Libby. 'It's beautiful!'

'Don't they just leave some buildings to rot away?' Pat made a face.

'They do, yes,' said Fran. 'They used to do that with the stately homes they couldn't afford. Before the National Trust, anyway.'

'Oh dear.' Libby looked at her. 'This gets worse and worse.'

'You said another couple of licensees retired,' said Fran, turning back to Pat. 'Would they talk to us?'

'They might – but why? They were both ready to retire and they had homes to go to.' Pat let out an unamused laugh. 'Sensible people.'

'What happened to their pubs?' asked Libby. 'Not that it matters, I suppose.'

'Change of use,' said Pat. 'Houses.'

'Right. But the police asked if they would talk to them, so would you ask them for us?' said Fran. 'That's a lot of theys and thems, isn't it?' She smiled at Pat.

'Yes, I suppose so. I'll send them both an email, if that's all right. Then they can answer if they want to, can't they?'

Libby looked as if she were about to protest, so Fran stepped in.

'Yes, we do that with our police contact,' she said. 'And what you've told us is very useful, thank you, Pat.' She looked around the comfortable bar. 'What a pity they couldn't do the same at the Fox and Hounds as you have here.'

'As I said, they haven't got a Sir Jonathan.' Pat glanced up as the door opened to let in more customers. 'I must go, I'm sorry. Did you want anything else?'

They both said no, and watched as she hurried to greet the new-comers, whom she obviously knew. One woman placed a shopping bag full of food on the counter, and another a pile of books. There was much cheerful conversation as these items were taken to the food bank bin and the bookshelves.

'You'd think this sort of thing would take place in the village hall, wouldn't you? Beth said that's where she holds services.' Libby peered hopefully into her mug.

'This is much friendlier than a village hall,' said Fran.

'And I expect the local council own the hall,' said Libby. 'They might charge.'

Fran nodded. 'Well, there's nothing else we can do here, so shall we go and find some lunch? If we have it here, Pat might think we're trying to put pressure on her.'

'OK – where? The only place I can think of on the way back to me is the Poacher.'

'Not exactly on the way,' said Fran, standing up. 'We could go and see Harry.'

'Or I could just do something at home,' said Libby, waving at Pat as they left.

'Not as much fun,' said Fran, surprisingly.

'What's got into you?' Libby gave her friend an assessing look. 'Fun?'

'The Coach, then. It's a pity the Pocket doesn't do food. We could have asked Simon a few questions.'

'Oh, yes! He lost his job at the Puckle Inn because his brewery sold it, didn't he?'

'That wasn't in the current round of sales, though,' said Fran. 'But he might know something about it.'

'He might know something about Marsham's,' said Libby. 'What a pity it's not the sort of pub you can go to for coffee.'

'Which is not actually the point of a pub,' said Fran.

'Well, I seem to have eaten out an awful lot over the past couple of weeks, so I'd be just as happy eating at home. We could buy sandwiches?'

'All right. I'll stop outside the eight-till-late, and you pop in and buy lunch while I turn the car round. OK?'

'OK,' said Libby.

Chapter Sixteen

To Libby's annoyance, Fran's manoeuvre in the middle of the high street was watched with amusement by Harry and Bob the butcher. Harry waved as she came out of the eight-till-late.

'My food not good enough?' he shouted.

Gritting her teeth, Libby crossed the road.

'We're going to mine to talk tactics,' she said. 'I can't keep going out for lunch.'

'All right, petal.' Harry patted her on the shoulder. 'I'll let you off.'

Libby ran up to the Smart car and climbed in.

'That was embarrassing,' she panted.

'I said we should have gone to Harry's,' Fran said smugly.

Back at number 17, Libby put the kettle on and brought her laptop into the kitchen. 'Easier to have a council of war at the table,' she said.

Fran nodded and laid her phone in front of her. 'And now we decide what we tell Ian.'

'Stan's number, for starters, if Pat gets him to agree to give it to us.' said Libby. 'And I wonder if there's a connection between Marsham's – or Roy, at any rate – and Jackie Stapleton.' She looked up. 'Or even Ricky's dad?'

The events of last year that had introduced them to their young friend Ricky and his dog Barney were still having repercussions in the area.

Fran frowned. 'Because they developed the oast houses and Foxhole Close, you mean? And Pat said the developers didn't want competition from the Fox and Hounds.' She sat back in her chair. 'That's worrying.'

'But again, nothing to do with Dickie.' Libby banged the table with her hand. 'It's so frustrating!'

'I wonder how far the legal business has got now? What about attachment of earnings, or whatever it's called?'

'Proceeds of crime?' suggested Libby. 'I don't know how these things work. And who was being prosecuted?' She shook her head. 'I wonder if Ricky comes in for any money, or if it was all whipped away by the courts? That's what you were thinking, isn't it?'

'Yes. I was just wondering about the Fox . . .' Fran got up to pour water into mugs.

'And if Ricky and his mum would buy it for the village? But what village? Shittenden, was it?'

'I never went there,' said Fran, 'but meetings used to be held there, didn't they?'

'Which are now held in the converted oast house,' said Libby. She opened her packet of sandwiches. 'I think it's a non-starter.'

'OK.' Fran sat down again. 'So what do we do next?'

'Go riding at Stella's farm,' said Libby, with a grin.

'By the way,' said Fran, opening her own sandwiches, 'I haven't heard anything of Ricky over Christmas. Isn't he coming to the pantomime?'

'He's been staying with his mum,' said Libby. 'She kicked up a fuss about him staying with Pete and Harry, so he gave in, although he's with them now. But his grandma's bringing him at the weekend.'

'Oh dear!' Fran grinned. 'The dreaded Linda, eh? Will you be polite?'

Linda had now moved to Steeple Martin and become friends with Hetty and Flo, joining the little group of friends who met regularly in Carpenter's Hall in Maltby Close.

'I've managed to avoid her so far,' said Libby. 'But Ricky's going to stay with Peter and Harry until he goes back to uni, so I expect I shall *have* to be polite.'

Fran nodded. 'Into each life . . .'

'And Linda isn't really much of a rainfall,' said Libby. 'But going back to the murder – what shall we do next? I feel we ought to meet Gina.'

'We ought to make up our minds whether we're investigating Dickie's murder or Roy's attack,' said Fran.

'They've got to be linked. But what else do we do? We've asked all the questions Ian wanted us to ask.'

'We could stop?' Fran didn't look hopeful.

'Oh, here we go again,' said Libby with a sigh. 'Look, Ian wanted help. And we're quite good at it.'

'I know.' Fran pushed the remains of her sandwich away. 'I just wish we weren't regarded as interfering old biddies.'

'We aren't!' Libby was shocked.

'Yes, we are. Even Harry calls you Miss Marple.'

Libby scowled. 'He doesn't mean it. And it just goes to show how little the general public know about murder. Books about people like us are called "cosy"! Did you know that? Anything less cosy I can't imagine.'

'I know – you've said it before.' Fran smiled. 'And I agree. Which is why I'm more hesitant than you about getting involved.'

'But we can't help it, can we?' said Libby. 'Because we've got a reputation, people come to us. Even the police.'

'All right, all right. So you think we should somehow engineer a meeting with Gina Marsham?'

'Well, we've heard that Roy was easily led and Dickie was protective of him. So that argues that Gina was doing the leading.'

'And she was shrewd enough to – what? *Ensnare* him after she'd been thrown out of her flat.'

'Yes, which is why I want to talk to Alanna.'

Fran nodded slowly. 'And there's another thing.'

Libby waited. 'And? What thing?'

'We've been told Roy had a gambling problem, and recently he's been selling off properties owned by his brewery. But that money would go to the brewery, not to him personally.'

'And,' added Libby, 'the sales would go through the brewery's accounts, so the Marsham's board would know about them. And as we – or I – have already said, they would have had to approve the sales. So the selling off of assets can't be anything to do with Roy personally.' She sat back with a triumphant grin on her face.

'Which makes Dickie's murder even less likely to be anything to do with Roy,' said Fran.

'Yes. So it must be something to do with his personal life.' Libby took a sip of cold tea and pulled a face. 'Which means the ex-wife?'

'Or Roy's ex-girlfriend.'

'Or the old friend who lives in Spain.' She stood up. 'Who else?' She filled the electric kettle. 'More tea?'

'Yes, please.' Fran put her head on one side. 'You never use your big kettle any more. You used to have it permanently simmering on the Rayburn.'

'This is quicker,' said Libby. 'And I don't use the Rayburn so much any more.'

Fran nodded. 'Energy costs,' she said.

'Anyway,' Libby carried on, 'the only other one I can think of is the girl they mentioned who used to go to the Poacher.'

'Who flitted in and flitted out?'

'That's the one. But that was years ago. I can't think she had anything to do with his life now.' Libby took the used mugs to the sink, rinsed them out and put in fresh teabags. 'In fact, it seems he'd been living over there in Bishop's Bottom for quite some time. You'd think he'd have made more of a local impact.'

'But wasn't it Sandra who said his life was mostly his work?'

'Oh, I can't remember now.' Libby poured boiling water onto the teabags. 'We need to talk to the old friend, too.'

'Libby, stop trying to link this murder to our – I mean Ian's – old cases. You've mentioned Stapleton, criminal expats . . .'

'And what about London villains?' Libby chuckled. 'After all, Edie's friend who found Dickie's body was married to a notorious London criminal.'

Fran laughed. 'Oh, I forgot that! Of course! He was left on her doorstep as a warning!'

'Course he was!' Libby put Fran's mug in front of her. 'But seriously, remember we've come across nasty organised crime in connection with other things where we wouldn't have expected it.'

'Yes, but there's absolutely nothing in this case to link to that sort of activity,' said Fran.

'True.' Libby sat down. 'Oh well. It'll be Alanna next week and hopefully Gina. If I can work out how to bump into her.'

'Pity she isn't coming to the panto,' said Fran. 'You could have put a spell on her.'

'But Alanna's coming tonight,' said Libby thoughtfully.

'You can't interrogate her in the theatre! Think how annoyed you were when Rachel tried to do that to cast members in a play when it was actually running!'

'OK.' Libby shrugged. 'But I can ask her if I can talk to her next week.'

'If you see her. They may not wait after the performance.'

'Of course they will!' said Libby. 'John and Sue will want to speak to me.'

Fran raised an eyebrow. 'Oh, will they now.'

Libby blushed.

The performance on Wednesday night was a little slow to get going after two days off, but by the end of the first scene, everyone had got back into their stride.

'I shan't be sorry to see the end of it, though,' Libby said to Judy in the interval. 'I don't know how I used to do it for months on end.'

'It was your job,' said Judy. 'And it was before you had children.'

'And I had more energy.' Libby shook her head. 'I look at Ian McKellen when he's doing his dame and wonder. I mean – he's older than all of us!'

'Old Brandon seems to be coping all right.' Judy laughed. 'He loves it over at the Manor – he's made quite a pal of Hetty.'

'Oh dear! Joe Wilson won't like that!' Libby grinned.

'He's the old boy we met when we did the concert in Canterbury, isn't he?' said Judy. 'Are he and Hetty a couple?'

'We don't know!' Libby laughed. 'Neither of them will let on.'

Libby went into the auditorium after the performance to find Ben talking to John and Sue, and Alanna talking to Cinderella, to whom Ben had obviously introduced her.

'Loved it!' Stella smiled fondly as Libby joined them. 'And she was most impressed by the lovely life-size picture of Cascade over there.'

Ben had managed to obtain cardboard cut-outs of Cascade and the coach to stand just inside the main doors.

'Oh, good,' said Libby. 'Sometimes at her age they pretend to be bored by panto.'

'It's all new to her,' said Stella. 'She'd never been to one before. We're gradually getting her thoroughly anglicised.'

'Not too much, I hope,' said Libby. 'Are her parents happy – settled – here now?'

'More or less. Her mother's very nervous still. But her dad's got a good job as a mechanic, and they've even loaned him a van so he can get to work from my place. Which is a bit out of the way, you must admit.'

'Oh, that's good.' Libby accepted a glass of wine from Ben. 'Do you think they'd mind if I asked her a couple of questions when I come over next week?'

The smile fell from Stella's face. 'What about?'

'Gina Marsham.' Libby glanced at her nervously. 'I won't . . . um . . . I'll be careful.'

Stella looked away. After a moment, she turned back.

'I'll have to be there.'

'All right. I just want to know what she thought of her. And' – Libby took a breath – 'I want to find out about their eviction.'

Stella looked surprised. 'There's not much to tell.'

'Maybe not,' said Libby, deciding not to go into it any further. 'But I'd like to know. You know I'm part of the protest group in Nethergate?'

'Oh, I see.' Stella nodded. 'Well, if it helps some other poor souls, yeah. But I'll still have to be there.'

Chapter Seventeen

The rest of the week passed in a blur of increasingly subversive pantomime performances. Libby wondered if there would actually be anything left of her script by Saturday night.

The auditorium was crammed for the final performance, completely against all health and safety rules. Various friends and relations without tickets packed the back and the side aisles, and the final curtain – without a physical curtain, of course – went on for a good fifteen minutes, with impromptu gags and songs from cast and audience alike. Libby slid off the stage and went to hide in the dressing room, knowing that if she didn't, she would be paraded around the stage to the strains of 'For She's a Jolly Good Fellow', an embarrassing situation particularly for the audience members who didn't know who she was, or indeed her connection with the pantomime. Apart from being the Fairy Godmother, of course.

Eventually, cast and crew assembled in the auditorium, saying goodbye to their audience.

Ricky and his grandmother, Linda, came over to Libby as soon as she appeared.

'It was great, Lib!' said Ricky, his face pink with excitement. 'Do you think I could join the company?'

Linda raised her eyebrows. 'But you're still at university, Ricky!' She turned to Libby. 'Excellent show, Libby. But I gather there were a few unexpected additions?'

'Oh, yes.' Libby laughed. 'Always happens on the last night.

And of course you can, Ricky – when uni allows, of course. What do you fancy doing?'

'Oh, one of the funny men, of course!' He looked thoughtful. 'And I really enjoyed the Shakespeare back in October. I wonder if—'

'Now, don't start saying you want to change courses,' said Linda, patting his arm. Libby hid a grin. Linda obviously knew her grand-son very well, as she, too, was certain that was what he'd been about to say. Ricky looked somewhat abashed.

Libby reported this conversation to Peter and Harry, who had come to the theatre after closing the Pink Geranium to join in the after-show party.

'He's still on a bit of a high,' said Harry. 'After being miserable for so long, he's now doing almost exactly what he wants, he's able to be the person he wants to be and he's got friends. He just wants to do everything.'

'I don't think Linda wants him to,' said Libby.

'Oh, she's not too bad,' said Peter. 'You haven't tried to get to know her. And she's been great with the family who live in the ground-floor flat.'

Linda had bought the penthouse flat in the converted Garden Hotel from Colin, and Libby had been worried about her attitude towards the families renting the other apartments.

'She has?' She raised her eyebrows.

'Yes – she actually babysits for them!' Harry gave her a dig in the ribs. 'Even picks the kids up from school and nursery sometimes.'

'Blimey!' Libby shook her head. 'All right, I'll make an effort.'

'She could be helpful to you.' Peter went behind the bar and topped up Libby's wine glass.

'Helpful? How?'

'She always asks what you're doing.' Harry leant on the bar.

'When?'

'She comes into the caff almost every day. Coffee in the mornings, usually.'

'I've never seen her in there!'

'No – she's an earlier riser than you are, petal. But I get the feeling that although she enjoys the meetings with Hetty and Flo and that lot, they're all a bit old for her. She's not that much older than you. And she'd love to get involved.' Harry grinned at her. 'Go on – give her a go.'

'I'll think about it,' said Libby dubiously.

Sunday was spent mostly clearing up the theatre. Libby was delighted to see Richard Brandon, Judy and Cyd joining in with the operation, although Cooper Fallon left as soon as he could after Hetty had provided breakfast.

'Busy, busy!' he said to Libby, when he put his head round the theatre door. 'Thanks for the . . . er . . . *opportunity*, Libby. I'll be seeing you.'

'No surprise there, then.' Brandon, wielding the theatre's industrial-sized vacuum cleaner, came up behind her. 'Not the most gracious performer, is he?'

Libby turned with a rueful smile. 'Not exactly. Although he surprised me the other year when we caught the *Puss in Boots* murderer.'

'Self-preservation, that was,' said Brandon. 'Anyway, I just wanted to say, Libby, I'd be happy to do anything down here, if you want me.' He looked slightly sheepish.

'You would?' Libby was surprised. 'But we can't always pay – or at least, not very much.'

Brandon gave her a lopsided smile. 'I was thinking of retiring,' he said. 'Although we never exactly retire, do we? But I've been looking round, and there's a nice little cottage down past your Ben's pub. Cuckoo Lane, is it?'

'Cottage?' Libby gasped. 'You're *moving* here?'

'Why not? I've really enjoyed these last two seasons, and I got

119

on really well with Hetty and her friends. I'm too old to fit in with all the youngsters in London, and I'm not rich enough to live in any of the posh areas. I just feel I fit in here better than I do up there.'

To the imminent danger of the vacuum cleaner, Libby gave him a delighted hug.

'Oh Brandon! That's brilliant!' she said. 'And you do know we do an end-of-the-pier show down at Nethergate every year? You know – in the Alexandria. You've done music hall, haven't you!'

'Oh, I know, dear!' He tapped the side of his nose. 'I came down to see it last year!'

'You didn't! Why didn't you tell us?'

'I didn't want to get in the way.' He gave himself a little shake and picked up the vacuum again. 'So, if you're sure you don't mind me butting in, I'll get on to the agent tomorrow and confirm. I didn't want to do anything until I'd spoken to you.' And he strode off towards the auditorium, almost, Libby thought, with unexpected tears in her eyes, with a spring in his step.

When they'd done as much as they could, Libby announced that she'd stand everyone a drink in the Hop Pocket.

'That's rash,' said Ben, as they locked up.

'They won't all come,' said Libby. 'But I hope Brandon will.'

'Why him especially?' asked Ben.

Libby explained.

'Well I never!' He grinned and shook his head. 'What's the betting we'll have a new addition to Libby's Loonies, then!'

Libby's Loonies was the rather unflattering name given by Harry to the group of friends who supposedly helped out with solving the various mysteries Libby and Fran got themselves involved in.

'I can't see old Brandon doing any sleuthing,' she said.

'Don't forget what a good actor he is. He could be an asset.'

'That's true,' said Libby, and fell quiet until they arrived at the Hop Pocket, where at least half the *Cinderella* cast and crew were already ensconced in the bar.

120

'I'm buying,' she said to Simon, who grinned.

'I know – they told me. I've made you a tab.'

'Oh good,' said Libby, looking resigned.

She and Ben squeezed onto a table with Cyd and Judy, who looked at each other a little nervously, then spoke together.

'We were wondering,' said Cyd.

'Brandon told us,' said Judy.

'Yes?' prompted Ben when they fell silent.

'Well, we like it here too,' said Judy.

'And we wondered . . .' Cyd looked at Judy, then Brandon, who'd joined them, and finally at Ben, 'if we could carry on renting Steeple Farm while we look around.'

Ben cocked an eyebrow. 'Look around?'

Libby smiled.

'I suppose you wouldn't sell it?' burst out Judy.

Ben and Libby laughed.

'No, I'm afraid not,' said Ben. 'As I think we told you, it's been very useful as a refuge and a stopgap for a lot of people over the years. And technically, it belongs to my aunt.'

Peter's mother, Millie, currently resided in an expensive home for the bewildered.

'I told you,' said Cyd. She looked at Ben. 'But could we carry on renting for a bit? Like Judy says, we've loved it here.'

'Don't forget how different it will be without panto,' warned Libby.

'That's why we thought we'd wait a bit. Look round, as we said.' Cyd nodded at her partner. 'Judy's a bit impulsive. I'm a bit more . . . er . . . *staid*.'

Judy laughed. 'Sensible,' she corrected. 'That's why you've still got a house and I haven't.'

'Steeple Martin would be pleased to have you,' said Libby. 'All of you.'

'As long as you don't upstage our regulars,' said Ben.

'Wouldn't dream of it,' said Cyd.

Several of the pub's regulars, including Dan and Moira Henderson and their dog, Colley – who was a golden retriever, despite his name – came over to congratulate the cast.

'Dan, Moira,' said Libby, 'this is Richard Brandon.'

'Oh, yes! The Demon King!' said Moira. 'You're not at all scary really, are you?'

Brandon looked embarrassed.

'He's going to be a neighbour of yours,' said Libby. 'Brandon, Dan and Moira live right at the end of Cuckoo Lane.'

Brandon beamed. 'That lovely house with the five-bar gate?'

'That's the one!' Dan held out his hand. 'Well, this a nice surprise. Welcome to Cuckoo Lane!'

Brandon and the Hendersons fell into conversation, while Colley collapsed on the floor. Libby bent down and stroked his head.

'I'd love a dog,' said Judy.

'Last I heard it was a cat,' said Cyd.

'And a pony,' said Libby.

Judy turned a pretty shade of pink. 'Oh, well . . .'

Simon appeared at Ben's shoulder.

'Could I have a word?' he murmured.

Libby's insides jolted.

'Both of us?' asked Ben, squeezing out of his chair.

Simon nodded, and they followed him to the side door.

'You're looking into Dickie Marsham's murder, aren't you, Libby?' he asked quietly.

'Sort of,' said Libby, casting a quick glance at Ben.

'I heard about it from Izzy at the Puckle.' Simon looked from one to the other. 'I told you I worked there a while ago, didn't I?'

'Yes.' Libby nodded. 'And when it closed, you lost your home.'

'That's right. It was actually a Marsham's pub,' said Simon.

'It can't have anything to do with the current round of closures, though.' Libby frowned.

'Well, no,' Simon agreed, 'it hasn't. But there was a terrific fuss about it at the time.'

'There was?' said Ben.

'Because the money didn't actually find its way into the Marsham's bank account.' Simon looked from one shocked face to the other. 'The accountant was sacked, and prosecuted.'

'Golly!' said Libby.

'But I still don't see what that's got to do with Dickie's murder,' said Ben.

'There are rumours now that the same thing's been happening,' said Simon. 'And somebody thinks Dickie was behind it.'

Chapter Eighteen

'Eh?' Libby's mouth fell open.

'But it's Roy who's in charge of estates!' said Ben. 'And we've heard various theories that . . . Well, I don't know, actually.' He looked puzzled.

'Exactly,' said Libby. 'Nobody's said that Roy's pocketing the money. Have they?' She was puzzled too.

'Look, I probably shouldn't have told you,' said Simon, 'but Izzy said you'd been talking to Pat Bailey at the George. Is that right?'

'Yes. Ian – you know? DCI Connell – he wanted us to find out about the people who'd lost their pubs recently.'

'In the May coup!' Simon smiled.

'Yes, I noticed that it all seemed to happen in May!' said Libby.

'It was almost wholesale. The Fox and Hounds, the George, Izzy's Crown and Sceptre and the others.' He shook his head. 'Now I don't know who's put it about that it was Dickie's fault, because I can't see that at all. As you said, Ben, Roy's in charge of estates.'

'Do you mind me asking where you heard this rumour?' asked Libby. 'Did Izzy tell you?'

'No. She'd heard it, but it came from within Marsham's itself. I know a couple of the reps.'

'Do breweries have reps?' Libby asked.

'Of course they do!' said Ben. 'And they told you?' he asked Simon.

'One of them did. He pops in here for a drink sometimes – he says it's nice to get away from Marsham's beer!'

'I don't get it,' said Libby. 'Did this rumour start before Dickie died? Or after?'

Simon looked surprised. 'I don't know. I only heard about it after he died, but it could have started before.'

'Makes sense if it did,' said Ben. 'That would provide the motive for his murder.'

Libby nodded. 'Of course!' She looked at her feet. 'I don't suppose your friend would . . . er . . . well, would he . . .'

'Talk to you?' Simon was amused. 'I'm sure he would. He was quite upset about the rumours.'

'OK.' Ben shook his hand. 'Thanks, mate. Anything that helps my old dutch here.'

'Oi!' said Libby, and smiled at Simon. 'Thanks, Simon. I'd better go back to my cast. And did you know you'll soon have a new neighbour?'

'Oh yes.' Simon lifted a hand to Brandon. 'He's been in here several times over the last two weeks.'

'That was surprising,' said Libby, as she and Ben walked home a little later.

'On all counts,' said Ben. 'I'm not actually surprised about Brandon, though. I found him in the kitchen with Hetty several times. And Flo and Lenny – and even Joe Wilson.'

'Perhaps he hasn't got many friends back in London,' said Libby. 'It's not an old man's game, is it? And he said he didn't fit in.'

'And what could be better than Steeple Martin?' Ben gave her a smile. 'Theatre, pub on the doorstep, people your own age, and a fair amount of peace and quiet.'

'Except for the odd murder,' said Libby.

As Fran had declined to go riding with her, Libby drove herself to Brooke Farm the following morning. The weather, although not

125

exactly sparkling, was at least dry, and she turned down Pedlar's Row to join the track across the marsh with a pleasurable sense of anticipation.

In the distance she could see the ruins of St Cuthbert's Church and the venerable yew that also bore its name. Slightly to her left was Hobson's, John and Sue's house, and further ahead and very slightly to the right, Brooke Farm. There was nothing else but a few sheep on the tussocky grass between her and the sea.

Stella met her as she parked in the yard.

'I guessed you wouldn't have a hat,' she said, handing one over. 'Nowhere near as nice as the old velour-covered ones, are they?'

'More like motorbike helmets,' agreed Libby. 'Now all I've got to do is remember how to ride.'

'Like riding a bike, as they always say,' said Stella. 'Come on, Alanna's tacking up Punch for you.' She stopped with a hand on Libby's arm. 'I thought, if you don't mind, I'd come with you, and you could talk to her while we're out. She might be more relaxed.'

'Of course – that's a very good idea,' said Libby. 'And she'll be in charge, which will make answering my questions a lot easier from her perspective.'

'Exactly.' Stella gave a satisfied nod. 'Come on, then.'

Alanna beamed happily at Libby from where she stood between a grey who could almost be called dappled and who stood, Libby thought, about fourteen hands, and a lively-looking Exmoor who was a little shorter. Stella went to lead out a more majestic bay with a Roman nose.

'Rajah,' she said. 'Punch is the grey, and Alanna's going to ride Charade, who can be very naughty.'

'How do you do?' said Libby, stroking Punch's nose. He curled his lip at her and butted her arm. 'I think I might need a mounting block,' she continued. 'I haven't climbed anything but stairs for years.'

Alanna fetched a small stool, and, with a little effort, Libby heaved herself into the saddle.

'Gosh!' she said. 'I'd forgotten how high it feels!'

126

Stella mounted Rajah with enviable ease, Alanna fairly flew into the saddle, and they moved off.

For the first fifteen minutes, Libby reaccustomed herself to the experience. Punch, she discovered, had a sensitive mouth, so she had to be careful to keep her hands low and still unless she actually wanted him to do something. But eventually, relaxing, she began to talk to Stella, who, taking her cue, eventually led the conversation in the direction Libby wanted.

'Where did you go to school, Alanna?' asked Libby.

'In Nethergate and then Canterbury,' said Alanna. 'I went to grammar school, but I didn't want to stay on, and anyway, we were living here by then and I could work for Stella.'

'Your English is perfect,' said Libby. 'You've been here a long time?'

'Six years?' Alanna looked at Stella, who nodded. 'And we've lived at Brooke Farm for . . . three years, I think.'

'Bit longer,' said Stella. 'You stayed with me while we had the barn converted, didn't you?'

'Yes.' Alanna turned to Libby. 'We lived in a house in Nethergate – in Marine Parade.'

Libby nodded.

'Only the people who owned it wanted it back. So we had to leave.' Alanna didn't look particularly upset about this, and Libby decided it must be because life now was far more to her taste.

'And Gina lived there, too?' she asked tentatively.

'Jean – yes. She was on her own – not with her parents, I mean. I used to go and talk to her in the evenings sometimes, if she wasn't out. She was nice, then.' Alanna looked thoughtful, but again, not upset.

Libby noted the name Jean.

'But you've seen her since?' she asked.

'Of course. She moved here with her new husband.' Alanna pulled a face. 'I don't like him. And he was one of the people who made us leave the house.'

127

'But Jean married him?'

Alanna laughed. 'Yes! That's why she changed her name. And then made him buy one of the golf club houses. I went there, you know. She's changed. She was like . . . you know . . . all . . .' She frowned.

'Puffed up?' suggested Libby.

'Superior?' said Stella.

Alanna nodded. 'Better than everybody else. Only she isn't.'

Libby and Stella grinned.

At this point, Charade, obviously thoroughly bored by trekking sedately across the marsh, performed a perfect fly buck, and streaked off in front of them. Luckily, Alanna was quick enough to bring him back under control, and wheeled him back to them.

'I'd let him have his head for a bit,' said Stella. 'Libby and I will follow. You OK, Libby?'

Libby, who had noticed certain signs of restiveness in her mount when his friend shot off, nodded. Punch had subsided almost with a sigh of relief that he wasn't going to be asked to perform such outlandish feats.

'Any help?' asked Stella, as Charade and Alanna disappeared into the distance.

'I'm not sure,' said Libby. 'I was interested to hear that Gina was originally called Jean.'

Stella nodded. 'And I did wonder, with her living on her own in a bedsit – at least I assume it was a bedsit – quite what she was doing. I know I'm probably jumping to conclusions, but from what Alanna and her mum said, she didn't seem to have a job.'

'I wondered, too,' said Libby. 'Quite unwarranted, I'm sure, but it's fairly inescapable.' She gently pulled Punch's nose away from a tempting-looking clump of vegetation. 'But she does seem to have got Roy into bad ways, which is what some people are saying.'

'They've been together . . . what?' Stella frowned. 'Three years? That was when the Nethergate building was put up for sale – or

128

turned into holiday lets, at any rate. They've lived in Links View for about eighteen months.'

'When there was all the trouble about the golf club,' said Libby.

'When the first people began to sell their houses, anyway. Not sure when they actually got married.' Stella shrugged. 'Ready for a bit of a trot?'

Libby grinned and nodded. 'The real test. Can I still rise?'

In fact, to her delight, she could, and, it turned out, was perfectly happy at a canter and even a brief gallop.

Back at the yard, Libby insisted she give Punch his rub-down herself. When she led him back to the paddock to join Charade, Rajah and Cascade, who looked slightly grumpy that he hadn't been out having a good time on the marsh, Alanna stopped her.

'I think Roy's a . . . a . . . well, not a nice person,' she said. 'And I don't think Jean is, either. And his brother's been killed, hasn't he?'

'Yes, I'm afraid he has,' said Libby.

'You don't think . . .' Alanna looked down at the muddy ground, then glanced up. 'I don't think Jean would do that, I really don't.'

'I'm sure she wouldn't.' Libby smiled at the girl, who seemed a lot younger than most sixteen-year-olds she had met. 'Now let's go and get Stella to give us a warm drink. It was a lovely ride, thank you, but I'm a bit chilly!'

Alanna allowed herself to be led into the farmhouse kitchen, where Stella assessed the situation in a moment.

'Hot chocolate?' she asked.

'Did she say anything else?' Stella asked, as she saw Libby out to her car.

'She said she doesn't think Roy's a nice man. And I think she has a shrewd idea of what Jean was getting up to in her bedsit.' Libby sighed. 'Poor Alanna, thinking she'd found a friend.'

Stella patted her arm. 'Don't worry about Alanna. She's got plenty of friends now, mostly the girls who come to ride And you were right – we had a lot of enquiries about riding Cascade! But we managed to give most of them the option of learning to ride on Punch.' She looked thoughtful. 'I'm thinking I might have to invest in another pony. Charade isn't suitable for a beginner, as you saw.'

'So will you start being a proper riding school?'

'I'll have to look into all the licences and police checks first.' Stella pulled a face. 'You can't breathe without a licence these days.'

Chapter Nineteen

Libby drove back off the marsh – or Heronsbourne Flats, as it was known to the locals – up Pedlar's Row and on to the Nethergate road. As it was now lunchtime, she decided to stop off at Fran's and persuade her to go to Mavis's for a sandwich.

'I'm on duty,' said Fran, discovered behind the counter at the gallery. 'You go and bring me one back. Guy's gone off to see someone about an exhibition.'

Libby hurried along Harbour Street to the Blue Anchor, which, predictably, was full.

'Need a drop more of your fundraising,' said Mavis gruffly, as she piled tuna mayonnaise onto brown bread. 'Got more than ever in 'ere now.'

Mavis opened the Blue Anchor to people who were either homeless or couldn't afford to heat their homes during the current economic crisis. She provided food for whatever they could pay, and if they couldn't pay anything, that was all right, too. The protest group that Guy, Fran and Libby were involved with had done some fundraising on her behalf.

'How about Kirsty and her family?' asked Libby. 'I don't see them here.'

'No – they actually got into the cottage they were promised. Before it all went tits up.' Mavis looked ferocious. 'Awful bloody business.'

Libby nodded. 'Our barrister – Philip, you know? – he thinks all the homeless people who were promised homes will still get them.'

'Good job too.' Mavis handed over the sandwiches. 'See you've met that Alanna?'

'Where did you hear that?' asked Libby, proffering her bank card to the machine. 'In the paper?'

'Don't get no papers!' scoffed Mavis. 'Saw it online, didn't I? For the panto.'

'Yes – I've just been over there now. She was telling me how she and the other tenants were turned out of their homes a few years back.' Libby waited, eyebrows raised.

'Yeah. Before all this present business.' Mavis nodded. 'Marsham's did that. They owned the building.'

'So I believe. I didn't realise they owned anything except pubs.'

'Owned half of Felling at one time,' said Mavis. 'Back in the old days. Started buying up places here. When the concert party was here. You know about that.'

'Oh, when Nethergate was becoming fashionable? Back in – what? The beginning of the last century?'

Mavis nodded again. 'That'd be about right. Them big houses on Marine Parade.'

'Yes.' Libby was thoughtful. 'So Marsham's was just turning the house back to what it had been before? Holiday property?'

'Yeah, but then it was just fer one family, weren't it?' Mavis shook her head. 'Don't wonder that bloke got murdered.'

'Dickie Marsham? But he wasn't the one who sold off the house on Marine Parade,' said Libby. 'At least . . .' She stopped, frowning. 'I don't think so.'

'You find out,' said Mavis. 'Now, I got to get on. How's that Ricky?'

'He's fine.' Libby smiled. 'And Barney.'

She walked slowly back along Harbour Street, thinking. To her left, the sea was a uniform iron grey, fretting angrily at the empty beach, the ever-present gulls staying noisily inland.

In the gallery, Fran had boiled the kettle ready for her coffee and Libby's tea, and settled down on her stool with her sandwich.

'So what have you got to tell me?' she asked.

'Well,' Libby began, 'first of all – did you know Marsham's owned loads of property back in Edwardian times?'

'I didn't know, but it stands to reason.'

Libby went on to relate what Mavis had told her, then what Alanna had said, and finally a recap on everything else they'd learnt over the past four weeks.

'Do you think Dickie might have been behind the sale of Alanna's building, then?' asked Fran, passing over Libby's mug. 'And Jean – or Gina – took revenge on him? Can't see it myself. It did her a favour, didn't it? Marrying her to Roy.'

'Yes.' Libby stared at one of her own small paintings on the wall behind Fran. 'I think it wipes her out as a suspect.'

'And what about all the dispossessed publicans?'

'The only one who would appear to have a grudge is Stan from the Fox and Hounds. And to be honest, I really can't see any of them being so angry they'd murder a member of the Marsham family.'

'I agree.' Fran dropped her sandwich wrapping in a bin behind the counter and wiped her fingers. 'In fact, the whole pub sale thing is a red herring in my opinion. I'm going to wash my hands. Mind the shop for me.'

Libby looked round the empty shop that formed the front of the gallery. The second week in January was never going to be prime time for selling prints, paintings and assorted merchandise.

'So,' she said, when Fran came back, 'you think we ought to concentrate on Dickie's personal life?'

'I don't think "we" ought to do anything,' said Fran, hoisting herself back onto her stool. 'That's what Ian asked you – us – to do, isn't it? Rob Maiden is looking after that while Ian looks into the police problems.'

'Mmm.' Libby took a sip of tea. 'It wouldn't hurt, then. After all, we got all the info about Dickie's school friend and the ex-girlfriend.'

'You've passed that on, though, haven't you?'

'Yes, of course. I'd still like to explore the Spanish connection, though.'

'As I've said, every one of our cases doesn't have to link up,' said Fran.

'Think about it,' said Libby. 'Number one – local well-to-do family, the Marshams. Number two – best friend. Both live in Felling.'

'We don't know that.'

'Well, all right, but in the area. St Aldeberge, maybe? What's more logical than that the best friend, at least, was part of that nasty little club? Especially as he's run off to Spain like the others.'

The nasty little club had been uncovered during a recent investigation.

'They didn't all run off to Spain,' Fran pointed out. 'And Colin went to live in Spain, too, don't forget, and he's as honest as they come.'

'Oh, all right. Well, what about the whole gambling thing?'

'What about it?' Fran shrugged. 'No one has attacked Roy . . . Oh. They did, didn't they?'

'But not very effectively,' said Libby, nodding portentously. 'But none of it makes any sense really, does it?'

'Not really.' Fran smiled. 'Perhaps we'll just have to stop.'

'Except . . .' Libby suddenly remembered, and grinned.

'What?' Fran looked suspicious.

'What Simon told us yesterday. I can't think why I forgot.' And Libby told Fran about the brewery rep's information.

'Well, that changes things a bit, doesn't it?' said Fran. 'And *Dickie* was suspected?'

'Yes, but that was some time ago. Anyway, I shall report that to Ian.'

'And there's nothing you can do about it, is there?' said Fran reasonably. 'So, as I said, we might as well stop.'

Libby drove home feeling decidedly frustrated. Much as she hated to admit it, Fran was right. There was nothing else they could do, and now there was no panto to occupy her either. Time to think of something else.

When she got home, she reported her minimal findings to Ian's voicemail, including Simon's information, and set about an inventory of her food stocks, sadly ignored and depleted over the past two weeks. This was what she had to do for the foreseeable future, normal day-to-day tasks and no ferreting about in unsavoury murder cases.

Over the next two days, she managed to do just that. She renewed Judy and Cyd's contract for Steeple Farm, checked that all was well with the hoppers' huts ready for the summer season, resisted doing the same for the rooms at the Manor, rather than risk Hetty's displeasure, and called a meeting of the Oast Theatre's board (Peter, Ben and herself) to finalise the coming year's programme. This took place at the Coach and Horses on Wednesday evening before Patti and Anne joined them after dinner at the Pink Geranium.

Libby had also asked Judy and Cyd to join them, and when Ben informed her that Brandon had booked a room at the Coach prior to moving into his cottage in Cuckoo Lane, invited him, too.

'After all, they joined us before the panto opened, didn't they? They're all friends.' she said to Ben after they'd agreed on the theatre programme.

'Who did?' said a new voice.

'Colin!' Libby turned delightedly. 'Haven't seen you for ages. And Gerry!'

Hugs and greetings were exchanged, and Gerry went to the bar.

'So are you just visiting, or is this landlord business?' asked Peter. 'Everything's all right with the Garden, isn't it?'

'Oh, yes, thanks.' Colin pulled up a chair. 'The rented flats are full of happy families, and Ricky's grandma is trying to take over the village from the penthouse.'

Libby laughed. 'No chance! In fact, I've hardly seen her. She came to the panto with Ricky, but she isn't interfering in anything, although she's joined *everything*.'

'Good.' Colin looked round as Gerry put his drink in front of him. 'Actually, we wanted a word before Ian comes in – if he does, of course.'

'Oh?' Libby, Ben and Peter pulled their chairs closer. 'What about?'

'Dickie Marsham,' said Gerry, causing gasps of astonishment from his listeners.

'*Dickie?*' repeated Libby.

'Yes.' Colin looked down, then back up, a frown on his face. 'We'd both met him, you see, out in Spain.'

'Ah.' Libby nodded. 'Was I right, then? Anthony Leigh?'

'Right about what?' Peter looked bewildered.

'Dickie's oldest friend was Anthony Leigh,' explained Libby, 'who went to live in Spain. I wondered if . . . well, if he was anything to do with the St Aldeberge business.'

'Was he?' Peter turned to Colin. 'Or is the old trout making bricks with straw again?'

Colin shook his head. 'Honestly, we don't know. But yes, Dickie used to come out to visit Anthony. And Anthony knew Nick Nash. Remember him?'

'How could we forget?' muttered Ben.

Colin took a deep breath. 'And Nick introduced me to Anthony because we came from the same area. So he introduced me to Dickie.'

'You didn't mention this when we saw you at the Christmas quiz,' said Libby.

'To be honest, neither of us had realised who it was then,' said Gerry. 'It was only when people started talking about his brother that we put two and two together.'

'Talking about Roy?' said Ben. 'Why?'

'Oh, his house was attacked on Christmas Eve – didn't you know?' said Colin. 'They were talking about it in the Fox.'

'Oh, yes, we know about that,' said Libby.

'Well, then we realised. And, well . . .' Gerry looked at Colin, 'we just thought, with everything that had happened before, perhaps we ought to mention it.'

'I'm not at all sure I followed all of that,' said Peter, 'but if it does have anything to do with, as our friend here says, all that St Aldeberge business, yes, you should mention it.'

'Right.' Colin let out a breath. 'We wanted to speak to you before Patti and Anne came in, you see.'

'Good idea,' said Ben, 'and just in time, as it happens.' He nodded towards the door, where Patti was manoeuvring Anne's wheelchair inside, followed by Judy, Cyd and, surprisingly, Brandon.

'Judy and Cyd invited me to dinner with them,' he explained, 'and we met up with these lovely ladies. If I'm intruding . . .?'

'Of course not,' said Libby. 'You've met everyone before, haven't you?'

'Not us,' said Colin, standing up and holding out a hand. 'I'm Colin, and this is Gerry. We used to live here, but we've moved to Heronsbourne.'

'And I'm just moving in,' said Brandon. 'Lovely to meet you.'

By tacit agreement, the subject of Dickie Marsham was abandoned and the conversation revolved around the more pleasant subject of moving to the area. Anne had just finished extolling the virtues of her little close off New Barton Lane, where, she said, there was a two-bedroomed bungalow for sale, when Harry burst through the door, followed by Ian.

'I need alcohol,' Harry announced. 'I am devastated by the lack of paying customers.'

'We were there!' protested Anne.

'But how many others?' He threw himself into a chair. 'Five of you for the whole evening. Wouldn't keep a cat alive.' He looked at Libby. 'Especially not your cat, petal.'

Ian, amused, went to the bar. Colin got up and followed him. Gerry and Libby exchanged looks.

'So,' said Patti, clearing her throat and sitting up straight, 'what's next at the theatre, Lib?'

Everyone smiled, and Anne unsuccessfully stifled a giggle.

'We've got a few one-nighters,' said Libby, 'an Ayckbourn in March, two visiting companies, and then the Glover's Men again in midsummer with the *Dream*. It's going to be a proper midsummer production, with a summer fair outside – you know, where we had the beer festival. Then we've got the end-of-the-pier show in Nethergate for the whole of August.'

'Can we be involved in that?' asked Cyd. 'I can do a great Marie Lloyd!'

'And I can do "The Night I Appeared as Macbeth"!' said Brandon.

'The more the merrier,' said Libby. 'And you're welcome to audition for anything else, obviously.'

'Which Ayckbourn is it?' asked Judy.

'*Woman in Mind*,' said Libby, looking wistful.

'And guess who wants to play Susan,' said Ben, with a grin.

'Who's Susan?' asked Patti.

'The main character,' said Judy. 'Absolutely brilliant part.'

Libby nodded, still keeping a wary eye on Ian and Colin at the bar.

'I shouldn't have moved away!' said Gerry, with rather forced brightness. 'I could have played one of Susan's sons!'

'She's not old enough to have you as a son,' said Colin, returning to the table.

'Got a minute, Libby?' said Ian, still standing by the bar.

Libby stood up, amid a sudden silence.

'What?' she said nervously, coming to stand next to him.

'It's all right.' He still looked amused. 'You haven't done anything wrong.'

'Oh.' Libby fidgeted. 'What is it, then?'

'Colin told you about meeting Dickie Marsham in Spain?'

'Yes.'

'And about his friend Anthony, who you told me about?'

'Yes.'

'And who you obviously thought might be involved in that unpleasant business connected to Patti's church?'

'Yes.' Libby fidgeted some more.

Ian smiled. 'Well, who knows? You could be right.'

Chapter Twenty

'Eh?' Libby blinked and stepped back.

'We – or rather, I – looked into everything you found out. And Anthony Leigh appears to be the archetypical Costa criminal.' Ian laughed at her expression. 'I know. It's too trite to be true, isn't it?'

'Oh, for . . .' Libby left the sentence unfinished. 'Next you'll be telling me he knew Chloe Vaughan's husband.'

'Mickey Vaughan? Quite likely.' Ian put his head on one side. 'See? Sometimes your wild theories can be right.'

Libby shook her head. 'I don't believe it.'

'No. I didn't either.' He sighed. 'But it might be as well if you stepped back now. The criminal fraternity won't take kindly to you – or us, for that matter – poking into their business, and it could put you in danger.'

'Do you think that's what happened to Dickie?' asked Libby.

'It's a possibility,' said Ian, 'but we've got a lot more digging to do yet.'

'What about the information about the brewery? Can you look into that?'

'We are, but so far we aren't having much luck.'

Libby was quiet for a moment.

'How much can I tell Fran?' she asked eventually.

'As much as you like. But be a little more circumspect with the others.' Ian looked round to where Colin was holding court. 'Although I think that horse has bolted.'

'They're all trustworthy,' said Libby.

'But the three newcomers are unknown quantities,' said Ian. 'Please be careful, Lib.'

'I don't think they've got connections with the criminal under-world,' said Libby.

'Although your friend Judy did end up losing her home as a result of debt, didn't she?'

'Yes, but we know who she was in debt *to*,' insisted Libby. 'She's all right. And she and Cyd are moving here.'

'So they must be all right, of course.' Ian chuckled. 'More additions to the Loonies.'

Libby smiled ruefully. 'I suppose so.'

'Let's go back to the others.' He took her arm. 'Do you need another drink?'

'Probably,' said Libby.

They returned to a table full of expectant faces.

'Very exciting living in Steeple Martin,' commented Brandon, draining his pint. 'Anyone for another drink?'

Libby silently blessed him for diverting attention and sat down next to Ben. Colin looked at her, then at Ian.

'I didn't tell them all of it,' he said. 'Just scratched the surface.'

'And that was enough,' said Anne. 'It's all connected to Patti's church, isn't it?'

Ian shook his head. 'No, it isn't. The only connection is that our most recent murder victim knew a typical Costa criminal, and we – or should I say you – have come across those before.'

'Suitably vague,' muttered Ben.

'Not all the criminals in Spain come from St Aldeberge and Felling,' said Patti. 'It's just a coincidence, isn't it, Ian?'

'It is, yes.' Ian smiled at her. 'The voice of reason.'

The conversation then returned to matters theatrical and became quite animated when Cyd suggested a trimmed-down version of the concert she and Judy had performed in back in the autumn. Brandon was particularly enthusiastic.

'He looks ten years younger, doesn't he?' Libby murmured to Ben. 'The energising air of Steeple Martin.'

'Coupled with the uplifting benefits of Ben's Best Bitter,' said her beloved.

'Not in this pub.' She gave him a dig in the ribs. 'He has to have that in the Pocket.'

'No, actually. Tim's taking a barrel or two of mine now. He says he'd lose even more custom if he didn't.'

'Oh, Ben!' Libby looked worried. 'Is he really bothered?'

'No, of course not.' Ben patted her arm. 'And we're already talking about sharing the beer tent at the summer fete.'

'Really? We're having a tent?' Libby's eyebrows rose in surprise.

Ben grinned. 'Don't take me so literally, Lib.'

'Oh.' She pulled an apologetic face. 'Sorry.'

As they were all making preparations to leave, Libby noticed Ian finishing a large whisky.

'Taxi?' she asked. 'Or Hetty?'

Ian often stayed at the Manor on his social visits to Steeple Martin.

'Peter and Harry,' he said. 'Harry's idea. He said he's got used to having visitors in the spare room now that Ricky comes so often.'

'Well don't completely ignore your room at the Manor,' said Ben, coming up behind them. 'Hetty would be heartbroken.'

Ian laughed. 'Wouldn't dream of it.'

'I must say,' said Libby, head on one side, 'you seem a lot more cheerful than you did before Christmas.'

'That's because I am.' He winked. 'I've finished investigating my slice of the police service. They all passed with flying colours!'

Libby and Ben laughed.

'Now there's a surprise!' said Ben.

'What did Big Bertha say?' asked Libby.

'Not a lot.' Ian grinned and followed Peter and Harry out of the door.

'He fudged it,' said Ben. 'Good for him.'

'I just hope it doesn't come back to bite him,' said Libby. 'The force is under such pressure at the moment.'

'Quite rightly. They aren't all as morally upright as our lot, by any means.'

'I know.' Libby sighed. 'Go and help Patti with Anne's chair. She's stuck again.'

The following morning, Libby phoned Fran to tell her about Colin's and Ian's revelations.

'And Ian wants us to step back in case we get caught up in dangerous criminal activity,' she concluded.

'By the sound of that, you don't intend to,' said Fran.

'Yes, I do! I just thought it might be interesting to chat to Edie's friend. You know, the criminal's widow.'

'How interesting?'

'You know – what was it like being part of that world . . .' Libby trailed off.

'And why was a dead body dumped on her doorstep,' snapped Fran. 'Honestly, Libby! You're incorrigible.'

'Oh, yes. I hadn't thought of that.'

'What do you mean, you hadn't thought of it? Edie told you right at the beginning that the police had thought of the connection between the body and what's-his-name Vaughan.' Libby could almost see Fran shaking her head.

'Oh, all right,' she said. 'I'll leave it alone.' She paused. 'Unless something else happens.'

Nothing else did happen over the next couple of days, at least nothing that concerned the police investigation into Dickie Marsham's death or the attack on his brother's house.

On Sunday, she and Ben wandered up to the Manor as usual for

Sunday lunch. They were not unduly surprised to find Flo and Lenny there, as well as Joe Wilson, Hetty and Lenny's friend from Nethergate, Edward, and Colin and Gerry. They were far more surprised to see, squashed in around the big kitchen table, Lewis and Edie Osbourne-Walker.

'I wanted to talk to you, Libby,' said Edie, after greetings had been exchanged. 'You remember I told you about my friend Chloe?'

'Of course,' said Libby, squeezing a chair in between Edie and Lewis.

'Well, she's a bit worried.' Edie shot a quick look at her son. 'Lewis don't think it's anything to worry about, but I think he's just saying that to make me feel better. But what I say is, Chlo's got no one around to help her, not like I have, so I ought to do my best.'

Lewis gave Libby a wry smile. 'And of course, she's right, my ma. She always is.'

'All right, Edie. So what's Chloe worried about?' Libby asked, accepting a glass of something red and expensive from Lenny.

'She's had a couple of these letters, see.' Edie chewed her lip.

Libby looked at Lewis. 'Letters?'

'Yes, those sort of letters,' he said. 'Not saying exactly anything, really. Just . . . you know . . . a friendly warning.'

'And she's got a cat,' said Edie.

Libby immediately understood the underlying meaning of this gnomic utterance.

'Has she spoken to the police?' she asked gently.

'No. She says that'll make it worse. You remember what those London gangs are like.' Edie shook her head gloomily. 'And Mickey Vaughan were in with the worst of 'em.'

'I think you should speak to the police, Edie. Ian's been looking into a London connection already.' Libby mentally crossed her fingers and hoped he had. 'Do you think she's safe in her little house?'

'No,' said Edie firmly.

Lewis gave in. 'All right. She can come to us. Cat and all.'

Edie and Libby both beamed at him.

'I'll give her a ring now,' said Edie. 'Can we pick her up on the way home?'

'It's hardly on the way home, Ma.' Lewis blew out a breath. 'Taxi down here?'

Edward leant across the table. 'Ian's coming from Canterbury. He could pick her up. Sorry for eavesdropping.'

'That's all right, luvvie.' Edie reached over and patted his arm. 'Good idea.'

'Shall I ring him, or will you?' asked Libby. 'I think it would be better coming from you.'

Edward laughed. 'I'll do it now. Warn your friend that a big bad policeman's coming to get her, Edie.'

After a good deal of resistance from Chloe, her transfer to Creekmarsh via Steeple Martin was set up, Ian being of the opinion that the quicker the better in the circumstances.

'So he thought it was serious?' asked Ben, when Libby returned to her seat next to him.

'I think he just thought she shouldn't take any chances,' said Libby. 'I wonder if they were real threats?'

'How do you mean, real?'

'If these people – criminals, whoever – really had something to do with Dickie's death, or if they're just using it to make sure Chloe doesn't step out of line.'

'Step out of line how?' Ben frowned.

'Well, she must know where *some* of the bodies are buried, surely? Metaphorically speaking.'

'Hmm.' He glared at his wine glass. 'You've got a tortuous mind.'

Colin and Gerry were bearing huge dishes of vegetables to the table, and Ben went to relieve his mother of the enormous joint of pork, supplied, of course, by Bob the butcher.

'I dunno how she does it, you know,' said Edie. 'She never knows how many she'll have round her table, does she?'

Flo cackled. 'Always gets enough for fifty. Leftovers feed 'er fer a week.'

'And me,' said Ben.

'Only for lunch,' said Hetty. 'Now sit down and let's get on with it.'

Lunch was over and the older members of the company had retired to Hetty's sitting room by the time Ian came into the kitchen.

'If you don't mind, Lewis,' he said, 'I suggest you go home straight away. There's a lady outside with a very angry cat in a basket.'

'Oh, bloody hell!' Lewis shot up from his seat at the table. 'I'll go and get Ma.'

'Thank you for doing this, Ian,' said Libby. 'Edie was obviously very worried.'

Ian gave her a tired smile. 'So was the lady herself. I wish she'd come to us straight away when she got the first letter.'

'When was that?' asked Libby.

'How many have there been?' added Ben.

'The first was before Christmas. Two since then. She's been working herself up into a state of terror ever since.'

'Oh, poor woman!' Libby turned from the dishwasher and grabbed a tea towel.

'No, Libby.' Ian put out a hand. 'Don't go interrogating her. She's already had to suffer me turning up on her doorstep and whisking her out of her safe place. Let her go home with Lewis and Edie and settle in. I've got all the details.'

Lewis reappeared in the kitchen doorway. 'Mum's gone straight out to the car,' he said. 'She said sorry not to say goodbye.'

'I'll come and wave you off,' said Libby, giving Ian a don't-you-dare-stop-me look.

'We all will,' said Colin.

Everyone trooped outside to see Ian go and speak to the little lady in the back of Lewis's car, then waved them off down the drive.

'Come and get yer dinner,' came Hetty's gruff voice from behind them.

Ian smiled and went to give his hostess a kiss. 'You're a life-saver, Hetty,' he said. 'And you lot, don't sit round watching me. Go off to the pub or Pete and Harry's or something. I'll join you later.'

'Well,' said Libby, watching him go back into the house. 'What about that, then?'

Chapter Twenty-One

There being too many of them to fit into Peter and Harry's small sitting room, they opted for the Hop Pocket, 'Although it doesn't feel right,' Libby complained. Harry having already closed the Pink Geranium, he and Peter joined them, and Libby filled them in on the surprising events of the last few hours.

'That was all a bit quick, wasn't it?' said Harry.

'And nobody knew anything about the situation beforehand?' asked Peter, as Simon's occasional helper, Gwennie, placed a tray of drinks on the table.

'Well, we knew that Edie's friend had found Dickie's body and that she was worried she'd be a suspect because of her late husband.' Libby regarded her glass of red wine with a worried frown. 'I'm not sure I should drink any more, you know.'

There were exclamations of astonishment from the entire company.

'We'll carry you home if necessary, petal,' said Harry.

'It does seem rather sudden,' said Ben.

'Ian must have thought it was urgent,' said Colin.

'Yes, but it was us who set it all in motion, once Edie had told us about the letters,' said Libby. 'I'd have said we were overreacting, but Edie wanted to ring Chloe straight away.'

'And I was the one who suggested calling Ian,' said Edward. 'Sorry.'

'No, you obviously did the right thing,' said Gerry. 'He wouldn't have agreed if, as Col said, he didn't think it was urgent.'

There were murmurs of agreement at this.

'And what about Anthony Leigh?' asked Colin. 'Did Ian do anything about that after I said we knew him?'

'No idea.' Libby shrugged. 'He told me to keep out of it, so I have.'

'Wonders will never cease!' said Peter, casting his eyes to heaven.

'So what are you going to do, Lib?' asked Edward. 'I can't see you leaving it there.'

'I don't know.' Libby looked round the table at her friends. 'Whatever I suggest, you'll all moan at me.'

'Too true,' said Ben. 'At the risk of being labelled a misogynistic old so-and-so, why don't you stay at home for a few days?'

'And do yer tatting,' added Harry.

Monday morning, and the pantomime seemed months away, normal service had been resumed. And Libby didn't know what to do with herself.

It appeared that various other people were expecting her to know what was going on in the investigation, if not expecting her to be actively involved. Sandra Farrow being the first.

'I just wondered if you'd heard anything more about Dickie?' she said. 'We haven't seen anything online, or on the local news.'

'No.' Libby let out a sigh. 'I haven't heard anything. The police know about his old school friend, and I spoke to his sister, Ruth. But otherwise – no, I don't know.'

'Oh.' Sandra sounded disappointed.

'Sorry,' said Libby.

'Well, never mind. We're coming over to the Hop Pocket on Friday for a darts match – did you know?'

'No!' Libby was surprised. She was still taken aback by the success of Ben's pub, and to tell the truth, still worried that he was taking custom from her beloved Coach and Horses. Sandra put her mind at rest.

'It was Tim's suggestion. He felt that the Coach wasn't quite the place for darts these days, so the Pocket is now in the league.'

'He still hosts the chess club, though,' said Libby, grinning to herself.

The next phone call was from Sid Best at the Poacher.

'Been to see my mate Jenny yet?' he asked.

'Jenny?' Libby frowned. 'Oh – at the Bell and Butcher! No, I'm still recovering from the panto, and the police don't need me any more.'

'Oh.' Sid went quiet. 'It's just . . .' he went on slowly, 'everyone's a bit worried.'

'How do you mean?' Libby's metaphorical ears pricked up.

'Tenants and managers. They can't seem to get through to anyone at Marsham's. I wondered if you knew what was going on.'

'No, I've no idea.' Libby thought for a moment. Was this to do with what Simon had told them? 'Perhaps I'd better try and find out.'

'Go and see Jen. She can tell you more.'

Libby thought about what Sid had said while she had her lunch, and decided to ask Fran to accompany her to the Bell and Butcher in the next few days. At least she now had something to do, she thought.

And then, just as she was about to call Fran, the landline rang.

'Libby, it's Edie.'

'Edie? What can I do for you? How's Chloe?'

'That's what I was ringing about, ducks. I wondered if you'd fancy popping over here to see her?'

'Really?' Libby felt a familiar lurch of apprehension somewhere under her ribcage.

'Well, she don't know much about police investigations.'

'I would have thought she did, with her husband being . . . um . . .'

'Yeah, I know, but that was more them turning up on the doorstep and hauling him away. No polite questions, an' that.'

'Oh, I see. OK. Will tomorrow morning be all right?'

'Er . . . yes. That'll be OK. Stay to lunch?'

'Actually, I was supposed to be going somewhere else for lunch,' said Libby, making up her mind to go to the Bell and Butcher.

'OK. We'll see you tomorrow, then.'

Edie sounded disappointed, thought Libby.

'I think she wanted me to go over this afternoon,' she said to Sidney, and peered out of the window. The sky was grey and lowering, and it would be dark by four. No, tomorrow morning would be better. She called Fran to tell her.

'Do you want me to come with you?' asked Fran.

'I thought maybe to the Bell and Butcher,' said Libby, 'but I suppose we'd better not overwhelm poor Chloe.'

'All right. We're not busy now, so Guy won't mind me having the afternoon off.'

'Oh, come on! He doesn't keep you working all day every day anyway.'

'No, I know. But now Sophie's not here all the time . . .'

'She's got this posh new job now, hasn't she?'

'At the Bullivant Museum in Canterbury,' said Fran proudly. 'That's where she met her new chap.'

'Oh yes – you never did tell me about him.'

'He's very nice, very studious, divorced with two kids.'

'Good Lord! Are we old enough for our kids to have divorced partners?'

'Scary, isn't it?' Fran laughed. 'Call me when you're on the way to the pub tomorrow and I'll meet you there.'

'At least you've got something to do now,' said Ben later, unconsciously echoing Libby's own thoughts.

'You don't mind, do you?' she asked anxiously, looking up from her shepherd's pie.

'I suppose not,' he said with a sigh. 'And I must say, I'm intrigued to know who killed the poor bloke. I would have said it was a mugging, given where he was found, but obviously the police don't think so.'

'That's a point,' said Libby. 'Nobody even suggested that, did they? Once they knew who it was. While we thought it was a homeless person, I suppose that's what everyone thought.'

'Edie's friend didn't recognise him, did she?'

'I wouldn't have thought so,' said Libby. 'Although her anonymous letters would suggest a connection. I don't know. I'll ask her tomorrow.'

'I wonder what the connection actually is?' Ben frowned. 'His brother's gambling debts?'

'That seems to be one theory, but why kill Dickie and not Roy?'

'Because while Roy's alive there's a chance of getting the money?'

'Maybe.' Libby stared at her plate. 'I wonder if Chloe's husband knew Wally Willis?'

'Who?' Ben looked startled.

'You remember. You met him when we had the *Pendle* ballet here.'

'Oh yes! Central casting London gangster, barathea coat and all.' Ben grinned. 'And Hetty sent him off with a flea in his ear.'

Libby laughed. 'Not scared of anyone, our Het!'

'Actually, of course, it's quite possible they knew one another,' said Ben. 'But I can't see that that's got anything to do with the Marsham murder.'

'No, I know. I just wondered.' Libby pushed her plate away. 'Finished?'

Tuesday morning, and the weather continued grey and threatening. Libby sent Lewis a text to say she would probably arrive between ten and ten thirty, tripped over Sidney on the way out, and set off for Creekmarsh.

On the way, she passed the Red Lion and Pedlar's Row and continued past the golf club and The Drive, where Colin and Gerry now lived. Turning off opposite the Fox, she drove down the little lane and past the disused church to Creekmarsh, where she was surprised to see Adam with a wheelbarrow.

'I didn't think you were working here at the moment,' she said, climbing out of the car. 'It's winter.'

'There are still things to do, Ma. Actually, we're restoring the orangery. Lewis wants to start growing pineapples.' He grinned at her. 'Going to grill the newest resident?'

'No – she's *asked* to see me, cheeky.' Libby grinned back.

Edie appeared at the door that led to the kitchen.

'Come in, love,' she called. 'Don't let that rascal hold you up!'

Libby winked at Adam and went into the house.

'This is Chloe,' said Edie, patting the elderly lady sitting at the kitchen table on the shoulder. 'Chlo, this is our Libby.'

Chloe peered up as Libby held out her hand. 'Can't see very well, dear,' she said. 'Sorry.'

'Don't worry about it,' said Libby. 'I'm not much to look at anyway.'

Chloe laughed a trifle uncertainly.

'Now, sit you down, Libby. Tea?'

'Yes, please, Edie. Lewis not here? I sent him a text.'

'Upstairs in his room,' said Edie. 'Thought Chloe would feel easier without him here. He says to pop up and see him before you go.'

'They've been so good,' said Chloe. 'Even Bertie's quite happy.'

And Libby saw she had a very large black fur ball on her lap.

'Wasn't too happy on the way down,' said Edie, putting a big enamel teapot on the table.

'Well, he'd been pushed into his basket without any warning!' said Chloe. 'He doesn't like change, you see.'

'Had to bring his litter tray, too,' said Edie with a grin. 'Your Ian had to put it in his boot. Not sure he was too pleased about that.'

'Yes, but I couldn't let Bertie out in a strange place, could I?' Chloe looked at Libby. 'Could I?'

'No, you couldn't. I've got a cat, too, and he doesn't like change either.' Libby smiled at Chloe and leant forward. 'I'm sorry we more or less kidnapped you yesterday. But it was for the best.'

'Oh, yes, dear – I quite understood. Edie told me on the phone, and that nice policeman explained it was for my own safety.' Chloe shook her head. 'I don't understand why I've been threatened, though.'

'Is that what the letters were? Threats?'

'Sort of, dear. See, when I found that body . . .' She stopped and closed her eyes. 'Well, that was horrible. And first of all I thought – oh, dear, they'll think it was me because of my Mickey.'

'Yes, Edie told me,' said Libby.

'And then the police left me alone, so I didn't worry. Until this letter arrived.'

'What did it say, exactly.'

'What was it, Edie?' Chloe peered across at her friend.

'Just be careful if you know what's good for you, wasn't it?' Edie poured out the tea. 'More or less. Typewritten, of course. Or done on a computer, anyway.'

'I see.' Libby nodded. 'And then you got more?'

'Yes. And they said much the same. Keep your mouth shut, sort of thing.'

'But they didn't say why? Had you recognised the . . . um . . . the body?'

'No, dear.' Chloe shuddered. 'Not that I looked very close, you know.' She paused to sip her tea. 'Thought he was asleep – or drunk – at first. I poked him with me stick.'

Libby tried and failed to stifle a laugh. She needn't have bothered. Edie and Chloe both giggled.

'Why didn't you tell anyone when you received the first letter?' asked Libby.

'Well, I thought . . .' Chloe looked down at her cat. 'I thought

154

it'd make 'em look at me more close.' She looked up. 'But then I got scared. So I told Edie.'

'Did you go up to London over Christmas?' asked Libby after a short pause.

Edie and Chloe looked startled.

'No, why?' said Chloe.

'She come here,' said Edie. 'Only she hadn't had the other two letters by then.'

'So no one would have seen you. No one you used to know, I mean.'

'No, dear. My kids wanted me to go to them, but I don't travel so well these days.'

'Oh? Where do they live?'

'Sharayne and her hubby live in Liverpool, and Kyle and his Kiala are in Spain.'

Chapter Twenty-Two

'*Spain?*'

Chloe looked thoughtful. 'Not that it isn't easier to get to them rather than Sharayne.'

Libby cleared her throat. 'Yes, I suppose it might be. Whereabouts in Spain?'

'Oh, down south. You know, the posh part.' Chloe smiled fondly. 'They've got lots of friends there.'

'I bet,' said Libby hoarsely.

Edie shot her a sharp look. 'We got friends who used to live in Spain, haven't we, Libby?' she said. 'Wonder if they know each other?'

'Oh, I shouldn't think so,' said Chloe. 'Big place, Spain.'

'You'd be surprised,' muttered Libby. She took another sip of tea. 'So why do *you* think you were threatened, Chloe?'

Chloe sat back in her chair, stroking Bertie. 'It must be because he – the body, you know – had something to do with my Mickey's mates. Don't you think so? That's what I told your policeman. He wondered why the first policemen hadn't bothered to find out.'

'But you hadn't had the letters then.'

'Yes, but like I said right at the beginning, I was a link, wasn't I? I was surprised when they didn't even come and ask me any questions.' She sighed. 'I'm used to that. But not to this sort of thing. It was more "Was Mickey at home that night?", not complicated stuff like this.'

'Mmm.' Libby swirled the remaining tea in her mug. 'So why would any of Mickey's old friends kill someone? I mean, would they actually go that far?'

'Oh, you didn't like to ask, dear,' Chloe said. 'My Mickey kept his nose clean. He used to say he mostly did admin and supplies.' She laughed. 'Still got him banged up, though.'

'Were they involved in gambling? That sort of thing?'

'Oh, yes, dear. Clubs and everything. And racing. Dogs and horses.' She hitched a shoulder. 'None o' this modern stuff, though. You know, people smuggling. Cruel, that.'

Libby blinked a little at this.

'So what Chloe wanted to ask you, Lib, was what you thought she ought to tell the police now,' said Edie. 'Should she give them any names? You know, of the people Mickey worked with?'

'To be honest, Chloe, I don't think you need to,' said Libby, after a moment. 'They know who you are and who you were married to. I would imagine they know exactly who Mickey was involved with. Let's face it, DCI Connell was worried enough to whisk you down here as soon as we told him about the letters. That means they've got a good idea where they came from – or at least the likely area.'

'I suppose so.' Chloe went back to stroking Bertie, who had stirred enough to pat her arm with a large black paw. Just to remind her he was there. 'I just wish I could go back to how I was.' Her voice cracked a little. 'Not that it isn't lovely being here, but . . .' She looked down.

'I know, ducks,' said Edie softly. 'Horrible feeling that something's hanging over you.'

Chloe looked up and smiled gratefully. 'And you must think I'm a silly old woman, Libby. I could've worked out everything you've told me myself, couldn't I?'

'You don't know that what you tell yourself is the truth, though, do you?' Libby said. 'You need someone else to tell you you *aren't* being a silly old woman. And you're not.'

'No.' Chloe looked down at her cat. 'And I was worried about him, see? You hear of such things. And he was used to going out. I had a job to keep him in. It's easier here.'

'Because it's not his home territory,' agreed Libby. 'So, is there anything else you want to talk to me about?'

'No, I don't think so, is there, Edie?' Chloe looked at her friend. 'It's awful nice of you to come all this way just to see me, dear.'

'Oh, it's never any trouble to come and see Edie!' said Libby. 'And now I'll just pop up and see Lewis. Won't be a minute.'

Upstairs, Libby found Lewis in his solar, with its beautiful view across the park and gardens.

'Done yer ministering angel bit, then?' he said, turning from his seat in the window.

'She just needed a bit of reassurance,' said Libby. 'It was all so sudden yesterday, wasn't it? And Bertie was upset!'

'Bloody cat!' said Lewis with feeling. 'I've still got the scars.'

'Well, I hope I've made her feel better.' She wandered over to look out of the window. 'Did you know her son lived in Spain?'

'I don't think so.' Lewis frowned. 'Oh. Now don't go linking him up with all the other Spanish villains!'

'Everyone keeps telling me that,' said Libby. 'It's just such a coincidence.'

'Look, Lib.' Lewis sat forward, hands on his knees. 'Lots of villains went to Spain back in the day. These days they all pole off to the Caribbean or the Seychelles. They don't all know one another, and they aren't all involved in the same dodgy dealings. It's just that you seem to get involved with a lot of criminals, so you think they're all connected.'

'Yes, yes, I know.' Libby turned back from the window. 'Now I'd better get off. I'm meeting Fran in Steeple Mount.'

'Steeple Mount? What's goin' on there?' Lewis looked surprised.

'We're going to the pub – the Bell and Butcher. Do you know it?'

'No. What are you going there for? Adding it to your list of Pubs I Have Known?'

'It's a Marsham's pub,' said Libby, 'and the landlady has something to tell us about the brewery.'

'Oh, Gawd 'elp us,' said Lewis, shaking his head.

Back downstairs, she bade farewell to Edie, Chloe and Bertie, who gave her a green-eyed stare and went back to sleep.

'Call me whenever you like,' she said. 'If there's anything I can do.'

'Find out who killed the poor bugger,' said Chloe. 'Edie says you're good at that.'

Libby drove away from the house and paused outside the church to ring Fran.

'I should be there by twelve,' she said. 'Early lunch?'

The road to Steeple Mount led off to the left from the main Steeple Martin road. The first thing to come into view was the mount from which the village took its name, topped with its ancient grey standing stone known as Grey Betty. On the other side of it, Libby knew, was a modern replica of a sacred grotto, and this side was a car park, but today she drove past them and down the short high street.

The Bell and Butcher was a typical village pub, probably eighteenth century originally, but 'improved' in the early twentieth. Perhaps when Marsham's took it over? Libby parked in the small car park behind it. She had just got out of the car when Fran arrived.

'How are we going to play this?' she asked.

'How do you mean?' said Libby. 'We just ask to speak to Jenny and tell her Sid sent us.'

'Just like that?'

'What else would we do? We don't need to pretend we're there for anything else.'

'Right,' said Fran doubtfully.

159

Libby regarded her with amusement. 'You're not usually worried.'

'No, but there seem to be proper criminals involved this time,' said Fran.

'Oh, and all the murderers we've come up against in the past weren't proper criminals?'

'Well, no. They were often people who got caught up in something by accident.'

'Hmm.' Libby pulled a face. 'Some accidents.'

Inside, the Bell and Butcher was quiet. A couple of men sat at a table with newspapers, two more sat at the bar and a solitary woman sat by the empty fireplace with a book. Libby went up to the bar.

'Jenny!' called one of the men sitting there. He turned to Libby. 'Don't get many customers during the day, see.'

'Thanks, Paddy.' A slim, brown-haired woman appeared from a doorway to their left and went behind the bar. 'Hello! What can I get you?'

Libby smiled at her. 'You're Jenny. Sid Best said we should mention his name.'

Jenny's face changed. Far from looking pleased, as Libby had expected, she looked worried.

'Yes?' she said. And waited.

'Didn't he tell you we might come and see you?' asked Fran, moving slightly along the bar away from Paddy and his friend's interested gaze.

'I . . . I don't know.' Jenny looked from one to the other. 'Who are you?'

'I'm Libby Sarjeant.'

'And I'm Fran Wolfe.'

'The two women who sorted out all that Morris business,' called Paddy. 'I know who they are.'

Jenny's face relaxed. 'Oh! Yes, of course.' She turned and gave him a smile. 'How come you always know everything, you old bastard?'

160

Paddy grinned.

'Sorry about that.' Jenny turned back to the two women. 'Can I get you anything?'

'Do you do food?' asked Libby.

'Only ploughman's or ham or cheese sandwiches, I'm afraid. We don't get enough custom to do anything else. We don't fill up till around half four, with the after-work crowd.'

They both opted for ploughman's, with coffee for Fran and tonic water for Libby, who didn't trust unknown pub tea. Jenny sent them to a table as far away from the bar as possible and promised to join them.

'That was an interesting reaction, wasn't it?' said Libby quietly, as they settled themselves.

'Who else was she expecting, do you think?' replied Fran. 'Someone from the brewery?'

'Well – it can't have been anything really nasty,' said Libby, staring at a poster for an upcoming music night, 'or we wouldn't have mentioned Sid.'

'That could have been a ploy,' said Fran.

'Hmm. But we would hardly be from the brewery if we mentioned Sid, would we? He's a free house.'

'Do they still have local Licensed Victuallers Associations?'

'According to Tim, most of them have stopped. I think there's a federation, or something.' Libby looked up as Jenny approached the table. 'Hi – we were just wondering about local Licensed Victuallers Associations. Are they still going?'

'Not like they used to be,' said Jenny, placing plates on the table. 'There's the federation, but the old LVAs are a thing of the past.' She sighed as she sat down. 'They were basically just social. Anyway.' She looked at them both in turn, and finally addressed Libby. 'Sid said you're looking into Dickie Marsham's death.'

'Yes – well, we were, but now that the police have moved their focus, we've stopped,' said Libby.

'Oh.' Jenny looked disappointed.

161

'But if you think there's something they need to know, please tell us. They do listen to us.' Fran gave Libby a grin. 'Even when they aren't supposed to.'

'Paddy was right.' Jenny leant back thoughtfully. 'I remember that whole Morris dancing scandal. You were involved in that, weren't you? And the ukulele band murder?'

'That's right,' said Libby. 'And we know an awful lot of pubs in the area.'

'You're Steeple Martin, right?' Jenny put her head on one side and squinted at her. 'You've got a new pub, haven't you?'

'That belongs to Libby's partner,' said Fran.

'Well, to his family's estate,' corrected Libby. 'He got the licence back and renovated it. It's called the Hop Pocket.'

'Of course!' Jenny slapped the table. 'Ben Wilde! We're allowed to have the occasional real ale, and we've started having Ben's Best Bitter. Very popular, it is!'

Libby went faintly pink. 'I'll tell him – he'll be pleased.'

'Sid said you had something to tell us about Marsham's,' said Fran, before the conversation could become too personal.

'In a way.' Jenny realigned a beer mat in front of her.

'How do you mean – in a way?' asked Libby, after a moment.

'It's just . . .' Jenny threw the beer mat down. 'They won't talk to us!'

Chapter Twenty-Three

Fran and Libby exchanged puzzled glances.

'Look,' said Jenny, sounding exasperated, 'a lot of us tried to get in touch with the brewery when we heard about Dickie. Well, we would, wouldn't we?'

'Of course you would,' agreed Libby.

'And none of us got a reply.' Jenny gave a sharp nod and sat back. 'So then we wondered about all the houses that have been sold off. So some of us tried to get in touch with Roy. And he didn't answer either. In fact, none of us have heard a word from the brewery since before Christmas.'

'What about deliveries?' asked Fran.

'Oh, they've been coming.' Jenny sniffed. 'They won't talk to us, but they take the money.'

'Are you a tenant or a manager?' asked Libby.

'Manager. Tenants have almost all gone. Ever wondered why there are so many free houses round here?'

Libby frowned. 'Well, there are a lot, but they weren't all Marsham's houses first, were they? I mean, the landlords we know have been in their pubs for years.'

'Not all of them, but several were. And Marsham's used to be a good brewery. It all seemed to change a few years ago.'

'When Dickie and Roy's father took over?' asked Fran.

'No, he'd been in the top job for years.' Jenny shook her head. 'Although it's all the boys these days. Boys! Huh.'

'So was it when he stepped aside, then?' asked Libby.

'I suppose it could have been. We – the houses, that is – weren't really aware of when that was. When it got really bad was when the pub sales started increasing.'

'We know about Pat Bailey and Izzy at the Puckle,' said Fran. 'Most of the sales seem to have been quite recent.'

'Yes. Oh, there were a few before last year, but mostly that was "natural wastage", as they call it. And everyone was doing it. But round about spring last year, it seemed that we were all hanging on by our fingernails.'

'You must have talked about it among yourselves,' said Libby. 'What did you make of it?'

'Some people just said that with the way things were – you know, the cost of living and everything – it wasn't surprising. But most of us couldn't make it out. It wasn't just pubs in villages where there wasn't much trade. It was places like the Fox and Hounds over near Harbledown – know it?'

Libby nodded.

'They had loads of clubs meeting there, really good restaurant trade – especially at weekends. Then *bang*. Closed.'

'A lot of the clubs went to the Oast community centre,' said Fran.

'Stapleton's place!' scoffed Jenny. 'We reckon he was behind that one.'

'Yes, so do we,' said Libby. 'And what about Pat Bailey's pub? That was a real community centre, wasn't it?'

'She was lucky. They had that Sir Jonathan backing them.'

'So Roy wouldn't talk to you,' said Fran after a pause. 'How long has he been in charge of the estates department?'

'Oh, he's been on that side of the business for years, but only in charge for the last two or three years, something like that. And no. He hasn't answered any emails, and his phone goes straight to voicemail. Even his direct business line.'

'Did you try Dickie before he died?' Libby finished the last of her ploughman's and pushed the plate aside.

'Yes. Some of us spoke to him. He promised he'd look into it.' Jenny stopped. 'Oh.'

'Yes, *oh*.' Libby's lips thinned.

'Don't jump to conclusions,' said Fran.

'Why not? Dickie promises to look into problems in the business – Dickie is suddenly murdered and no one will talk about it. It isn't far to jump.' Libby scowled at her friend.

'No evidence,' said Fran. 'What do you think will happen now, Jenny?'

'We don't know.' Jenny shook her head. 'That's what we want to find out. Is the brewery going bust or something?'

'Surely if it were in danger of doing that it would have been reported in the financial papers by now,' said Fran.

'But we don't read those!' said Jenny.

'No, but if it *was* reported there, it would also have been reported in your trade press,' said Libby. 'Is that online now?'

'There's *The Brewer's Journal*,' said Jenny doubtfully.

'And what about your salary? Other automatic payments? Are they being made?' asked Fran.

'Well, it's not quite as simple as that,' said Jenny, 'but there haven't been any refused payments.'

'Sounds as if they're running scared and trying to regroup,' said Libby. 'I wish I knew more about financial matters.'

'But it's not exactly a small company,' said Fran. 'They've got pubs everywhere – even London. Didn't someone tell you that, Libby?'

'Yes. It is peculiar. I mean, there'll be a wages department, won't there? And personnel – or HR, or whatever it's called now. And then there's the actual brewing part of it. They use the creek, don't they?' Libby looked at Jenny.

'They used to, for cooling. I don't know much about the brewing process. But they still brew their own.' Jenny gestured towards the bar. 'There's Felling Creek, that's a pale ale, Marsham's Strong and Dunton Bitter. They buy in a lager from Germany.'

'So there must be dozens of employees,' said Libby. 'Have they told them all to keep quiet?'

'We – that's the managers – we've all tried to get in touch with employees. But none of us know any of them.'

'What about . . . what's it called? The pub in Felling? The Gate, that's it.' Libby quirked an eyebrow. 'Surely they'd know.'

Jenny laughed. 'Believe it or not, it isn't a Marsham's pub! It's tenanted, but I don't know them. That's the trouble – Felling's rather stuck out on a limb, isn't it?'

'Well, someone must know,' said Fran. 'I think, if you don't mind, Jenny, we'll tell our friendly policeman about it. They haven't been concentrating on the local angle, so perhaps it's time they did.'

'Did you actually know Dickie?' asked Libby.

'Yes.' Jenny smiled sadly. 'He was nice. Quite quiet, and seemed to be very – what d'you call it? Focused, that's it. Loved the business. Didn't seem to have much of a social life – not like his brother. Roy was a right tearaway before he got married.'

'Did you hear that Dickie was suspected of pocketing funds at some point?' Libby said tentatively.

'That was rubbish. Dickie just wasn't like that. If you'd said Roy . . . except that he isn't clever enough.'

'Oh?' Libby looked at Fran. 'And what about the sister? Ruth?'

'I didn't know there was a sister,' said Jenny, looking surprised.

'Well.' Libby sat back and smiled at her. 'As Fran said, I think we ought to tell DCI Connell what you've told us. Don't be alarmed if someone else comes to talk to you – what you've said is very helpful.'

'Thank you,' said Jenny, looking relieved. 'I just don't want to lose the old Bell. It's been my home for over fifteen years, and the regulars are like my family.'

'That's how all good publicans feel, isn't it?' said Fran.

'Yes – that's why it's so hard when you have to leave. I feel so sorry for poor Stan.'

'From the Fox and Hounds? Yes, so do I,' said Libby.

Outside in the car park, Libby wandered over to the fence, which looked out at the other side of the mount and Grey Betty.

'Despite being so worried, they haven't tried very hard to find out what's going on, have they?' she said.

'Not everybody is as nosy as you are, or as good at ferreting things out,' said Fran. 'But I agree. And I can't understand why the police didn't find all this out right at the beginning.'

'Oh, don't say there was another rogue cop,' said Libby. 'There couldn't have been! Ian said Rob Maiden and Rachel were running the investigation.'

'And Superintendent Bertram was overseeing *his* investigation,' said Fran. 'Could she have put a spoke in?'

'But why?' Libby turned away from the view. 'To prove a point? But *what* point?'

'Oh, I don't know!' Fran made an impatient sound. 'And now I'm going home. Will you report to Ian later, or do you want me to do it?'

'Do you want to?' Libby looked surprised.

'No, but you've done it all so far.' Fran shrugged. 'Just thought you might want a break.'

Libby frowned. 'No – he asked me in the first place. Come on, what's going on?'

'Nothing! But I was wondering . . .' Fran turned back to Grey Betty. 'Well. Remember Fred Barrett?'

'Oh, *yes*! What a good idea, Fran – and he always liked you better than me.' Libby beamed and patted Fran's back.

Fred Barrett had been a reporter on the *Nethergate Mercury* some years ago and could occasionally come up with priceless nuggets of information.

'All right. I'll give him a ring and see if he knows anything.' Fran grinned back at Libby. 'And you can ask Ben and Tim if they've been in touch with the Gate since the Christmas quiz.'

'Oh, yes, we mentioned it then, didn't we. Right, I'll do that.

Funny it isn't a Marsham's pub.' Libby went to unlock her car. 'I'll ring you later.'

Libby drove slowly home, thinking over everything she'd learnt in the last few hours. There was in fact very little from Chloe, as she'd said to Lewis, it was reassurance that was needed there. Jenny did actually need help, although Libby was pretty sure she and the other publicans could have pressed for information themselves. Or perhaps they were worried that if they did, it would bring them to the notice of their bosses and they too might end up losing their pubs. It was a very weird situation.

At home, she left a long message on Ian's voicemail, made a cup of tea and called Ben.

'Did you find out whether the Gate was joining in the quiz league?' she asked.

'Oh – nice to hear from you too!' he said.

'Sorry – the name came up when we were talking to Jenny at the Bell and Butcher.'

'Of course it did.' Ben was silent for a moment. 'No, I don't think we did. We ought to ask Tim. Why?'

Libby explained. 'But what's weird is that it isn't a Marsham's pub. It's the only one in Felling, isn't it?'

'I don't know!' said Ben, sounding surprised. 'I'd be surprised if it was. I know Felling isn't a large town, but you'd think there'd be more than one.'

Libby was searching on her laptop. 'Yes, there is,' she said. 'Two. The Star and the Shipwright's Arms. That makes sense. There was shipbuilding there, wasn't there?'

'Couple of hundred years ago, yes. So are either of them Marsham's?'

'Hang on.' Libby tucked the phone under her chin and carried on searching. 'Yes,' she said finally. 'They both are. Why don't we know about them?'

'Don't ask me!' said Ben. 'I'll give John Newman a ring and find out.' John Newman was the son of the former licensee of the Hop Pocket. 'Maybe they've both been closed, too.'

'Oh, goodness, yes! All the more reason to get in touch with the Gate, then. You played a couple of bat and trap matches over there during the summer, didn't you?'

'Yes, Libby. When do you want to go?'

'Really? You'll come with me?'

'Well, as you said, I do know them – very vaguely, but I do.' He paused. 'Tell you what, I'll pop in to Tim's on the way home and ask about quiz fixtures, and we can talk about that when we go as an excuse. And bat and trap, of course.'

'Can I meet you at Tim's?' asked Libby.

'I won't be staying long,' said Ben. 'I want my dinner. And I don't want to trail over to Felling tonight, either. I suggest tomorrow lunchtime, then if you learn anything and Ian comes to the pub tomorrow, you can tell him all about it.'

Chapter Twenty-Four

'I don't know why it didn't come up on your search,' said Ben when he arrived home after his visit to the Coach and Horses, 'but Tim tells me both the pubs you found have been closed for years.'

'Really?' Libby pulled out her phone. 'I'll have another look.'

'Don't bother, I'll tell you.' Ben peered into the pan on the Rayburn. 'Is it nearly ready?'

'Might be.' Libby sat down at the table and fixed him with a glare. 'Carry on.'

Ben grinned and sat down. 'Right. Both the Star and The Shipwright's Arms were closed a few years ago due to a lack of custom. Marsham's were consolidating, apparently. However, they retained the Shipwright for their own use, although Tim doesn't know exactly what use that is. The Star is now a private dwelling.'

'I wonder what they use the Shipwright for?' Libby stood up and fetched plates. 'Extra office space?'

'Maybe. We'll ask at the Gate tomorrow. Tim says they haven't joined in the quiz league, but we're to find out if they would like to. And I spoke to John Newman. He's meeting us there.'

'Is Emma coming?'

'I don't think so.' Ben carried the pan from the stove to the table. 'I don't think she likes us any more than you like her.'

Libby gave a small sigh of relief. 'That'll make things easier.'

★

Wednesday morning was wet. By the time Libby and Ben left for Felling, the rain had been falling steadily since before breakfast. Sidney was not pleased.

Ben drove them via Bishop's Bottom, through drowned fields and sodden hedgerows sheltering miserable-looking sheep. Eventually, the Sand Gate, the only accessible approach to Felling from the road, loomed into view, and once through, beside it stood the Gate Inn. Ben parked at the back beside the bat and trap pitch and they ran for the door.

'Ben!' John Newman stood up to greet them. 'And Libby. Lovely to see you.' Tall, with bushy greying hair and matching eyebrows, he was, nevertheless, a rather retiring individual, in thrall, Libby felt, to his ostensibly meek and fluttery wife.

'How's Emma?' she asked, to counteract her lurking feelings of guilt.

'Oh, fine, thank you.' John looked sideways at the bar. 'She's sorry she can't be here. Work, you know.'

'Oh, yes,' said Libby, who didn't.

'What will you have, John?' asked Ben, approaching the brightly smiling young woman behind the counter.

'So, do you know the landlord here?' Ben asked, when they were settled at a table by the window. Like the Bell and Butcher the day before, there were only a few customers, who looked as though they'd taken root. 'I've only ever met the members of the bat and trap team. I expect the landlord was watching, but I've never been introduced.'

'Zack, yes. Known him for years.' John looked over his shoulder, rather nervously, Libby thought. 'I'll ask Ellie to call him, shall I?'

'Not yet,' said Libby. 'We want to know what you know about Marsham's brewery first.'

'Oh, yes, Ben said.' John looked down into his pint. 'Well, I don't know much, to tell you the truth. I know they were approached to sponsor the bat and trap league in the centenary year, but they refused. Said it wasn't played at any of their pubs.'

'Oh, well, I suppose that's fair enough,' said Libby. 'But they're a Kentish brewery. You'd think they'd have a few teams, wouldn't you?'

John shrugged. 'I don't know.'

'But this isn't a Marsham's pub, is it?' asked Ben. 'That's why they have bat and trap. And we want to ask if they'll join the quiz league. Tim in Steeple Martin said he's asked, but they haven't replied yet.'

'Oh, I'm sure Zack will want to do that,' said John. 'But . . . as to finding out about Marsham's . . . They keep themselves to themselves a bit. Except for running the FBCG.'

'FBCG?' repeated Ben and Libby.

'Sorry – Felling Business Community Group.' John looked over his shoulder again.

'Oh? What's that?' Libby asked.

'What it says, I expect,' said Ben. 'Local businessmen? Solicitors, accountants, that sort of thing?'

John nodded. 'A bit like Rotary. Only . . .'

'More secretive?' suggested Libby.

'I was going to say "exclusive",' said John. 'It's more like a club. You have to be proposed and seconded.'

'They don't meet in the Shipwright's Arms, I suppose?' said Libby, whose synapses had been working overtime.

John looked surprised. 'Yes – how did you know?'

'Lucky guess. Is Zack a member?'

'I'm not sure.' John was still looking neervous. 'This isn't a Marsham's pub, as you said, Ben, so maybe not.'

Ben sat back and looked at him, head on one side. 'What are you worried about, John?'

A faint flush rose up John's neck. 'Nothing.'

'There's obviously something,' said Libby. 'Please don't tell me this is a hangover from Nasty Nigel Preece's ill-doings?'

'Of course not!' John sat up straight. 'No one here would have anything to do with . . . well, with that sort of thing.'

Sir Nigel was a disgraced MP who had crossed Libby's path a couple of years before.

'No.' He swallowed almost half his pint. 'They're . . . well, they're just quite private. Look, I'll get Ellie to call Zack. He knows more about them.'

'I thought you said you weren't sure if he was a member,' said Ben.

'I don't. But he'll know about them.' John got up and went to the bar.

'Sounds like the Masons,' Libby muttered to Ben.

'What I was thinking,' said Ben.

John returned to the table. 'Just coming,' he said, and within seconds, a small, slim man with sandy hair was approaching, a broad grin on his face.

'Hello, I'm Zack!' he said, thrusting out a hand. 'And I know you – you're Ben. You're in the bat and trap team from Steeple Martin.'

'That's me,' said Ben. 'Pleased to meet you, Zack. First of all, I have to ask you if the Gate would be interested in joining our quiz league? Tim from the Coach and Horses says he has asked you . . .'

'And I never got back to him – yes.' Zack sat down. 'Can I get you another drink?' He turned to the bar. 'Ellie, my usual, please.'

They all refused, and Ellie brought Zack a bottle of low-alcohol beer.

'Right,' he said. 'Sorry I never replied – it completely slipped my mind, and yes, we'd love to. Can you get Tim to give me a ring?'

'Yes, of course,' said Ben.

'Now, John tells me you're after information about Marsham's?'

'Yes – if we're not being too intrusive,' said Libby.

Zack looked at her shrewdly. 'Not at all. This'll be about Dickie, I take it?'

'Yes. I . . . er . . . I've been . . .'

'Helping the police with their inquiries?' Zack grinned. 'See,

173

we all know who you are. Couldn't fail to, really, after all that business before.'

'They want to know about the FBCG,' John told him.

'Well, actually, we didn't know about it until John mentioned it,' said Ben. 'But we wondered if it – the FBCG – would know why the managers of Marsham's houses can't get in touch with the brewery.'

Zack exchanged resigned looks with John. 'I'm sure they do. I'm not a member, although I do attend some of their events.' He sat forward, leaning his elbows on the table. 'You see, they're basically a sort of gentleman's club, and they look after one another.'

'I said – like the Masons,' growled Libby.

Zack smiled at her. 'Not really. Oh, they do charity events, but they're mostly anonymous. The organisation facilitates them – makes it easy to donate or help out without being seen, if you get me.'

'Oh.' Libby and Ben looked surprised.

'The reason I don't belong is I'm not rich enough.' Zack held up his hands. 'And that's not like it sounds. They need to have enough money to help people, you see.' He shook his head. 'It's daft, really. We all know who's behind it if we hear about a family being given somewhere to live, or a child being sent to the States to have an operation, but we have to pretend not to. And of course, we don't know the individuals involved, although we all know who the members are.'

Silence fell round the table while Ben and Libby reflected on this surprising information.

'So you think they might know what's going on at Marsham's?' said Libby eventually.

'Dickie was a member,' said Zack. 'I expect they've closed ranks.'

'The group, or Marsham's?' asked Ben.

'Both, probably, although why Marsham's aren't communicating with their landlords, I can't think.' Zack frowned and shook his head.

I can, thought Libby. Aloud, she said: 'How could we find out?'

'I don't know. The group don't welcome outsiders, and I can't imagine that Marsham's would either at the moment.' Zack played with his bottle. 'I did hear they were having some internal problems, so they're probably trying to sort those out just now.'

I expect they are, thought Libby.

'Do you think they could be connected with Dickie's death?'

'I wouldn't like to say.' Zack said. 'But maybe that's why they aren't talking to their landlords.'

'Hmm. Well, you've certainly given us some useful information,' said Libby.

'You have,' agreed Ben. 'But I'm still not sure I understand about all the secrecy.'

'I think,' said John slowly, 'they use each other's services under the counter, if you know what I mean. You said solicitors and accountants, didn't you?'

Libby nodded. 'A little bit of creative accounting, perhaps, and legal advice – or get-outs.'

'All quid pro quo,' agreed Ben.

'What do brewers put into the mix, though?' asked Libby.

'Beer!' exclaimed all three men.

'I wonder,' said Libby, when they'd all settled down again, 'if sister Ruth's husband is a member. He's an accountant, isn't he?'

Zack's eyebrows rose. 'He is indeed. Have you met Ruth?'

'Yes.' Libby looked puzzled. 'And I don't think she was aware of what was going on at Marsham's, so perhaps the FB whateveritis doesn't know.'

'Or her husband hasn't told her,' said Ben.

'But she's an accountant herself,' said Libby. 'What about Roy? Is he a member?'

'No!' said John and Zack together.

'Oh!' Ben and Libby looked at one another. 'That was definite,' said Ben.

'Roy's always been a . . . well, not exactly a black sheep, more a sort of dirty grey,' said Zack, laughing.

175

'But he's a member of the local Rotary, isn't he?' said Libby. 'He was at a meeting with them the night Dickie was killed. At Heronsbourne Golf Club. And how do they – the Rotary – get on with the FC-whatsit?'

'Fine.' Zack shrugged. 'Lots of the same people are members.'

'But not Marshams,' said Ben. 'Apparently, Dickie wasn't a Rotary member.'

'Actually,' said Zack thoughtfully, 'I think he was. He just didn't attend very often.'

'So are Marsham's looking into the sale of their houses?' asked Libby carefully after a short pause. 'Everyone we've spoken to thinks it's odd, to say the least. And Roy's in charge of estates, isn't he?'

'So I'm told,' said Zack, 'but you've got to remember, I'm not supposed to know anything, not being a member of the group or an employee of Marsham's. And I guess that's what the internal trouble is about – not necessarily Dickie's murder. Although,' he looked from Ben to Libby, 'I suppose they could be connected. Is that what you're thinking?'

'We wondered, but I don't know about the police,' said Libby. 'And how *do* you know, not being a member or an employee, as you said.'

Zack looked smug. 'I have friends.'

Ben heaved a resigned sigh. 'And you won't tell us.'

'What about the Shipwright's Arms?' said Libby. 'Marsham's have hung on to that, John tells us. Why?'

'Because it's much nicer to meet there than in the conference room at the brewery, I expect,' said Zack. 'It was a lovely old pub. The landlord was a friend of mine.' He winked. 'He's now the steward.'

'Ah! All is explained,' said Ben with a smile.

'I said nothing,' said Zack, looking innocent.

Half an hour later, having learnt nothing further, Ben and Libby left, promising to return with the quiz and bat and trap teams in due course.

'So what do we think about all that?' Libby asked as they got back into the car.

'I'm not sure there was anything new, was there?' said Ben.

'I'm not sure,' said Libby. 'But it did seem to confirm that there's something wrong inside Marsham's, which is why they aren't talking to anyone. I'll have to think about it, and speak to Ian tonight.'

'Better hope he comes, then,' said Ben.

Chapter Twenty-Five

'You know what,' said Libby some hours later, when Ben came back from a visit to his brewery, 'I think it's all bricks with straw again.'

'You do?'

'Well, I was thinking.' She made herself comfortable on the sofa. 'I was flattered when Ian asked me to help. Especially when we both went to see Pat Bailey at the George and Dragon. And I was keen to help because Ian was having to look into corruption in the force.'

'Which he isn't now?' said Ben.

'Apparently not.' Libby frowned. 'But I think he's keeping that quiet. After all, it's a very sensitive issue, isn't it?'

'It is. But go on. What's made you think you've made bricks with straw?'

'Everything we've found out is all just nosing about into Roy and Dickie Marsham's lives. Dickie's old friend, darts at the pub, being fond of Roy's ex. And Roy dumping the girlfriend and marrying Gina, possibly gambling, and selling off some of the Marsham's pubs. I mean, he can't be selling them off to pay gambling debts, can he? The money goes into Marsham's coffers, not his. The only really reprehensible thing we could find out about him was that Alanna's family and Gina were kicked out of their homes when Marsham's sold their building. There really isn't anything else. And all this secret squirrel stuff about the FC-whatsit is just big boys playing games.' She made a harrumphing sound. 'And as for Anthony Leigh – well, I think you're all right. I'm trying to make everyone who moves to Spain into a criminal. Even though Ian says Leigh is.'

'Including poor Chloe's son? Or was it daughter?' Ben smiled. 'It's an excellent summing-up, and put like that it does all seem rather pathetic. But Ian has been seriously worried. First when he asked you to help, and second when he kidnapped Chloe. So there must be something in among all that random information. And you know what they always say in the TV crime dramas – it's the smallest detail that provides the answer.'

Libby heaved a great sigh. 'I know they do, but I'm not sure I'm the person to find it.'

'Let's hope Ian turns up tonight and can put your mind at rest.' Ben held out a hand. 'Come on, let's go and find something for dinner. Then I need to have a shower. I always seem to get so dusty in the brewery.'

The small bar in the Coach and Horses was still empty when Ben and Libby arrived.

'So, what did Zack at the Gate have to say?' Tim asked as he came to serve them.

'He's sorry he hasn't got back to you, but yes, they'd love to join the quiz league. Would you give him a ring to sort out details,' said Ben.

'And was he helpful in the investigation?' Tim turned to Libby.

'In a way – perhaps,' said Libby, picking up her glass.

'She's having mid-case doubts,' Ben explained.

'Oh?' Tim raised his eyebrows. 'Well, perhaps a nice conference round the table will cheer you up, Lib. Can't have you giving up on the job.'

Libby gave him a half-hearted smile and went to sit down.

It was another half an hour before the door crashed open and Anne's familiar hoots of laughter were heard as Patti manoeuvred her wheelchair inside. Ben grinned, put away the quiz fixture sheets he'd been perusing and went to help.

'I'm glad you're here,' said Libby. 'I was beginning to think we'd be all on our own this evening.'

'No chance!' said Anne. 'Come famine or flood, we'll always be here on a Wednesday. So what's up with you?'

'Ben calls it mid-case blues,' said Libby. 'I just think I've been finding completely irrelevant stuff and being nosy.'

Patti smiled. 'In a way, you probably have. But I expect it'll all be useful. You'll see, Ian will tell you.'

'If he comes,' said Libby.

Ben came back to the table with drinks for Patti and Anne. 'You can't cheer her up,' he said. 'She's beyond help.'

Just then a head appeared round the door from the other bar.

'Can we come in?' asked John Cole.

'Oh, yes, please do!' said Ben. 'We don't often see you on a Wednesday.'

Beth and John emerged and took their seats at the round table.

'I know you've always said we'd be welcome, but we don't like to intrude,' said Beth. 'Hello, Patti, Anne. How are you?'

'Trying to cheer Libby up,' said Anne. 'She's not enjoying her latest investigation.'

Ben rolled his eyes and began to speak to John about the quiz league.

'It's not that, exactly,' said Libby. 'I just feel it's all been a bit of a waste of time.'

Beth regarded her closely. 'Hmm. Don't they say that half the stuff the police have to investigate is wasted? But they have to go through it all anyway in case they miss something?'

'That's what Ben says,' said Libby. 'I just feel all I've done is be nosy.'

'That's because you're not official,' said Anne. 'Except that Ian asks you to help, so you are.'

'Oh-oh.' Ben caught the end of this. 'Now she's going to start

180

imagining that Ian's been asking for her help to keep her out of the way. How many times has that happened?'

'Well, now you can ask him,' said John, nodding towards the door.

Ian came into the bar, followed by Edward and Peter.

'Ask who what?' he said, fixing Libby with a gimlet eye.

'Oh, take her away and give her a grilling,' said Ben. 'She's depressing everyone.'

Ian came to stand beside Libby. 'What's up?' he asked quietly.

She shook her head and stood up. 'Let's go over there,' she said, and led the way to the little table beside the fireplace. Ian carried her drink over for her and went back to fetch his own from the bar.

'Now,' he said. 'What have you been up to that's made you miserable?'

So Libby told him.

Ian sat staring into the fire when she'd finished.

'Well, say something!' she said eventually.

He looked up and smiled ruefully. 'Perhaps you're right,' he said.

Libby gasped.

'Sorry, I put that badly.' He leant over and patted her hand. 'What I meant was – perhaps I shouldn't have involved you. Especially while there's an internal investigation going on.'

'Oh – it still is, then?'

'Yes. But, as it should have been from the start, by another force.'

'What's happened to Big Bertha?'

'I'm afraid she's under investigation along with everybody else,' said Ian. 'It's all rather depressing and not conducive to a good work ethic.'

'I can imagine,' murmured Libby.

'So what I can tell you is that everything you've found out would normally have been found out by teams of detectives. What

181

your friends have said is true – *and* what the TV dramas say. Everything has to be investigated, however intrusive it may seem, because somewhere in there is the tiny detail that will lead to the solving of the case.' He gave her a wry smile. 'Not that I can see it at the moment, I confess, but I'm sure it's there.'

Libby sat looking at him in silence.

'Well?' He picked up his drink.

'So I haven't been wasting my time?' she said slowly. 'And it all means something?'

'Not all of it, perhaps, but certainly some of it.' He leant back and crossed his ankles. 'What does Fran say?'

'Not a lot. Ben was actually very helpful, coming to Felling with me today. But honestly – all this Boy's Own club stuff down there . . .'

Ian laughed. 'I know what you mean. Making themselves important.'

'That's what it seemed like to me. And John Newman was actually nervous about speaking to us! What did he think they could do to him?'

'Oh, ban him from the pub or something probably,' said Ian. 'Don't forget they're probably still smarting from all the previous problems. Not just your Nasty Nigel, but the St Aldeberge business, too.' He shook his head sadly. 'Poor Patti's had more than her fair share of worry since she got that parish, hasn't she?'

'She has.' Libby turned to look at her friend at the other table. 'Come on, let's go back. They're all dying to know what we've been talking about.'

'Let me tell it, then,' said Ian. 'I know what to leave out.'

He was halfway through his precis of events when Harry crashed through the door demanding alcohol.

'Listen,' he said, leaning across the table and poking Ian on the arm. 'I've just had Randy Roland in the caff.'

'Who?' asked Ian amid general laughter.

'Roland Ritter. I know – daft name, isn't it? Well,' said Harry

182

settling back and accepting his drink from Edward, 'he's an accountant. Not my accountant, but an accountant anyway.'

'Yes, yes – he's an accountant. Get on with it,' said Peter.

'I take things at my own pace,' said Harry, with an indignant sniff. 'Randy Roland knows someone in the Marsham's accounts department. Or something.'

'And?' prompted Ian.

'He reckons there's been something dodgy going on.' Harry gave a decisive nod. 'And he said he couldn't understand why the police weren't investigating the company.'

All eyes turned to Ian.

'We have been,' he said in a tired voice. 'It just isn't always broadcast to the nation.'

'Oh? And what have you found out?' asked Harry.

'You know I can't tell you that, Hal, but if you sit still and shut up, I'll carry on telling you all what Libby's been unearthing for me.'

'Oh, well done, petal.' Harry raised his glass to Libby. 'Carry on, then.'

When Ian had finished, everyone began to talk at once, and, as always, everyone had a theory.

'So what do you think?' Ben asked him. 'A spot of creative accounting?'

'We wondered if the accountants in the Felling Boy's Own Club did a bit of that for their members,' said Libby.

'That's what Simon's information seems to suggest,' said Ian. 'But we need some kind of proof before we send in the forensic accountants. And proof that it had something to do with Dickie's death, too.'

Libby nodded and fell to scrutinising what was left of her drink.

'Let me get you another one,' said Ian, and stood up, just as his phone began to ring. He cursed.

'I'll go,' said Ben.

Libby watched as Ian answered his call and wandered over to

the door. She was still watching when he turned sharply and spoke.

'I'm sorry, I've got to go,' he said. 'Patrol car's picking me up – you'll have to have the cab on your own, Edward.'

'What's happened?' Libby stood up.

'Chloe Vaughan's home's been ransacked.'

Chapter Twenty-Six

'Remind me – who's Chloe Vaughan?' asked Anne in a stage whisper.

Ben explained while Libby went across to Ian.

'Is it linked?'

'It may not be – house obviously empty and in the centre of Canterbury, it could easily be an opportunist thief. But somehow I don't think so.' Ian looked at his watch. 'And I haven't got an overcoat. Damn.'

With that, he disappeared.

'I don't suppose,' said Edward thoughtfully, his eyes still on the door through which Ian had gone, 'he was supposed to tell us that.'

Ben, Peter and Harry all nodded.

'He's not supposed to tell us anything,' said Peter.

'Which just goes to show his lack of faith in the force,' said Harry. 'Poor bugger.'

'I rather thought,' said Libby, 'that he'd asked for a watch to be put on Chloe's flat.'

'So either someone is countermanding his orders, or they're just being ignored,' said Beth. 'That's not good.'

'What worries me,' said Libby, 'is that he'll lose his job – or worse.'

'What's worse?' asked John.

'He'll be prosecuted,' said Libby, with an involuntary shiver. 'I think there's something nasty going on, and they'll try and pin it on him.'

'Why did they ask him to investigate the local force, if that's the case?' said Peter.

'Under the aegis of Big Bertha, don't forget,' said Libby.

'Um – Big Bertha?' Beth made a face. 'I think my memory must be going.'

'Superintendent Bertram,' said Ben. 'Libby and Fran came up against her when Lewis had all that trouble at Creekmarsh. We didn't know you then.'

'She was moved sideways at the time, but brought back to oversee the internal investigation, as far as I can make out,' said Libby.

'And what makes you think they'll make him a scapegoat?' asked Anne.

'You remember the homeless person who was murdered last year?' said Ben.

'Who wasn't – yes.' Anne nodded.

'The DI who was in charge of that was trying to derail the investigation,' said Edward, 'and Ian asked Fran and Libby to help. He didn't stick to the rules and was suspended – briefly – because of it.'

'Someone else was trying to do the same during the Constance Matthews case,' said Patti. 'Weren't they?'

'And we found that someone was passing information back when there was that investigation into Colin's friend,' said Harry. 'Or so Petal tells me.'

Petal grinned. 'And I tell you much more than I should!'

'So there's endemic criminal behaviour in the local force?' Anne was frowning. 'But we trust them to keep us safe and protect us. No wonder Ian's fed up.'

'And he, Rachel Trent, Rob Maiden and the others do just that,' said Libby. 'I think they ought to form their own little agency.'

'And they'd be stamped on by the authorities immediately,' said Peter. 'Much better to fight it from within. Which is what Ian's trying to do.'

'No wonder they don't like him asking for help from you two,' said Patti. 'It's already exposed some of the bad apples.'

'And it looks as though it'll expose even more,' said Edward. 'He's really worried. And he isn't sleeping. Sometimes I get up in the night and his light is on.'

'He needs a good woman,' said Harry, lounging back in his chair. 'I could offer.'

The laughter this provoked dispelled the sombre mood, but Libby couldn't stop thinking about it.

'You know we found out about the policeman who was actually part of the St Aldeberge business?' she said to Ben on the way home. 'Well, do you think the same thing's happening this time? Someone in the Felling group, perhaps?'

He looked at her in surprise. 'But they're supposed to be good guys. Charity work and being nice to people.'

'Could be a cover. After all, that's what the Masons are supposed to do, and they've got loads of bad apples, as Patti calls them.'

'Yes, but it *is* only bad apples,' protested Ben. 'They aren't an inherently bad organisation. I'm not one, although I've been approached more than once.' He smiled. 'Being an architect, I suppose it was a foregone conclusion.'

Libby sighed. 'Yes. And I expect any organisation can be used for . . . I don't know . . . *nefarious* purposes.'

'What a lot of big words we're using,' said Ben, as they turned into Allhallow's Lane.

'Must be the beer,' said Libby.

On Thursday morning, Libby waited in vain for Ian to update her on the break-in at Chloe Vaughan's house. When her mobile did finally ring, it was Fran.

'I'm sorry I haven't called,' Libby said. 'I was leaving both phones free in case Ian rang.'

'Why? If he didn't get a reply on one, he'd try the other. And he'd leave a message.'

'But I couldn't ask questions that way,' said Libby.

'That's why he often leaves a message,' said Fran. 'So tell me what's happened.'

Libby explained.

'And what are the thoughts of the Wednesday Night Murder Club?' asked Fran.

'We were mainly discussing the investigation into corruption in the force.'

'And I wonder if this break-in isn't part of that?'

Libby sat down with a thump.

'Wha . . .?'

'To distract him?'

'But how?'

'Well, suppose Ian's on the trail of Dickie's killer and he's getting close. The killer might stage the break-in to focus his mind somewhere else.'

'But . . .' Libby stood up and went into the kitchen. 'What trail? It seems to be all over the place at the moment.'

'Someone knows he was concerned enough to spirit Chloe away. And why did he do that?' Fran was sounding positively bouncy.

'Hold on, hold on,' Libby said suspiciously. 'Have you had a "moment" you aren't telling me about?'

'No!' Fran was laughing. 'It just seemed to fall into place. Go on – why was Ian concerned about Chloe? It was because of her husband's connections, wasn't it?'

'Well – yes.' Libby frowned as she filled the kettle. 'Because they might have had something to do with Dickie's death.'

'Why did he think that?'

'I don't know! Why *did* he?'

'Was it something to do with Roy's gambling debts?'

'Maybe, but I thought we discounted that.'

'We did, but did Ian? He still doesn't tell us everything, you know.'

'I think that might take us down another rabbit hole,' said Libby, with a sigh.

'So might your theory about scandalous doings in the business community,' said Fran. 'What evidence have you got for that?'

'None. And Ian mentioned the lack of hard evidence yesterday.'

They both fell silent while Libby waited for the kettle to boil.

'Do you know,' she said eventually, as she poured water into a mug, 'I think I've lost track of it all.'

'I don't think I can bear to go over it all again,' groaned Fran.

'All right, I'll do that on my own,' said Libby. 'But I don't know what Ian wants us to do. If anything. Does he want us to go and talk to some more people? And if so, who?'

'Well, you could work that out yourself,' said Fran.

'Not Chloe,' said Libby, 'despite the break-in, because if you're right, she won't know who it's likely to have been.'

'No. What about the publicans?'

'But it isn't Dickie who sold their pubs.'

'But what if the creative accounting theory is right? And he found out about it?'

'Yes, but that's one of the things Ian says we need hard evidence for. Then he could send in the forensic accountants.'

'What about sister Ruth?'

'What about her? Oh – she's an accountant. But she doesn't work for Marsham's.'

'No, and if she did, she'd have blown the whistle already, or else she'd keep quiet because she was involved. But she – or her husband – could look into it, perhaps.'

'I don't see how,' said Libby. 'Marsham's wouldn't let anyone else see their books.'

'No, they wouldn't. I have the feeling that Roy's gambling has something to do with the whole thing, that's all.'

'Simplest idea would be that Dickie disapproved of the gambling and Roy got angry with him,' said Libby.

'And lashed out? Maybe. But that's what the police thought right at the beginning. It's why Roy was taken in for questioning, isn't it?'

'Starting me off on the trail,' said Libby, with a short laugh.

'But it was Ian coming to the pantomime that really set you off,' said Fran.

'It wasn't just me,' said Libby. 'He wanted you, too.'

'Yes.'

Silence fell once more as they both contemplated the double meaning of Libby's last statement.

'Oh well. I suppose I'll just wait and see what happens. Last time I did that, I got two phone calls that set me off again. Perhaps that'll happen this time too.' Libby added a splash of milk to her tea and carried it into the sitting room.

'Do you honestly want to be set off again?' asked Fran. 'Wouldn't life be simpler without murder, mystery and mayhem?'

'Oh, maybe. What should I do instead?'

'What you usually do at the end of a case,' asked Fran. 'Normal stuff.'

'Yes, but that's when we've solved the mystery, not left it hanging,' said Libby. 'I need a new project.'

'Oh, hell,' said Fran.

It wasn't until halfway through the afternoon that Libby got her phone call from Ian.

'I was sure you'd be dying to know what was going on,' he said.

'Well, only if you want to tell me,' said Libby.

'Goes without saying,' said Ian, still sounding weary.

'So do you think the break-in was something to do with Dickie Marsham's death?'

'Tangentially, possibly.'

'How do you mean?'

'I think it was meant as a distraction.'

'No! That's exactly what Fran said!' Libby bounced in her seat. 'You must be getting close to the killer. Is that what you think?'

'Slow down!' Ian was laughing. 'Did Fran have a "moment"?'

'No, she worked it out logically. Although I'm not sure how.'

'Well, there's no evidence pointing to any of Chloe's late husband's former associates.'

'How would you know?' asked Libby. 'They'd hardly leave a calling card, would they?'

'If it was meant as a warning from them, yes – that's exactly what they would do.'

'But I thought you had a watch on the place?'

'We did. But Chloe's flat is tucked down a tiny alley, so unless we have a poor officer standing outside all the time, we have to make do with patrol cars doing a drive-by.' Ian paused. 'Anyway, what I wanted to ask you was do you know if Chloe knows anyone in the area apart from Edie and Lewis? Who might know she wasn't at home?'

'Only us, I think,' said Libby. 'Do you want me to find out?'

'Yes, please, if you don't mind. Because if it was meant as a distraction, then it must be the killer – or someone the killer's paid. It's such a complete muddle.'

'That's what I said,' said Libby smugly. 'All these odd people. I said so last night, didn't I?'

'And as *I've* said, we have to investigate every little detail. So go off and do your thing. But be careful. Or Ben will have my guts for garters.'

As soon as Ian had rung off, Libby called Lewis.

'Hello, Lib, what can I do for you? I'm in the middle of a production meeting right now, so . . .'

'Oh, sorry. I'll call the Creekmarsh landline. I wanted Edie, anyway'

'They've gone into Nethergate. I've got a cab picking them up from the Blue Anchor at five. You can try Mum's mobile – if she's remembered to take it with her.'

'I'll go and meet them at the Blue Anchor and bring them home,' said Libby. 'Cancel the cab.'

''Ere! What you up to? What's happened?'

'Nothing. I need to talk to Chloe.'

'About last night?'

'Sort of. Thanks, Lewis.'

After quick calls to Fran and Ben, who offered his car and himself as driver, Libby collected her bag and her warmest coat and waited for him outside.

'What's up, then?' he asked, as he pulled out of Allhallow's Lane. Libby told him about Ian's phone call and her offer to pick the ladies up from the Blue Anchor.

'What he really wants to know is how did someone know Chloe had gone away. Who did she tell,' said Ben.

'Yes – or who did *we* tell. It could have been any of us making an unwise comment.' Libby frowned. 'And that's a worry.'

Chapter Twenty-Seven

It was dark by the time Ben parked behind the Blue Anchor. Edie and Chloe were sitting at a table with two of Mavis's regulars, Karen and Nora, who greeted Libby as an old friend.

'And how's Miss Dorothy?' asked Libby, sitting down with them. Dorothy Barton, owner of Temptation House, just outside Nethergate, was the women's landlady and great-aunt to Libby's friend Hannah.

'Well, that's what we were just talking about,' said Nora, leaning forward confidentially.

Edie gave Libby a smug smile.

'Oh?' Libby looked from one to another and Karen laughed.

'Nothing serious,' she said. 'But we've lost a tenant at Temptation House.'

'Ah!' Libby began to see the light.

Ben arrived at the table with two large white mugs of Mavis's strong tea.

'Mavis introduced the ladies,' he told Libby.

'After I told her about Chloe's trouble.' Edie nodded. 'Good sort, Mavis.'

'I didn't know you knew each other,' said Libby.

'Course we do. I always come in 'ere when Lewis and me come to Nethergate.'

'Mavis said she was thinking about Marine Parade at first,' said Ben.

'So you came here because you want to move, Chloe?' asked Libby.

'Well, I don't feel safe there anymore, see, dear.' Chloe looked apologetic. 'Not after last night.'

'Thank goodness you weren't there, dear,' said Nora, patting Chloe's hand. Ben and Libby refrained from saying that if she'd been there, it wouldn't have happened.

'Of course, there's the house on Marine Parade that . . .' Libby stopped. Perhaps mentioning the house from which Gina and Alanna had been evicted wasn't exactly tactful.

'There's several.' Mavis loomed over the table and began to collect empty plates and mugs on a tray. 'Up by Skinner's Alley. And Slaughterman's Alley.'

'Ooh,' said Chloe. 'I wouldn't fancy living there.'

'They were alleys that led up from the harbour,' said Ben. 'Skinner's is just over there, between two cottages on Harbour Street, and links up with Marine Parade, and Slaughterman's goes from Marine Parade to Slaughter Yard. You can guess what their purpose was.'

The ladies shuddered.

'All to do with the smuggling history,' said Libby. 'Nothing like that goes on now.'

'Hmm,' said Mavis, with a darkling look.

'Anyway, Chloe, our nice policeman wanted me to ask you who you might have talked to about going to stay with Edie,' said Libby, grateful to change the subject. 'Who might have known the house was empty?'

Chloe looked surprised. 'Why, no one, dear. Only you and your friends. The only other people I would have told would have been the nice people at the Goods Shed – you know? I used to go there in the mornings – but of course, I left in such a hurry I didn't get a chance to see them.' She looked regretful. 'I shall miss them.'

Libby looked at Ben and pulled a face.

'Don't worry, Chloe,' he said, 'we'll take you up there to see them. Libby likes the shops in Canterbury too. And you've never met me, have you? I'm Ben.' He held out a hand.

Chloe positively glowed. 'Oh, I'm ever so pleased to meet you!' she said.

'So is that what you think, luvvie?' Edie asked Libby in an undertone. 'Someone who found out Chlo had gone away? What about the London lot?'

'Ian doesn't think it was them,' said Libby. 'But he needs to know how someone found out she wasn't there. If she had been, I don't think it would have happened. It wasn't so much a warning to her as a distraction for the police.'

Edie looked thoughtful. 'So someone local, then. Who d'you reckon?'

Libby sighed. 'We haven't got any idea. The man who was killed seemed to be a fairly ordinary businessman with no enemies. His brother was another matter, but he's still alive and kicking.'

'Oh, I know who he is,' said Edie. 'Roy Marsham. He come in the Red Lion with that wife of his when we was over there for the quiz.'

'That's right. You know them? Lewis didn't say.'

'Musta slipped his mind. They come to a do at the house a few months back. Some club or other.'

That wouldn't have been the Felling lot, thought Libby – Roy wasn't a member – and the Rotary appeared to use the golf club for their events.

'Would Lewis remember what the event was?' she asked.

'Might do. You could ask 'im. And now we better get goin', if you don't mind, duck. Tomorrow we're goin' over to see this Miss Barton. Chlo'll be better off with her.'

'Well done,' Libby said to Mavis as they left. 'We should put you up for an award or something. You're a whole community department on your own.'

Mavis grunted and went pink.

★

Back at Creekmarsh, Lewis had finished his production meeting with the television company, who had packed their traps and departed.

'New series with the orangery,' he told Ben and Libby, while Edie and Chloe went to take off their coats. 'Starring role for your boy, Lib.'

'Oh, there'll be no talking to him,' said Libby. 'Listen, Lewis. Do you remember a do a few months back that Roy Marsham came to? Your mum mentioned it.'

Lewis frowned. 'Hang on . . . Oh!' His face lightened. 'Yes, I remember! Nethergate Round Table – their summer do. They've been coming for about three years. I forgot Marsham was here. And his bleedin' wife.'

'Oh dear.' Libby quirked an eyebrow. 'Not popular?'

'Complained about everything and upset the waiting staff. Cow.'

'Right. You don't know anything else about them, then?'

'No. Don't want to.'

With further promises to take Chloe and Edie to the Goods Shed, Ben and Libby left.

'Want to pop in to see George as we're here?' asked Ben, to Libby's surprise.

'Oh, yes, please!' She gave him a kiss. 'Thank you.'

'I just thought he may have heard something about the problems at Marsham's, too.' Ben drove up the little lane past the church. 'Or we could try the Fox?'

'No, George, please. I don't really know them as well.' Libby stared thoughtfully out of the window. 'What do you think about Chloe going to live with Dorothy Barton?'

'I think she'd probably be safer there, and she'd have more people to talk to, other than the people in the Goods Shed,' said Ben.

'And do we think that Roy's been pocketing the proceeds from the sale of the pubs?'

'Things seem to be pointing in that direction, but don't most people think he wouldn't be capable? I don't see how he could do it. He isn't in the accounts department, is he?'

'No – that's the problem.' Libby frowned. 'It would be convenient if he was the killer, but I really can't see it. I think there *is* something going on to do with the sale of the houses, but how and who by I have no idea. We don't really know anything about Marsham's, do we, despite all this digging.'

Ben drew up beside the Red Lion. 'Shall we see if George is doing food this evening?' he said. 'After all, you haven't eaten out in the last couple of days.'

Libby kissed him again. 'What a good idea,' she said.

George was flatteringly pleased to see them.

'Darts match at your place tomorrow,' he said to Ben, 'and the quiz at the Poacher on Sunday, isn't it?'

'Unless Sid's swapped with Zach at the Gate,' said Ben. 'Would that upset your team?'

'The Gate's coming in, is it?' George looked surprised. 'Keep 'emselves to 'emselves over in Felling usually. But no – team'd be pleased. Not so far to go.'

'Yes, we went there to talk to Zach,' said Libby. 'Nice place.'

'It is. You over there about the Marsham murder?' asked George, placing two half-pints in front of them. 'Not a Marsham house, though, is it.'

'No, but it's in Felling,' said Libby. 'Are you doing food tonight, George?'

'Sorry, Lib, no. No call during the week. Just Saturday and Sunday lunchtimes now.'

'Yes, Jenny at the Bell and Butcher said much the same.' Libby sighed. 'Oh well, I'll have to cook.'

Ben took out his phone. 'I promised you a meal,' he said. 'I'll call Hal.'

'So you've been to see Jenny,' said George, resuming his usual seat at the end of the bar. The few customers were being adequately attended to by the bright young woman they had met before Christmas.

'Yes. Sid Best told us to talk to her.'

'Because Marsham's aren't talking to anybody.' George nodded. 'It's an open secret. Can't understand why the police aren't all over 'em.'

'I think they're trying, but they need hard evidence that something illegal's going on,' said Libby.

'Woulda thought the CEO being murdered would be enough, wouldn't you?'

'Yes,' said Libby. 'I would. I wonder why it isn't.'

Ben put his phone away. 'Hal says will we please not be later than eight thirty.'

'So he can go home early!' said Libby. 'That's—'

'I know,' said George. 'Your mate with the veggie café.'

'George was just saying why is Dickie's murder not enough for the police to go investigating inside Marsham's,' Libby told Ben. 'What do you think?'

'Perhaps because there hasn't been any hard evidence to link the murder to the brewery,' suggested Ben. 'Or anyone working there. They would have gone into that right at the beginning, wouldn't they?'

'That's true.' George nodded. 'What about Trisha? Talked to her, I s'pose.'

'Trisha?' echoed Ben and Libby.

'Oh, not that she'd know anything about Marsham's. But she knew both the brothers, didn't she?' George raised enquiring eyebrows.

'Trisha . . .' Libby stared at him. 'Oh, of course! Roy's ex-fiancée! Ben, I told you! Why haven't we followed her up?'

'Because,' said Ben, amused, 'I seem to remember you saying the police would be better at finding her.'

'Not difficult to find,' said George with a grin. 'Used to be a regular here. Till Roy the Boy moved in over the road.'

'No!' Libby gasped. 'Where is she now?'

'Canterbury. Comes over to see her mates and pops in now and then. Shall I tell her you've been asking?'

'Better not, George,' said Ben. 'I expect the police have talked to her.'

'She'll be cut up.' George got off his stool and went to pour himself a glass of tonic water. 'Dickie was always good to her, especially after Roy . . . well, you know.'

'I heard she blamed Dickie for the break-up,' said Libby.

'Oh, she were just lashing out,' said George. 'Very fond of Dickie, she was.'

Libby was surprised. 'That's not the impression I was given.'

'Who by?'

'Well, the sister, for a start.'

'Ruth?' George shook his head. 'They didn't get on. Mind, I don't think Ruth'd get on with anyone the boys wanted. Hated Ronnie, and that Gina, o' course.'

'Ronnie?'

'Veronica – Dickie's wife.'

'Oh, the one who slunk off to the Caribbean after he was killed.' Libby nodded.

'Did she now.' George frowned. 'Not the nicest person, Ronnie. Trisha was the best of the lot, if you ask me. I wouldn't put anything past the other two. Surprised there wasn't a proper cat fight when Roy went off with Gina.'

Chapter Twenty-Eight

'Well!' said Libby, when they'd left the Red Lion. 'So George knew the family a lot better than we thought.'

'To be fair,' said Ben, 'we – or you – never even considered him as a source of information. The only connection with Herons-bourne you knew about was the fact that Roy had moved to Links View – and that was quite recent, wasn't it?'

'And he was at the golf club the night his brother was killed,' said Libby. 'And Christmas Eve, when his house was fired.'

'And they came into the pub on the night of the Christmas quiz,' Ben finished. 'But to be honest, it takes you no nearer the killer.'

'No. And surely the police know all about the wife and the girlfriend by now. I don't suppose I'm learning anything star-tlingly new, frankly.' Libby fastened her seat belt and turned to Ben. 'It was very nice of you to humour me by driving me today. Thank you.'

He smiled and pulled out onto the road. 'I'd never see you if I didn't occasionally join in.'

'I'm sorry.' She put her hand on his arm. 'I'll stop.'

'Don't be silly.' He sent her a sideways look. 'You wouldn't be you if you weren't solving problems. Don't forget, you were doing it when we first got together, so it's part of you, as far as I'm concerned.'

Libby squeezed his arm, suddenly not knowing what to say.

★

Ben dropped Libby at the foot of the Manor drive, while he went on to park at the top. Libby pushed open the door of the Pink Geranium and was greeted by her son.

'Harry says sit on the sofa until your table's free,' he said.

Libby looked round at the half-empty restaurant. 'There are lots of tables free,' she said. 'Well, three, anyway.'

'But not the window table,' said Adam. 'Humour him.'

Libby smiled and went to sit on the sofa in the left-hand window, while Adam went to fetch a bottle of wine and glasses.

'I'm assuming this is what you want?' he said.

'Yes, please.' Libby looked up at him as he opened the bottle. 'Am I being spoilt for some reason?'

'Hal said you're not very happy at the moment.' Adam poured wine. 'What's up, Ma?'

'As they were all telling me last night, it's mid-case blues,' said Libby with a sigh. 'And I feel a bit of a prat, to be honest.'

'You do?' Adam looked surprised. 'Why?'

'Oh, too involved to tell you now. Go and finish seeing to customers and I'll speak to you in a bit.'

At this point, Ben came in shaking his head like a wet dog. 'It's started raining again,' he said.

'Sit down,' said Adam. 'Wine?'

Harry appeared from the kitchen and waved at them. 'Leftovers?' he called. The other diners looked round, startled. Adam hurried off to reassure them.

'I take it that means we get what's left rather than ordering from the menu,' said Ben.

'I think so. And I think he wants a bit of a heart-to-heart. He's put us on the window table.'

'So he and Adam can come and sit with us.' Ben nodded. 'He has an infallible nose for your moods, doesn't he?'

'Don't you?' Libby raised her glass to him.

'Yes, but I actually live with you. I can't avoid it.' Ben took a healthy gulp of wine. 'Ah, that's better.'

'So come on. What's the problem?' asked Harry twenty minutes later, when he'd seated them at the window table with a selection of leftovers.

'Why should there be a problem?' asked Libby, with wide-eyed innocence.

'Because there usually is.' Harry sat down. 'Go on, Ben – what is it?'

'Basically the same as it was last night,' said Ben. 'Nothing's going right, according to Libby, and she's going to give up.'

'I didn't say that,' Libby muttered.

'Yes, you did. You said, "I'll stop." Didn't you?'

'Yes, but . . .' She felt warmth creeping up her neck. 'Oh, all right. It's a horrible muddle and I haven't added anything to it. I'm pretty sure that everything Fran and I have found out is stuff the police already know themselves. I say this every time, don't I?'

'Yes, but there are also little gems people tell you that the police would never find out in a million years,' said Harry.

Adam arrived with two more glasses and sat down next to his mother.

'He's right, Ma. That's why Ian and that Rachel person ask you to help. Oh, I know they shouldn't, but they do. And you are running the risk of becoming boring.'

'What?' Libby reared back, while Ben and Harry laughed.

'Out of the mouths of babes,' said Harry, pouring wine for himself and Adam. 'If our Fran had continued with her writing career and written down all our adventures . . .'

'Our?' said Libby.

'. . . *our* adventures,' repeated Harry, 'her readers would be saying, "Wow, she's annoying, that Libby! Says the same thing every time. Can't make up her own mind." And they'd be right.'

'That's a bit harsh, Hal,' said Ben.

'But he's right.' Libby forked up a mouthful of vegetarian stew. 'I do it every time. And yet I can't help diving in the next time something comes up.'

'Ian wouldn't have found out a lot of the stuff people have told you over the last four weeks,' said Adam. 'I haven't even been following the case, and I know *that*.'

'Where have you been this afternoon – evening, I should say – and what did you find out?' asked Harry. 'And did Ian ask you to do it?'

'Yes, he did,' said Ben. 'We went to ask Chloe Vaughan – you know, the lady whose flat got ransacked – who she'd told that she was going away.'

'That makes sense,' said Harry. 'Except that I bet she didn't tell anyone apart from us lot.'

'Exactly,' said Libby. 'Which means someone knows what's going on with the case. Someone who shouldn't, I mean.'

'Or someone who should, but shouldn't be using it for the wrong reasons,' said Adam.

'Have you told Ian?' asked Ben.

'No.' Libby looked surprised. 'I forgot. And he hasn't asked.'

'He probably didn't expect you to go haring off the minute he phoned.'

'True. Shall I ring him now?'

'Go on then – text,' said Harry. 'And tell him he can stay here if he wants to come over.'

Libby fished out her phone and did as she was told.

'Give me a recap,' said Adam when she'd finished. 'I'm very behind on this case. Dickie Marsham, MD or CEO or whatever of Marsham's brewery, was killed and dumped in a back alley in Canterbury. And his brother Roy, who also works for the firm, was arrested and let go.'

'Not actually arrested,' said Libby. 'And he's got an alibi – he was at a Rotary Club meeting when Dickie was killed. But he's been selling off the Marsham's pubs, so the managers have all lost their homes.'

Adam raised his eyebrows. 'If they were only managers, why didn't they have their own homes?'

'Some do – Simon did when he was a manager, but his wife kept it when they separated,' said Ben.

'The more I hear about marriage, the more I'm determined it will never happen to me,' said Adam, shaking his head.

Ben and Libby exchanged glances and Harry chuckled.

'Anyway, that means there is some bad feeling about Marsham's, both from managers and tenants and inside the company, we think, because they won't talk to anybody,' said Libby.

'So someone's been on the fiddle, whether it's Dickie or his brother,' said Adam. 'Who are the other suspects, apart from Marsham's employees?'

'Not really sure,' said Libby. 'There's Trisha, who was engaged to the brother until someone called Gina snatched him away.'

'Gina's a bad lot, presumably?'

Libby laughed. 'People seem to think so. And then there's Dickie's ex-wife, Veronica, who'd been milking him steadily since they split up.'

'Does she benefit?' asked Adam. 'That's usually the prime motive, isn't it?'

'Oh!' Libby sat back in her chair. 'I never thought of that.'

'I expect the police have,' said Harry.

'There, see,' said Libby, pushing her plate away. 'They'll have found out all about that, while I'm just pottering around in the mud.'

The three men made sympathetic noises.

'Have some more wine,' said Harry.

Libby's phone buzzed. She read the message and turned the screen to face Harry.

'"On my way",' he read, and grinned. 'So you'll have to stay until he gets here.'

'I wonder where he is?' mused Libby. 'Canterbury? At Chloe's flat?'

'Or the police station,' said Ben.

'I shall call my beloved,' said Harry, standing up. 'If we're in for a session, he needs to be here.'

Peter arrived within ten minutes, and the discussion of suspects and motives was resumed, without, as Libby said, coming to any sort of conclusion. The second bottle of wine was almost finished when Ian opened the door and looked in. 'Can I come in?'

Room was made for him at the table, and Harry offered whatever he could find in the kitchen.

'No, thanks, Hal.' Ian sounded even more tired than he had yesterday. 'I had something from the canteen earlier. I could do with a drink, though.'

Ian having been supplied with a large whisky, Harry shooed him and Libby off to the sofa and bore Peter, Adam and Ben to the kitchen.

'Harry's in his pastoral mood,' explained Libby. 'And Adam has turned himself into his apprentice.'

'Pastoral apprentice?' Ian was amused. 'And I take it this is because you've been complaining?'

'Yes. Apparently I'm becoming boring.' Libby smiled nervously. 'Because I . . . um . . . I . . .'

'Complain. Yes, I get it. Because you get in a muddle.'

'I wouldn't be believable in a book, I'm told.'

Ian laughed. 'No, I wouldn't believe you. Anyway. What do you want unravelled?'

'It's more what have the police discovered while I've been pottering around? At your request, of course.'

'Not a lot.' Ian was suddenly serious. 'We are currently investigating inside Marsham's, but although we suspect some kind of fraud has been going on, we can't find hard evidence. I told you that, didn't I?'

'Yes. What about Dickie's ex? Veronica? And Roy's ex?'

'Trisha Hadley – yes, We've looked into both of them. Why, have you got any more information on them?'

'George at the Red Lion said the sister, Ruth, couldn't stand

205

either of them. And we wondered – or Adam did, actually – does Veronica benefit from Dickie's death?'

'Ah – the obvious motive.' Ian sat back and looked at the ceiling. 'Yes, to an extent. She's already got the house on the other side of Felling, and she gets part of the residue, but the rest goes to the business.'

'The business? Not the brother or sister?'

'They both get a nominal amount.' He looked at her. 'Not worth murdering for.'

'Oh.' Libby pondered. 'So not really suspects, then.'

'No. And Trisha Hadley is still in the area. I'm surprised you haven't found her, actually.'

'How would we have found her? No one's talked about her much. I didn't know her name until George told us this evening.'

'Maybe not, but you've heard of her father.'

'How – is he famous?'

Ian smiled. 'Not exactly. He's the former landlord of the Fox and Hounds.'

Chapter Twenty-Nine

'*Stan?*' gasped Libby.

Ian nodded. 'Stan Hadley. I'm pretty sure I said we needed to speak to the dispossessed tenants, didn't I?'

'Did Pat Bailey give you his details, then? She didn't give them to me,' said Libby, somewhat hurt.

'She did. Sensibly, I thought. And although the sale of the pubs was Roy's doing, I'm sure it had something to do with Dickie's death.'

Libby nodded slowly. 'Yes, Fran and I thought the same. But when Pat told us that Stan had gone to live with his daughter, I somehow assumed the daughter was married with a family.'

'No, she has a flat in Canterbury. Luckily, it's got two bedrooms, or Stan really would be stuck.'

'Did she live at the pub when she and Roy were together? Is that how they met?'

'I don't know, but it seems a safe bet,' said Ian. 'It also explains why that particular pub was on the hit list, doesn't it?'

'Because Roy and Trisha had fallen out? Maybe. Except that it hasn't been sold – it's being left to rot,' said Libby, 'which seems at odds with the whole picture.'

'It is rather odd,' agreed Ian. 'I wonder if Roy had an attack of conscience and hoped somehow to open it again and let Stan take over.' He frowned. 'That bears looking into.'

'Except that it's nothing to do with Dickie's murder,' said Libby.

'No.' Ian smiled at her. 'So that's another job for Sarjeant and Wolfe, isn't it?'

Libby smiled back. 'We can try. But meanwhile – suspects for the murder.'

'Well, we're going back over everything to try and find someone who saw the victim on the night he was killed. Pathology now has the time of death in the early hours of the morning. Apparently he was moved soon after death, or rigor would have prevented him being positioned as he was. So he must have been out somewhere that evening.'

'Not at home?'

'He could have been, but there was no evidence of a struggle or of intensive cleaning at his house; just a couple of dishes in the dishwasher, which looks as though he'd had supper before going out. So where did he go?'

'And why?' Libby peered into her empty wine glass. 'You'd have heard if he went to the Poacher, wouldn't you? Where else did he spend his spare time?'

'At the business, we think. It looks as though the Shipwright's Arms wasn't just used for meetings, but as a sort of private club.' Ian patted her arm. 'Thanks to you and Ben for unearthing that little nugget.'

'I can't understand why you didn't know about it already.' Libby shook her head. 'You'd been looking into the brewery, hadn't you?'

'Yes, but not its inner workings. That's only come up very recently.'

'Is it worth asking the Rotary Club?'

'Why?' Ian raised an eyebrow. 'As far as I can see, they only come into it because Roy was at a meeting with them the night Dickie died.'

'Well, to see if he really was there. And if so, for how long.' Libby leant forward, suddenly excited. 'If Dickie wasn't killed until after midnight, Roy could have done it!'

'We still come up against the problem of location,' said Ian. 'I think we may have to rely on you stumbling over another essential clue.'

'Don't mock,' said Libby, with a sniff.

'I'm not. I have great respect for your stumbles.'

'In which case,' she said with a lowering glare, 'may I stumble over and interview Stan Hadley?

'You may.' Ian smiled and lifted her glass. 'Another?'

'I don't think I ought to have any more,' said Libby, rather half-heartedly.

'I think Harry's opened another bottle,' said Ian. 'And by the way, I wouldn't go telling Rachel or Rob you're going to see Stan.'

'Oh?'

'They're still duty-bound to abide by the rules at present, until this whole investigation is finished.'

'The one into the force? Or the murder?'

'The former,' said Ian. 'Now let's go and get you another drink.'

'What did he say?' Ben asked on the way home.

Libby told him.

'So now I'm going to go and see Stan Hadley,' she said. 'And I do feel somehow we ought to try and get the pub back for him.'

'Unless he's a killer,' said Ben.

'Obviously. But I wondered . . . if Marsham's still own it, perhaps they'd let him back in. And you know all about licences and stuff now, don't you? I bet he could make a go of it. And I bet some of the oldies who used it – what were they called? – would love to go back there rather than the community centre in the oast house.'

'You'd better find out what the situation there is, too,' said Ben, fishing out his key. 'The ownership might be in doubt.'

'Of the oast? Yes, I thought of that. Actually, we wondered if Ricky and his mum had inherited anything from his stepdad. Or if it had been claimed by the state as proceeds of crime, or something. I don't know how these things work.'

'No, and you can hardly ask Ricky,' said Ben. 'Now, I take it you don't want a nightcap?'

On Friday morning, it was still raining. Libby called Fran as soon as she felt it was polite to do so.

'All right,' said Fran. 'Will Ian give you Trisha's address?'

'He did, last night. It's off the Sturry road – you know where the new student village is? Somewhere near there. Shall we pop over on the off chance?'

Fran laughed. 'You mean make an expedition of it. You want to go today? We could do some supermarket shopping at the same time.'

'Then it wouldn't be a wasted journey if we can't see him,' said Libby happily. 'What a good idea.'

'I'll pick you up, shall I? What time?'

'You tell me. You're the one doing the driving.'

They settled on as close to half past ten as Fran could make it, and Libby did a quick internet search on Trisha Hadley, the Fox and Hounds and Stan.

'Couldn't find anything on Trisha,' she told Fran, when she arrived, 'but the Fox and Hounds has a lovely website, and there's a picture of Stan.'

'I wonder why it's still up?' said Fran.

'It's like Marsham's still own it,' said Libby. 'I'm sure there must be a reason. Roy had a change of heart, or something stopped him?'

'Isn't that more likely?' Fran said. 'The firm stopped him selling everything off.'

'If they did that, why haven't they told the police? And why is Roy still employed by them?'

'Because he's the only remaining Marsham in the business?'

'Oh, yes.' Libby frowned out of the window. 'What happens in that sort of case, do you suppose? Do they have an election or something? Of the board directors?'

'Or maybe Roy automatically becomes CEO? I don't know. But I suppose he owns the company now.'

'Is it a limited company? Shareholders? Don't they have a say in these things?'

'Probably. You ought to ask sister Ruth. She might be part owner now.'

'Yes, she'd know. And if she is, I suppose that constitutes a motive for murder.'

'Meanwhile,' said Fran, 'what are we going to ask Stan?'

By the time they'd arrived in Canterbury, negotiated the ring road and found their way to the modern block of flats where Trisha Hadley lived, it was almost midday.

'Quite a convenient place to live,' commented Libby, as they got into the lift. 'Walking distance from two major supermarkets.'

'Not to mention a DIY superstore,' said Fran, with a grin. 'But not so close to the bars.'

'Well, that's a drawback,' agreed Libby, laughing. 'Here we are. What number did I say?'

Fran rang the bell, and after a few moments, the door swung open and a surprised-looking man peered out at them.

'Yes?' he said.

Libby took a deep breath and opened her mouth, but Fran stepped in smoothly.

'Mr Hadley? I'm Fran Wolfe and this is Libby Sarjeant. We're helping the police looking into the murder of Dickie Marsham.'

'Eh?' Stan Hadley took a step back. 'What're you talking to me for, then? I'm nothing to do with Marsham's any more.'

'No, we know,' said Libby. 'That's why we wanted to talk to you.'

'You say you're working with the police?' He peered at them suspiciously. 'How do I know that? Where's your identification?'

Slightly thrown, Fran looked at Libby.

'It was Pat Bailey who gave us your name. She might have told you?' Libby cursed herself for not having thought this through. 'We're friends of Sir Jonathan, who—'

'Oh, I know who he is,' Stan interrupted, his face relaxing. 'Pity we didn't all have a Sir Jonathan.' He stepped back. 'You'd better come in.'

Sighing with relief, Libby followed Fran into the narrow hallway, which opened into a surprisingly spacious living area.

'What do you want to know, then?' he asked, sitting down in the corner of one of the two overstuffed sofas and indicating the other. The women sat too.

'We wondered what happened when Marsham's announced they were closing your pub,' said Libby. 'I went there last year and someone told me it was shutting. It seemed such a pity.'

Stan's face darkened. 'Pity? It was a f . . . flaming disaster. They chucked me out, closed the pub and just left it.'

'That's what we couldn't understand,' said Fran. 'The other pubs, like Pat Bailey's and the Crown and Sceptre, were all sold.'

'How much do you know about my pub?' He narrowed his eyes and looked from one to the other.

'Libby knows. I've never been there,' said Fran.

'We know Stapleton converted the oast houses into accommodation and a community centre called the Hop House Centre,' said Libby, noticing Stan's automatic wince at Stapleton's name. 'And we know that your pub was the only one in Shittenden and you hosted various groups there, including the Vintage Drinkers.'

'Which all went to the centre,' growled Stan. He was a small man, with grey hair and a wrinkled face, which Libby imagined was usually cheerful.

'Yes,' she said. 'So why wasn't your pub sold?'

He paused, obviously thinking about his answer.

'If it helps,' said Fran, after a moment, 'we know that your daughter was once engaged to Roy Marsham.'

He sighed, nodded, and sat back against the cushions. 'Yeah. Would have been my son-in-law. Hilarious that, isn't it? But not

212

selling the Fox had nothing to do with that. If he felt guilty, he wouldn't have closed it and chucked me out, would he?'

'No,' agreed Libby. 'It's such an odd situation.'

'Yeah,' said Stan again. 'And if I'd been going to kill anybody, it would have been that bastard.'

Both women nodded.

'So why did you want to talk to me? Pat said you'd spoken to her.'

'And Izzy at the Puckle Inn, and Jenny at the Bell and Butcher,' said Libby.

'The Bell? They selling that, now?' Stan looked startled.

'No, but Jenny said everyone's worried, and Marsham's won't talk to them – the landlords, I mean.'

'I heard that.' Stan nodded. 'I tried to get in touch to see if they'd let me open up the Fox again, and I've had nothing. Phone calls just go to voicemail and emails aren't answered. I reckon the business is going tits up.' He looked sheepish. 'Sorry – language.'

'Don't worry about it.' Libby grinned. 'We've heard a lot worse.'

'Have you talked to the other landlords?' asked Fran. 'Does anybody know anything for sure?'

'Nah. Just guesses.' He sighed. 'Sorry – didn't even offer you a cuppa. Fine "mine host" I am.'

'That's all right,' said Libby. 'We'll leave you in peace in a minute, but before we go, can you tell us if and when it would be convenient to speak to Trisha?'

'What for?' He tensed again. 'She's got nothing to do with the murder – or what's going on in the business.'

'No, but she knew Dickie and Roy,' said Fran. 'It's just background, really.'

'Hmm.' Stan looked down at his hands. 'Give us a number and I'll get her to call – if she wants to.'

'That'd be great, Stan!' Libby beamed at him. 'Fran's got a card.'

Fran pulled out her wallet and extracted a card. 'That's my husband's gallery – I work there.'

213

'Oh!' Stan looked at it with interest. 'I know that place. I bought some prints there for the pub. OK, I'll tell Trish.'

Libby stood up. 'We'll be off then,' she said. 'And let us know if there's anything we can do — I really feel you ought to be back in that pub.'

'So do I, but I don't see it happening.' Stan got up to see them out. 'I don't reckon I've helped much, have I? If you're looking into Dickie's murder?' He paused with his hand on the door frame. 'He was all right, was Dickie. Really mad with his brother when he took up with that Jean. I always thought he was a bit fond of Trisha himself.'

'Someone else told us that,' said Libby. 'Ruth, was it?'

'Ruth Baxter?' Stan sniffed. 'Never got on with her. She didn't like Trisha. Or Dickie's ex, either.'

'Or Jean,' put in Fran. 'She thought Roy should have married Trisha, even if she didn't like her.'

'You want to find out why she didn't like other women.' Stan nodded. 'Be in touch.'

Chapter Thirty

'Really?' Fran said, as they waited for the lift. 'Ruth?'

'Sounded like sour grapes to me,' said Libby.

'Why?'

'Well, Stan's bound to champion his daughter, even if he didn't like Roy, and if Ruth didn't like her, he wasn't going to like Ruth, was he?'

'Bit tenuous,' said Fran. 'Now, which supermarket? Asda, Sainsbury?'

All the way round Sainsbury's, Libby thought about Stan's last surprising statement. He was quite right when he said he hadn't helped much in the search for Dickie's killer, simply confirmed what they already knew, but she was intrigued by his comments about mild-mannered Ruth Baxter.

'We should have told him we were really there to look into the sale of the pubs,' said Fran when they were loading the car, 'rather than Dickie's murder.

'I don't see that would have made any difference.'

'He might have been friendlier.'

'He was all right in the end,' said Libby. 'And I still want to know what's going on with Ruth Baxter.'

'You know we were talking about the ownership of Marsham's?' said Fran as she pulled out of the car park. 'Well, wouldn't it make sense if all the siblings had shares in the company?'

'Yes, of course.' Libby frowned. 'But what about other shareholders?'

'Suppose there weren't any? Suppose it was just the family?'

'OK, but so what?'

'It means that Ruth would be able to vote on company policy and presumably be able to look into financial matters. We said – or you did – that she wouldn't be able to do that, but if she was on the board she would.'

'And so would her husband, in that case,' said Libby. 'She wouldn't keep the details from him.'

'No. And they might have wondered about the sale of the pubs.'

Libby half turned in her seat to look at her friend. 'What are you thinking?'

'This whole business about selling the pubs has obviously got something to do with the murder, and it's looking increasingly as though Roy had some kind of plan to cream off the profits. But at least one person has said he wasn't clever enough.'

'So you think Ruth or her husband was helping him? Blimey!' said Libby.

'I don't know, but I would have thought it was worth looking into.'

They were approaching Steeple Martin when Libby said, 'I bet the police have thought of that already.'

'What?' Fran darted a sideways look.

'Ruth or her husband being involved.'

'Oh. Yes, I suppose so.'

'Ian did say they were pretty sure some sort of fraud had been going on. They just hadn't got hard evidence.'

'You think they'd have looked at the Baxters?'

'Of course,' said Libby. 'Family members and accountants. Obvious.'

'Hmm.' Fran waited to cross over into Allhallow's Lane. 'But murderers?'

'I don't know. Ruth didn't seem the type, and she was very keen to talk to me about the murder.'

'Could have been to find out what you – or the police – actually knew,' said Fran, pulling up opposite number 17, where Sidney sat in the window making soundless miaows.

'I don't suppose you want to come in for lunch?' Libby asked as she undid her seat belt.

'I've got frozen stuff in the boot,' said Fran. 'If I think of anything else, I'll ring you. Do you want me to call Ian, as it was my idea about the Baxters and the fraud?'

'Go on then. I'll wait to hear from one or other of you.'

Fran helped load Libby's shopping onto her doorstep, then got back in her car.

'Enjoy your darts match!' she called.

'Oh, bother,' said Libby to Sidney as she struggled in with the bags. 'I'd forgotten that.'

After putting the shopping away, foraging for lunch and endeavouring to put all thoughts of murder from her mind, Libby decided to ring Maria Stewart, as the only person who actually knew the Baxters.

Ron answered.

'We're coming to the darts match tonight,' he said, sounding surprised, 'if that's what you were ringing about.'

'No, I wasn't, actually. Are you on Sid's team?'

'Yes – I thought you knew.'

'No. I don't play darts, so I don't know much about the teams. I know the match is at the Pocket tonight, though.'

'You could hardly avoid it,' said Ron, sounding amused. 'So what can we do for you?'

'We-ell,' said Libby. 'You know Maria introduced me to Ruth Baxter?'

'Yes?'

'I wanted to find out what she knew about her. About them both.'

Ron sighed. 'I'll get her. Why didn't you ring her mobile?'

'Because your landline's the number in my phone,' admitted Libby. 'I'll put Maria's in now.'

'You'll already have it,' said Ron. 'She called you about Ruth before, didn't she?'

'Oh, yes,' said Libby, feeling foolish.

'Anyway, here you are. She's hovering at my elbow.'

There was a pause, then Maria said, 'Lib? What's up?'

Libby recounted George's and Stan Hadley's remarks about Ruth Baxter.

'And I wondered what your opinion was. Is she vindictive? And what about her husband?'

'Quentin? A bit full of himself, and thinks he's irresistible to women. At least that's the impression he's always given me. And with a name like Quentin, he's got something to live up to, hasn't he?' Maria laughed. 'Ruth just seems to do the equivalent of rolling her eyes and saying "Here he goes again."'

'So she isn't a jealous person, then?'

'I don't know her well enough, really, but I can't see why she would be jealous of Trisha and Veronica. Or Gina, come to that. They were all attached to her brothers, not her husband.'

'Perhaps she wanted to be the only woman in their lives?' Libby shook her head at herself. 'No, she doesn't seem that sort at all. Did her husband flirt with them all, maybe?'

'Given what I've seen of him, quite likely,' said Maria, 'but none of them reacted to him. Or not as far as I know.'

'No.' Libby frowned. 'It's odd, though, that both George and Stan had the same impression. She seemed quite mild to me.'

'Yes, although devoted to Dickie, I thought. Not so much to Roy. I'll ask Ron what he thinks, although he didn't have much to do with her.'

'But he might have an opinion on her husband,' said Libby. 'Although Quentin hasn't come into the equation before, so perhaps he's a red herring.'

'Where have you got to in the investigation so far?' asked Maria. 'Are you still the police's unofficial informers?'

'Ian's, yes,' said Libby. 'Given all the fuss about the service at the moment – and the investigations into corruption – he's keeping us very much below the parapet.'

'Well, between you I'm sure you'll get to the bottom of it,' said Maria. 'And we'll see you tonight. You will be there, won't you?'

'Oh, of course,' said Libby, who until Fran had mentioned it hadn't even thought about the darts match. 'I'll see you later.'

'Were you going to the darts match anyway?' Libby asked Ben when he came in later in the afternoon.

'Anyway? How do you mean? Yes, of course I was. I'm first sub.'

'Oh, are you?'

'Yes.' He beamed proudly. 'And I'm delighted that the Pocket's hosting the league.'

Libby smiled fondly at him. 'Of course. I'll be there to cheer you on.'

'Mainly because friends of yours will be there.' Ben cocked an eyebrow.

'They're your friends too.'

'Yes, but at the moment . . .' He leant over and gave her a kiss. 'I'm going to have a shower and change. Get the dinner on, woman.'

Most members of the three teams taking part in the darts match were already assembled by the time Libby arrived at the Hop Pocket. Ben had gone ahead, ostensibly to help Simon should he need it.

'It's actually because he loves playing at being a landlord,' Libby confided to Maria, who'd saved her a seat at her table. 'He's very proud of his pub.'

'So he should be,' said Ron. 'And the Coach and Horses hasn't suffered, has it?'

'Not at all, although I worry sometimes. Tim's still hosting the quiz league – that's on Sunday, by the way, at the Poacher.'

'Yes, we'll be there too,' said Maria. 'Our lives seem to revolve around pubs these days.'

'So many rural communities do,' said Libby with a sigh. 'That's why it's so sad that so many are closing down.'

'And often with no reason,' said Ron.

'Exactly. Fran and I have seen some at first hand. Like Trisha Hadley's dad's pub.'

'Oh – at Shittenden!' said Maria. 'That was a lovely pub. And the heart of the village.'

'Until old Stapleton forced the closure,' said Ron, scowling into his pint. 'With his community centre and all those new houses.'

'Well, actually,' said Libby, leaning forward, 'I'm not sure it was Stapleton himself.'

Maria looked interested, but just then Simon called the company to order and Ron got up to join his Poacher teammates, while the Pocket's first player took his place at the oche. Luckily for Libby, who had minimal interest in darts, John Cole was a member of the Pocket's team, and shortly after the beginning of the match, Beth joined her and Maria.

'So how's the investigation going?' asked Beth.

Maria looked amused. 'You can't get away from it, can you, Lib?'

Libby pulled a face. 'It's my own fault. I ask too many people questions.'

'Well, believe it or not, someone else has asked me a question this week,' said Beth. 'Although more pastoral than criminal.'

'What – to do with the Marsham murder?' Maria leant forward. 'I'm Maria, by the way – I think we met briefly when this place opened.'

'We did,' agreed Beth, 'and your husband performed for us.'

'So did yours,' said Maria. 'He's a dab hand on the piano.'

'Go on, Beth – this question?' interrupted Libby. 'Who was it?'

'The little girl who came over with the lovely pony before the panto. Alanna.' Beth put her head on one side. 'You know?'

'Yes!' Libby was surprised. 'How does she know you?'

'She doesn't really, but her family are churchgoers.'

'Oh, Patti's flock, then? She does Heronsbourne, doesn't she?'

'No, they attend the Catholic church in Nethergate. Anyway, she asked the priest there if there was a church in Steeple Martin, as apparently she didn't want to ask . . . Stella, is it? . . . how to get hold of you.' Beth smiled. 'Luckily, the priest didn't force her to talk to him and just gave her my name and number.'

'And what was the question?' Libby was getting impatient.

'She wanted to know if she should tell you something about . . . Jean, I think she said?' Beth looked a question.

'Yes – Jean, or Gina, Marsham. Roy Marsham's wife.'

'She wanted to tell you she thinks this woman is a sex worker. Of course, she called her a prostitute.'

Chapter Thirty-One

Libby sat back with a puff. Maria, wide-eyed, gasped.

'Stella and I both guessed she was,' said Libby. 'Poor Alanna. She was still a child when she made friends with Jean. She must have felt disloyal.'

'She did. We only spoke on the phone, so I couldn't see her body language, but she obviously felt guilty.' Beth shook her head. 'She's been thinking about it since she talked to you. She said you went riding with them?'

'That's right – and I hope to do so again,' said Libby. 'She did tell me she thought Jean wasn't a nice person, but she also said she would never kill anyone.'

'Yes, that's what she said to me. I said I'd tell you. She sounded relieved.'

'Does that help the investigation?' asked Maria.

'I don't see how,' said Libby. 'And please, Maria, don't spread this around – especially not to Ruth.'

'Of course not!' Maria looked indignant. 'As if I would.'

'Who's Ruth?' asked Beth.

Libby gave her a brief rundown of the Marsham family, then sat back to finish her drink and ponder the new information.

At half-time, Libby, Ron and Maria were delighted by the arrival of Ricky and Barney. Colley the golden Labrador belonging to Dan, a member of the Pocket's team, rushed over to greet them, to the imminent danger of several drinkers and their drinks.

To Libby's surprise – although she admitted later to Ben that it wasn't really such a surprise – Ricky was followed by Brandon, trying, and failing, to be unobtrusive.

'I had a meal with Harry and Peter,' he explained, having been introduced to Maria and Ron, 'and this young man had just arrived for the weekend, so we decided to come over together.' He looked round the crowded pub with satisfaction. 'I'm so pleased I decided to make the move.'

Libby explained about the cottage in Cuckoo Lane.

'I'm beginning to think we ought to move here, too,' said Ron, quirking an eyebrow at his wife.

'Don't you dare,' said Libby. 'What would Sid and my cousin do without you?'

A little later, Ricky sidled up to Libby and perched on the windowsill beside her.

'Lib, the lads have been telling me about this new case of yours.'

'Oh yes?' said Libby warily.

'Something to do with pubs being closed?'

'Yes.' She was still wary.

'Well, there was one that my nan knew. Over near that place with the converted oast houses.'

'Yes. The Fox and Hounds.' Libby relaxed. 'It wasn't sold, though. Just closed. Great shame.'

'Yes. I just wondered if . . .' Ricky looked distressed.

'Nothing to do with you, Rick.' Libby mentally crossed her fingers. 'Don't worry about it.'

'Oh, OK.' He didn't look convinced. 'I'd hate it if what happened was still hurting someone.'

It still is, thought Libby, but it wouldn't do Ricky any good to worry about it. 'I'll let you know if I think there's anything you can do,' she said. 'Do you want another drink?'

'Interesting evening?' Ben asked as they walked home.

'Very,' said Libby. 'Was yours?'

'You know what I mean.' Ben linked his arm through hers. 'I saw you talking to Maria and Beth, and then Ricky.'

Libby related their conversations.

'I think Ricky was wondering if he could somehow make restitution,' she finished up. 'We wondered about that before. I don't know how he and his mother were left financially.'

'Comfortable, I would think,' said Ben. 'You could ask Philip what he thinks.'

'Thing is, Marsham's still own the Fox and Hounds. I can't understand why they don't reopen it.'

'Ian said they were looking into possible fraud at the brewery, didn't he? They'll find out.'

'I'm beginning to wonder if the Baxters have got something to do with that after all. Ruth might still have shares in the company . . .'

'Let Ian's forensic accountants worry about that,' said Ben. 'You can go ferreting about in Gina Marsham's past.'

'Not sure about that,' said Libby. 'But I will try and get to talk to young Alanna on her own. See what she's got to say.'

'You know who might help there?' said Ben. 'Alice Gedding. She's nearer in age to Alanna.'

'Than me and Stella? Yes, but she's still got at least twenty years on her.'

'But she's got young kids,' said Ben. 'Give her a ring.'

'All right,' Libby agreed. 'Tomorrow. Although I expect Edward will be there.'

'What difference does that make?' Ben opened the door to number 17. 'Talk to Fran about it first.'

Early on Saturday morning, Libby phoned Fran and reported her latest findings, together with Ben's suggestion.

'That's a very good idea,' said Fran. 'Ring Alice this morning. If Edward's there for the weekend, she won't want to do anything until Monday, but then she might invite Alanna to her farm and you can see her there.'

'Remind me why I need to do it?' said Libby.

'Because Alanna thought it was important enough to tell you – and probably the police. I expect she's nervous of the police because of her family's history.'

'Yes, of course. OK, I'll let you know what happens.'

It wasn't until she sat down at the kitchen table to ring Alice that she realised she didn't have her number. Muttering to herself, she found Edward's instead.

'I'll tell her to call you,' said Edward. 'I'm here now, but she's got a couple of ewes early lambing, so she's in the shed, I think. Speak later.'

Giggling to herself over the image of the elegant Edward in a lambing shed, Libby put the kettle on for yet more tea. Then her phone rang.

'Libby? It's Alice. You wanted me?'

'Oh, Alice – I'm sorry to interrupt when you're so busy.'

'No worries. I was just checking. Both the girls are fine.'

'Girls? Oh – the ewes. Oh, good.'

'What did you want? It wasn't to do with Alanna, was it?'

Libby jumped. 'How did you know?'

'I guessed. She was over here the other day – she gives me a hand when Stella doesn't need her – and she was talking about you. She said she'd spoken to a priest. Was that Patti?'

'No, it was Beth, our vicar here in Steeple Martin. Thing is . . .' Libby paused, wondering how to frame her request. Alice saved her the trouble.

'If you want to speak to her privately, I can ask her over here. For some reason she's worried about telling Stella.'

'That would be brilliant, Alice.' Libby heaved a sigh of relief. 'Beth said she seemed worried about speaking in front of Stella. I can't think why. Stella's no more a fan of Gina Marsham than Alanna is.'

'She thinks of Stella as a sort of grandmother figure and doesn't want to shock her, I think,' said Alice. 'Which is mad. I can't think of anyone less shockable than Stella.'

'Yes – I've only just met her, but I agree! Anyway, when would be convenient? I don't suppose it's urgent. I can't see that it's got anything to do with the Marsham murder – not that the police seem to have got very far with that in any case.'

'Do you want to come today? I can ask her over to help with the kids – she loves doing that. And then I can go to the pub with Edward!'

Libby laughed. 'Excellent! When?'

'After lunch? I'll send you a text when I know she's on her way.'

Libby abandoned her tea and called Fran and Ben to let them know of her plans. Ben approved, but asked that she be back in time for dinner, and Fran said she could call in to Harbour Street on her way home if she had time.

The sky had brightened by the time Libby was driving down Pedlar's Row on her way to Alice's farm. She felt slightly guilty for bypassing both John and Sue's house and Brooke Farm, but consoled herself by promising to pay a non-murder-related visit to both of them next week.

Edward answered her knock at the kitchen door, clad in un-Edward-like jeans and a hooded sweatshirt. He laughed at Libby's surprised look.

'It's a different world out here, Lib!' he said, ushering her into the kitchen. 'And I'm getting to be a dab hand at being a farmhand.'

Alice was wiping her hands on a tea towel and waved it towards the door to the hall. 'The kids are in the sitting room,' she said. 'I'll get Alanna to come out.'

'I thought you were going for a drink?' said Libby.

'We are, later,' said Edward. 'Alanna's got a late pass to babysit this evening.'

'Actually, she's going to stay over,' said Alice. 'It makes a change for her. Her parents can be a bit . . .' She stopped and looked at Edward.

'A bit claustrophobic,' he helped out. 'They haven't quite got used to the fact that in this country, young women don't have to stay at home under their father's control.'

'But they let her help Stella? And you?'

'They feel obliged to Stella for "saving" them,' said Alice, putting the word in air quotes. 'And she vouches for me, so . . .'

'Alanna's one of the lucky ones, isn't she?' said Libby. 'Stella said she's actually made some friends among the girls who come to ride the ponies.'

'Yes, more than she did at school.' Alice nodded. 'And here she is!'

'Hello, Alanna,' said Libby, giving the girl what she hoped was an encouraging smile.

Alanna smiled shyly back. 'Hello, Mrs . . . Libby.'

'Will you take Libby to see the new lambs?' asked Alice. 'And meanwhile, I'll put the kettle on.'

Libby and Alanna escaped gratefully, and Alanna led her round the corner to the large shed, which, Libby discovered, held several individual pens. Four of these were occupied, two by ewes with their lambs, tiny little things with floppy ears and spindly legs, which made Libby want to take an immediate vow to become vegetarian.

'What did you want to tell me, Alanna?' she said, leaning over to stroke a little black and white lamb, who took refuge behind his large and suspicious mother. 'Was it something to do with Jean?'

'Yes.' Alanna looked at her feet. 'I told you I didn't think she was a nice person.'

'You did.'

'Well, I think she . . .' The girl cleared her throat. 'I think she . . . had men,' she finished quickly.

'When she lived in the same house as you?'

'Yes.' Alanna straightened up. 'I think she was a . . . a prostitute. And that's wrong, isn't it?'

227

Now there's a minefield, thought Libby, wondering how to answer.

'So I told the priest,' Alanna continued without waiting. 'I think perhaps she . . .' She swallowed hard. 'I think she might have . . . I think Mr Marsham might have . . .'

'Mr Marsham? Her husband?' said Libby, wondering where this was going.

'No, the other Mr Marsham. I saw him.' Alanna turned away and leant on the fencing round the pen.

Libby stared. Then: 'Do you mean you saw the other Mr Marsham at Jean's flat in Nethergate?'

'No. I saw him go to her new house.'

Chapter Thirty-Two

Libby took a deep breath.

'Oh, well,' she said carefully and without emphasis, 'I suppose he was her brother-in-law. And he could have been visiting his brother.'

Alanna shook her head firmly. 'No. The car was gone.'

'Jean couldn't have taken it?' Libby suggested tentatively.

'No. Jean cannot drive.' Alanna gave a tight little laugh. 'She said she liked taking a taxi whenever she went out.'

That fitted with what Libby had heard about Gina Marsham.

'So,' she began, leaning nonchalently against the sheep pen. 'When did you see Mr Marsham visiting Jean's house?'

'The week before he died.' Alanna nodded. 'And a few weeks before that.'

'So he was a regular visitor?'

'I don't know. I saw him twice. The first time, Jean's husband was there. I was walking home from the bus stop.'

'You go home down that road, then? Not down Pedlar's Way?'

'It's quicker by the golf club.' Alanna grinned, the first sign of lightness she'd evinced since they came outside. 'But you're not supposed to go that way.'

'Right.' Libby grinned back. 'And you were on your way from the bus stop the second time?'

'Yes.' Alanna nodded. 'I go to the library in Nethergate. Sometimes Stella takes me, but I don't like to ask her all the time.'

'No, of course not.' Libby desperately wanted to offer to drive Alanna anywhere she wanted whenever she wanted. 'But you didn't see him the night he was killed, did you?'

'I don't go out on Saturdays,' said Alanna, a little forlornly.

'Well, you've been a great help, Alanna.' Libby straightened up and stretched her back. 'And you've done absolutely the right thing. Can I tell my friend the policeman?'

'Yes, please. I wanted to tell them, but my parents are worried about the police.'

'I understand.' Libby smiled and wished she could think of something more reassuring to say to the girl. 'Let's go in and see if Alice has made tea. And I must arrange to come and ride again soon, mustn't I?'

It was getting dark by the time Libby left the farm, even though it was barely four o'clock. Thanking her own forethought in putting a casserole in the slow cooker before she left home, she headed for Nethergate and Coastguard Cottage.

'Do you think she's right?' asked Fran, when Libby had told her Alanna's surprising story.

'About Gina being a prostitute – sorry, sex worker – yes, we'd already thought that, but that Dickie was one of her clients? Can't see it myself. Especially not visiting her at her new home.'

'No, it does seem unlikely.' Fran gazed into the glowing wood burner. 'She didn't say anything about seeing him at the house in Nethergate?'

'No. And to be honest, whatever Dickie thought of Roy's marriage and the fact that he'd dumped Trisha, it's perfectly natural that he should be visiting, isn't it? After all, they both worked for the family firm.'

'I was thinking.' Fran sat back and clasped her hands in front of her. 'What if they were all members of the board and there was a . . . well, a contentious issue. And they weren't all in favour.'

'What – selling the business or something?'

'Perhaps. Would that be a motive?'

'Yes! But I bet the police have gone into that. Shall I ask Ian?'

'Yes – but I was thinking that could be why Dickie was visiting. And if Alanna's right, and he visited Gina on her own, it could have been to persuade her to get Roy to vote the right way.'

'Maybe.' Libby thought about it. 'But that situation makes it even odder that Ruth should have asked for my help. She would have known all about what was going on.'

'But did she *actually* ask for your help? Or did she just want to know how far the police had got?'

'Yes, that was it,' said Libby, much struck. 'What did I know about Dickie's death, she asked. And she was quite insistent about it being something to do with the business.'

'To distract from it being something personal?' asked Fran.

'I didn't think of it like that,' said Libby. 'But Ian had asked us to find out about Dickie's personal life, so that was bound to be part of the conversation. Oh, I don't know – I'm muddled now.' She glared at Fran. 'And don't say "What's new."'

'It is a muddle,' conceded Fran. 'I think you should just dump the whole lot in Ian's lap. It gives him the opportunity to go and question Gina – and Roy, of course – and maybe he'll get something out of it.'

'Mmm.' Libby nodded. 'I wish I knew who Gina's clients were, though. Surely there's got to be some sort of motive there?'

'If she was married to Dickie, yes, but she's married to Roy.'

'But if Dickie *was* one of her clients . . .'

'Stop it, Lib! Go on – go home and spend a pleasant domestic evening with Ben, and I'll see you tomorrow.'

'You will?' Libby was surprised.

Fran sighed. 'I'm still on the quiz team, remember? Tomorrow night? The Poacher?'

'Oh yes.' Libby smiled sheepishly. 'Too much going on in my head, that's the trouble.'

'Course there is,' said Fran with a grin.

Libby went home.

Ian called halfway through Saturday evening, while Ben and Libby were watching an obscure drama they'd found on one of the streaming channels.

'Am I interrupting anything?' he asked.

'No,' Libby told him. 'There's never anything on television these days.'

'Apart from the thousand and one channels you can now choose from.'

'Yes, well. I liked TV as it used to be. Did you want to know what I found out?'

'Well, your text was suitably vague. Fran advised you to tell me everything and leave it to me, I gather.'

'Dump it all in your lap was what she actually said.'

'Indeed. A way with words, your friend. Carry on then.'

Libby told him everything Alanna had said, and her own thoughts.

'I agree with you about Dickie Marsham. I don't think he would have been one of Gina's clients, if, indeed, she had them.'

'Don't you think she did, then?'

'Oh, I'm pretty sure she did, but we have no proof.'

'And what about him visiting the house in Links View?'

'As you said, a perfectly normal thing for him to do.'

'OK. And what about Fran's thoughts about the family being board members?'

'If you're wondering about Ruth – yes, she is. The three of them and the non-executive director, whom we have just discovered is Quentin Baxter.'

'So why didn't she know what was going on when she spoke to me?' Libby was indignant.

'I think the brothers rather kept her out of the loop. Quentin, as far as we can determine, was brought in for his financial expertise.'

'But Ruth's an accountant – why didn't they rely on her?'

'They needed an independent opinion, probably.' Ian sounded impatient. 'In fact, they've been so secretive about the business I feel inclined to lock up the whole boiling of them.'

'Shall I talk to Ruth again?' Libby asked hopefully. Ben sighed in the background.

'I doubt if it would help. And frankly, I'm not sure it has any bearing on her brother's murder. I doubt Gina Marsham does, either.'

'So that's that,' Libby said to Ben, after she'd rung off. 'There's nothing left for me to look into.'

'That's probably a good thing,' said Ben. 'Ready for a drink?'

Libby nodded absently. 'But Dickie's murder's still unsolved, and we still don't know why Roy sold off all those pubs.'

'Could it possibly be the obvious reason? They were losing money – particularly over the last year or so?' Ben came back from the kitchen with two whiskies.

'But they weren't. The Crown and Sceptre wasn't, and neither was the Fox and Hounds. And Pat Bailey's George and Dragon was doing really well. They were all real community pubs.'

'What about the Puckle? Simon worked there – and that was sold.'

'But that was ages ago. And it's doing well now.' Libby frowned at her whisky. 'I wish I could find out. I'm sure it's got something to do with Roy's gambling.'

'Is that proven now?' asked Ben, sitting back down.

'I don't know. Oh!' Libby shook her head furiously. 'There's so much I don't know!'

'Anyway, it isn't anything to do with the murder,' said Ben. 'Perhaps, after all, it was a random mugging.'

'What was he doing in Canterbury, in that case? And why was he left on Chloe's doorstep?'

'Was he, though? I thought he was just *near* her flat.'

'Hmm. I still think he was left there because someone knew who she was and it would throw suspicion elsewhere.'

'But neither you nor the police could find anyone who knew both Dickie and Chloe to link them up, could you?' Ben stretched out his legs. 'I think that was a coincidence.'

Libby sighed. 'Maybe. Do you want to watch the rest of this . . .' She waved a hand in the direction of the television.

'Not if you've got any other ideas?' said Ben, and took the whisky from her hand.

The following day being Sunday, Hetty cooked her usual enormous roast dinner. Even Harry and Peter were there, Harry having decided the Pink Geranium could stay closed on Sundays for at least the rest of January. Edward was still with Alice, but to Libby's surprise, Ian arrived, looking even more tired than he had been last time she saw him. Flo buttonholed him as soon as he appeared.

'So we not goin' to see that Edward any more?' She fixed him with a formidable glare.

'Well, certainly not so much,' said Ian. 'Alice can't really leave the farm and the children.'

'Hmm. What about her ma?'

'Her mother? I don't know if she's got one!' said Ian, surprised.

'Course she 'as. Must 'ave.'

'Maybe her mother doesn't live near here,' said Libby.

'Or she could be dead,' said Harry. 'She only came to the farm because of her husband, didn't she?'

'Hmm,' said Flo again.

'Edward comes over in the week,' said Hetty quietly. 'You can see him then.'

'It's serious, then? With Edward and Alice?' asked Peter.

'Looks like it.' Ian gave him a tired smile. 'I might be losing my neighbour soon.'

'No!' said Libby. 'You think he'll move in with her?'

'Surely he'd keep Grove House while he's still at the university,' said Ben. 'It would be too far to commute from the farm.'

234

'I don't know – I haven't discussed it with him,' said Ian. 'It's very personal, after all.'

Hetty pushed a bottle of wine towards him. 'You stayin' tonight, then?'

'No thanks, Hetty.' Ian smiled at her. 'I'll go and support the quiz team at the Poacher this evening, and it's almost on my doorstep.'

'You could talk to Maria, then,' said Libby.

'Why?' Ian raised his eyebrows. 'I thought you'd mined that seam already.'

'Well, yes.' Libby looked down at her hands. 'But you could speak to Ron, too.'

'And Mike and Cassandra, no doubt,' said Ian. 'No, it's fine, Lib. I shall have a well-deserved full day off.'

The usual post-lunch meeting in Peter and Harry's cottage was forgone as they were all going in the minibus to the Poacher that evening, and Libby declared she needed a couple of hours alcohol-free.

'Who stole Libby and put this clone in her place?' asked Harry, as they parted at the end of the Manor drive.

'She'll be back later,' said Ben, and ducked.

'Has Ian given up, then?' Libby asked him as they walked back down the high street. 'It sounded like it.'

'As you said last night, there isn't much left to look into, is there? It must be so frustrating for them.'

'It must.' Libby nodded. 'I feel sure there must be something I could do.'

'That's not what you said yesterday,' said Ben. 'I'd just leave it, if I were you.'

'Oh, all right.' She tucked her arm into his. 'I'll be good.'

Ben said nothing.

Chapter Thirty-Three

The Poacher was fuller that evening than Libby had ever seen it. She waved to Sandra and Alan Farrow, and went to say hello to Mike and Cass and Ron and Maria. Fran and Guy arrived on the heels of the Steeple Martin contingent and Ian came in quietly and found a seat near Ben.

'No Red Lion this evening?' he asked.

'No, this is the first heat of the new season,' explained Ben. 'The Red Lion is playing the Fox at Creekmarsh next week.'

Libby appeared by Ian's side.

'Mike's got something to tell you,' she said quietly. 'Do you want to speak to him here or outside?'

Ian frowned. 'Really?'

Libby nodded. 'Really.'

He sighed and stood up. Mike caught his eye and followed him outside.

'What was that about?' Ben asked. Fran leant across and raised an eyebrow.

'Mike saw someone hanging around Dickie Marsham's house this afternoon. He challenged him and the person said he was looking for Dickie. Mike didn't know what to say.'

'What *did* he say?' asked Fran.

'That there was no one there just now – something like that.' Libby shook her head. 'But this person kept asking. Well, I suppose he would – Mike said the police tape's still there.'

Mike and Ian reappeared, Ian with his phone to his ear. Mike made a face at them and returned to his table.

'What's happening?' Libby asked, as Ian came back to his seat.

'Nothing you need worry about,' he said. 'A patrol's going to check out the house. We didn't feel it was worth keeping a guard on the place after all this time.'

Unsatisfied, Libby sat back and tried to concentrate on the picture quiz, which had just been left at their table by one of Sid's regulars.

At half-time, Sandra Farrow made her way across to the Coach and Horses table.

'Any news, Libby?' she asked. 'About Dickie?'

'I'm afraid not,' said Libby with a smile. 'All the ends are dead ones.'

'Ah.' Sandra looked thoughtful. 'Only Alan actually had a phone call from that friend of his I told you about. The old school friend?'

Libby's mouth dropped open.

'Anthony Leigh?' she managed eventually.

'I think that was the name.' Sandra looked puzzled.

'What did he want?' Libby was trying surreptitiously to attract Ian's attention.

'To know about Dickie's murder, I think,' said Sandra. 'Is it important?'

'I think so,' said Libby, relieved that at last Ian had noticed and was coming over.

She told him what Sandra had said. 'And I thought, with the person Mike saw . . .'

Ian smiled. 'Yes, all right. Mrs Farrow, isn't it?' He turned to Sandra. 'I think we met over the ukulele club problems.'

'Oh, yes.' Sandra, looking flustered, sent Libby a pleading look.

'Could I speak to your husband, then?' asked Ian. 'Before the next round?'

Libby watched as they went over to the Poacher team's table.

'Now what?' said Ben.

'It's the Spanish connection,' said Libby.

There was no further opportunity to discuss this possible new development with Ian during the rest of the evening, or even with Fran, so Libby had to contain her soul in patience, making do with grumbling to Peter, Harry and Ben in the minibus on the way home.

'Oh, stop it, Libby,' said Philip eventually. 'We won! First time in ages! And you're depressing everyone.'

Monday morning, and Libby had sent several text messages before she'd even had her second cup of tea.

'Give it a rest, Lib,' groaned Ben. 'You'll find out soon enough. Somebody will call you – if only to find out what *you* know!'

Eventually she retired to the conservatory and tried to concentrate on a new painting for Guy. This, naturally, failed to hold her attention. At last, her phone rang.

'I knew you'd be eaten up with curiosity,' said Ian, 'so I thought I'd better ring before you drove everybody mad.'

Uneasily aware that this was very true, Libby said nothing.

'Well, it's another red herring, as far as I can see. There was no trace of a mysterious stranger at Marsham's house, and no reply from Anthony Leigh's phone. We have, however, wasted more of the force's budget trying to find out whether he's entered the country in the last few days.'

'And has he?'

'Not as far as we can see.'

'Oh.'

'What are you thinking?' asked Ian suspiciously after a pause.

'Nothing. Is Roy actually going to work at the moment?'

'Eh?'

'Well, I mean . . . Marsham's are under investigation, and Roy was selling off the pubs, and now his brother's dead – I would have thought he might be staying at home.'

238

'I don't know!' Ian sounded surprised. 'I think he was told to stay away at first. Whether he's gone back now, I don't know.'

'But you *should* know! You're in charge!'

'It's Rob's case – I told you.'

'Yes.' Libby went quiet again.

Ian sighed. 'Come on, out with it.'

'Roy's gambling. Is that definite?'

'Gambling debts? Yes. And we looked at connections with Mickey Vaughan's associates. Nothing.'

'What about Anthony Leigh? You said he's a typical Costa criminal.'

Now Ian went quiet.

'Ian? What about it?'

'I'll look into it,' he said slowly. 'But I can't honestly see that it has anything to do with Dickie's death, can you?'

'I just feel there must be a link,' said Libby. 'And I think Fran does, too.'

'So,' said Libby to Fran, after she'd made a cup of tea and sat down to call her. 'How do we find out?'

'We can't,' said Fran. 'Unless we go storming up to Roy and Gina's house and demand answers.'

'Well, we could.'

'Don't be daft, Libby. We'd be thrown out before we got a word out.'

'In that case,' said Libby, 'I'm going to call Ruth Baxter. I've still got her card.'

'What for?'

'She knows more than she's letting on. Ian knew all about her being on the board and her husband being a non-executive director, so the police questioned her after I saw her.'

'What do you mean?'

'She won't know how much I know, so I might be able to kid her into telling me something important.'

'What will you say?'

'I'll ask her why she didn't tell me about her involvement in the company – hers and her husband's. She spent most of her time trying to steer me away from the family and imply it was something to do with the business, so I reckon she knows something was up at the brewery.'

'And what do you think that is?' asked Fran.

'Well . . .' Libby took a reflective sip of tea. 'Roy had debts. Roy sold the pubs. Did he somehow divert the profits from those sales into his own pocket? Ruth and her husband are both accountants – in fact, she told me she started off with Marsham's. So did she find out about it?'

'The problem there, as we've already been told, is that Roy is simply not clever enough to do that. Besides, he doesn't appear to have anything to do with the financial side of things.'

'Mmm.' Libby frowned. 'I'm still going to talk to her.'

It wasn't, however, as easy as she had hoped. The number on Ruth Baxter's card rang out without even going to voicemail. She looked the practice up online and found another number, which was answered, but by an employee who informed her that Mrs Baxter was out with a client, and could anyone else help? Libby thanked her and tried to decide what to do next.

She called Maria.

'Do you know where the Baxters live?' she asked.

'In Felling,' said Maria, sounding surprised. 'Why?'

'I can't get hold of Ruth at the office or on her mobile, so I thought I might pay her a visit.'

'Libby! You can't do that! You don't just turn up on people's doorsteps!'

'Why not? Canvassers do it all the time!'

'And everybody hates them,' said Maria. 'Why do you want to speak to her, anyway?'

'I think she's got more to tell us.'

'Then let the police talk to her. Anyway, I haven't actually got their address. I just know it's in Felling because she said it's near the brewery.'

'Oh. Perhaps I'll have to try Gina instead.'

'Gina? You mean Roy's wife? Have you met her?'

'No. But I'm sure I could think of something.'

'Libby, you're poking your nose in again, aren't you? Does DCI Connell know what you're planning?'

'No.' Libby pushed her mug away. 'All right, I'll give up. But I'm sure Ruth knows something. And Trisha's dad said we should look at her.'

'Trisha's dad?'

'He's a former Marsham's landlord. One of the ones who lost his pub.'

'Oh.' Maria was obviously thinking. 'Well, why don't you ask him about Ruth, then?'

Libby paused. 'Yes. Why don't I? Brilliant, Maria! Trouble is, I shall have to turn up on his doorstep. I don't think I've got his number.'

And, she thought, after she'd ended the call, Stan had hers – or Fran's at least. But Trisha hadn't been in touch. She checked the time, took a biscuit from the tin and collected keys, bag and coat. She was going to see Stan Hadley.

This time, she and Stan met in the foyer. He was carrying two shopping bags.

'Hello again!' he said. 'Are you coming to see me?'

'I'm sorry to turn up unannounced again,' said Libby, pressing the lift button, 'but I haven't got your number.'

'Oh, that's all right.' He stood back for her to enter the lift. 'I haven't got much to do. I'm usually here.'

'Except for the shopping,' said Libby, indicating the bags.

'Very handy living here,' he said. 'Although I'd still rather . . . Well, you know.'

'Yes, I know.'

They fell silent until the lift reached Stan's floor.

'So what did you want?' he asked, dumping his bags on the floor in the smart little kitchen area. 'More questions?'

'Only one, really,' said Libby, watching him unloading his shopping. 'You mentioned Ruth Baxter and the fact that she didn't like women. You said we should ask ourselves why.'

'Yeah.' Stan looked up at her under his eyebrows. 'Well, why d'you think?'

Libby watched him in silence for a minute.

'Because she was jealous of them being with her brothers?' she said eventually.

Stan laughed, shut the fridge door and picked up the kettle. 'Want a brew?'

'Tea would be lovely,' said Libby.

'Right, well, you're nearly right.' He filled the kettle and switched it on. 'Far as I could see, and this goes back way beyond Trisha and Roy hitching up, Ruth always wanted her brothers' attention. She used to get mad when Dickie got Roy out of trouble. He was always in trouble.'

'Was this before Roy started working for the company?'

'Oh, he was family, so he was on the board. Not that he did much, not when he was younger. I'd had the old Fox for years, since their dad was in the chair, so I almost watched 'em grow up. Ruth used to be the little queen, see. And when the boys took up with women, she didn't like it.'

'I see.' Libby nodded. 'That's why she didn't like Trisha or Veronica.'

'Or Jean.' Stan glowered at the mugs he'd put beside the kettle. 'But that wasn't the worst of it.'

'Oh? What was it, then?'

Stan sighed. 'She got married.'

'Yes, but that must have been years before Roy and Trisha?'

'Not that many. Ruth always loved being the only woman in

242

her family's lives. She was her dad's little princess.' He made a face as he poured water onto teabags. 'Not that she was a beauty young Ruth. So she didn't get married till well after Dickie and Veronica got married, when she realised she was losing her place in the family. See, her dad had trained her up to be an accountant and he wanted her to run that side of the business.'

Libby gasped. Stan looked up and grinned.

'Oh yeah. But then she met Quentin Baxter. I reckon she thought he was the answer to her prayers.' He waved a milk bottle at her. Libby nodded. 'But it wasn't as simple as that.' He passed over a mug and waved at the sitting area. They went across and sat down.

'So what was the problem?' asked Libby.

'Quentin was.' Stan leant back. 'Course, I was on the outside, but I saw enough. Especially when he used to visit. Checking the books.'

'Oh, he'd already been made a director?'

'He was running the accounts department. That's how he met Ruth. Before they set up their own business.'

'But why was he a problem?' Libby persisted.

'Women.' Stan gave her a considering look. 'You haven't heard? Anything in a skirt, our Quentin. That's why Ruth hated other women.'

Chapter Thirty-Four

'Ah!' Libby sat back and stared. 'How did you know about that?'

'Common knowledge. He went after Trisha, but by that time she was seeing Roy.' Stan looked thoughtful. 'Actually, he and Roy were quite thick, I always thought.'

'Why hasn't anyone else mentioned this?' asked Libby. 'The other landlords, I mean. If it was common knowledge.'

'If you've been asking about Dickie's murder, why would they? Quentin being an idiot with women don't have no bearing on it.'

'Maybe not, but he was running the accounts department!'

'Well, what's that got to do with anything?' asked Stan, surprised.

A way for Roy to appropriate funds, thought Libby, although she couldn't quite see how just at the moment.

'So Ruth got mad about Quentin going after other women, although someone else told me she wasn't jealous. She obviously was.' said Libby. 'But that wouldn't have made her kill Dickie. Would it?'

'No,' said Stan reluctantly. 'S'pose not.'

'Well, it all helps.' She put down her mug. 'At least, I think it does. But it doesn't explain what's going on inside Marsham's at the moment.'

'Well, I don't know if Quentin's got anything to do with the accounts now,' said Stan. 'Although I reckon he could get into them no trouble if he wanted. But Ruth's still on the board – course, it's just her and Roy now. They'll come in for a pretty penny.'

'Only if they sell the brewery,' said Libby. 'Dickie only left them a nominal amount in his will, apparently. And if the brewery's not doing well . . .'

Stan nodded. 'Unlucky family, that. Their mum died when she was in her forties – cancer. Then the old man went doolally. He died, as well. And now Dickie.' He shook his head. 'Glad now that Trisha didn't end up married to Roy, although she was upset at the time.' He stood up. 'More tea?'

'No thanks, I'd better be getting back,' said Libby. 'And don't forget, if Trisha's got anything to tell us – or the police – you've got Fran's number.'

Stan saw her out.

'Reckon I'm going to try and get the Fox back,' he said. 'Dunno how, but I'm going to try.'

Libby pondered Stan's last statement as she drove home. Of all the dispossessed landlords she'd either met or heard of, he was the most upset. Was that a motive? But no. Killing Dickie would do him no good, and he had apparently thought Dickie was a good sort. So who actually *would* benefit from Dickie's death? That was the main question as far as Libby was concerned. Means and opportunity didn't come into it. She, Fran and the police had considered everyone over the past few weeks, but nothing had jumped out at any of them.

'I suppose,' she said out loud to herself, 'opportunity also includes Dickie's whereabouts on the Saturday night.'

And where was that? He hadn't been at home – the police had confirmed that wasn't a crime scene. And presumably he hadn't been at the brewery, either. Libby frowned as she drove past Cattlegreen Nursery towards Steeple Martin. Where did Dickie spend his time? What did he do with himself when he wasn't working? So far, the only evidence of his leisure activities were the reports of him being a regular at the Poacher. And even that seemed to have fallen off recently.

But, she remembered, as she waited to cross the junction into Allhallow's Lane, there was Anthony Leigh. An old friend who had been nosing around in the past few days. She pulled up outside number 17. What did that mean?

'Although,' she said to a surprised Sidney, as she let herself in, 'we don't know that it actually *was* him sniffing round the property. Or even if it was really him phoning Alan Farrow.'

And what difference did it make anyway? He was hardly coming to spend quality time with his old friend, was he?

She went to forage in the fridge for something for a rather late lunch.

'Quentin!' she said, as she pulled out a packet of past-its-sell-by-date ham. 'He's obviously a bad lot. We should be looking into him.'

'But,' said Fran when applied to with this theory, 'I still don't see what motive he had for killing Dickie.'

'No, neither do I, unless Dickie was going to tell Ruth about his . . . er . . . philandering.'

Fran laughed. 'Lovely word! But Ruth already knew about it, according to Stan. And yes, I know you want to speak to her, but I still don't see how you can.'

Libby pondered. 'You know, that conversation I had with her at Maria's was the most telling.'

'How?'

'For a start, she refused to call Dickie anything but Richard.'

'That doesn't mean anything.'

'No, but she was . . . odd about the company. She mentioned the board without saying "us" or "we". And about the whole Gina thing. And despite what Stan told us, she seemed to be standing up for Trisha. The whole conversation was strange.'

'So what does that mean? If anything?'

Libby thought for a moment. 'I think,' she said slowly, 'I think she knows something about Dickie's death – or *thinks* she does.'

'*Thinks* she does?'

'Suspects something.' Libby bounced in her chair. 'And it reflects on her. She was scared.'

'Well, I still don't see how you can ask her. Unless Maria's willing to set up another meeting.'

'No, all right. And Maria's already started telling me off like everyone else. But we've got to be able to find out somehow.' Libby scowled at Sidney, who twitched his ears.

'Or Ian has.'

'OK, or Ian has. And I wonder what's happening about Big Bertha? Apropos of nothing.'

'What put her into your head?'

'Ian said she was being investigated, too, and she was overseeing Rob and Rachel's team, wasn't she?'

'I don't know – I've lost track,' said Fran. 'Ian seems to be back in charge now, though, doesn't he?'

'I think so, although I'm not really sure what he's looking into – or what Rob and Rachel are doing either,' Libby said. 'Perhaps he'll tell us on Wednesday.'

'If you don't start bothering him before then,' said Fran.

'Do you mind if I go for a ride tomorrow?' Libby asked Ben later over dinner.

'Why should I mind?' Ben looked surprised.

'Because it's . . . I don't know. Not productive.'

'Oh, for goodness' sake! What are you on about?' He laughed. 'Go and have a ride. And you can ask young Alanna more questions at the same time, can't you?'

Libby felt her cheeks getting hot.

'There, see? I knew you would.' Ben tucked into his chilli. 'And I shall go off and see that chap with the hop garden near Whitstable.'

'OK.' Libby restrained herself from asking why, when he had a perfectly good hop garden of his own.

'So what are you really going to do when you go over to

Heronsbourne?' Ben rested his elbows on the table. 'Who have you got in your sights now?'

Libby opened her mouth and shut it again.

'Come on, out with it. You wouldn't have asked me if I minded if you hadn't got an ulterior motive.'

She bit her lip. 'I want to find out about Gina and Roy.'

'Find out what?'

'What Gina's really like – could she have killed Dickie and set fire to her own house.'

'She and Roy were together when that happened. And you've heard nothing more about it, have you? So it was obviously not considered serious.'

'Hmm.' Libby stood and picked up their empty plates.

'Well, don't go pestering young Alanna too much,' said Ben. 'Let her get on with her new life without interference.'

And anyway, Libby told herself as she loaded the plates into the dishwasher, it was actually Ruth and Quentin she wanted to know about, and frankly, she couldn't see Alanna helping her with that.

Libby called Stella early on Tuesday morning to ask if it was convenient to come over and borrow Punch for an hour, and was assured it would be a pleasure to see her.

'Alanna might come out with you, if that's OK,' said Stella. 'She doesn't really like going out on her own for some reason, and we've got no youngsters booked in until the weekend.'

'No, that's fine,' said Libby, feeling slightly guilty. 'I'll be over about eleven – is that OK?'

She was just going out of the door when her phone buzzed in her bag.

'Hello?' She didn't recognise the number.

'Is that Libby?' asked a rather breathless voice.

'Yes?'

'It's Chloe Vaughan here! Sorry to disturb, but I just thought you'd want to know.'

Libby's heart gave a little jump.

'I'm moving into Temptation House!' Chloe was almost yelling, she was so excited.

'Oh, that's wonderful, Chloe!' Libby smiled to herself as she closed the door. 'Are you going today?'

'I am! Dear Lewis has organised some firm to go into my old place and pack everything up – not that there was much – and he's taking me over there to make sure it's all OK.' Chloe sniffed. 'He's such a lovely boy!'

Libby grinned at the thought of middle-aged Lewis being a boy, but supposed he was to Chloe. 'That's brilliant,' she said. 'I'll come and see you when you're settled. And don't forget we're going to take you to the Goods Shed.'

There was a scuffling sound at the other end of the phone.

'Lib, it's me. Chloe's told you her good news, then?'

'Yes, it's great. The police haven't been able to find out who broke into her flat, then?'

'You haven't heard anything?' Lewis sounded hesitant.

'No – why?'

'Well, I had a sort of idea.'

'What?' Libby's heart jumped again.

'Mum told you that Marsham couple had been to a do at our place, didn't she?'

'Yes, and you hadn't mentioned it,' said Libby.

'I'd forgotten. Well, then I remembered that one of our casuals knew the wife. She was talking to her that evening.'

'Waiting staff?'

'Yeah. Well, you know, we've got quite a lot we can call on. This girl – she's good, actually, reliable – she used to live near this Jean. Marine Terrace, is it?'

'Nethergate, yes. Not now, though?'

'No, she's got a place near Hannah and Gary. The old nuns' place.'

Libby grinned. 'I know. So what do you think? This girl just went up to Gina – Jean – and told her that Chloe Vaughan was staying with you and her flat was empty?'

'Put like that it sounds bollocks, doesn't it? It's just it was the only connection I could think of that wasn't us lot. I dunno what that Jean would have to do with it anyway. I can't see her dumping a body, or breaking into a flat.'

'I only caught a glimpse of her at the quiz that time, but she's glamorous, isn't she?'

'And a squirt. Five foot soakin' wet.'

'Right. I see what you mean. Oh well, as long as no one's after Chloe, it's all right, isn't it?' Libby sighed. 'I'll see you soon.'

I wonder if it was that house, she asked herself as she drove towards Heronsbourne Flats. The same one that Gina and Alanna lived in. And now the girl was living in St Mary's, the converted nunnery behind the Red Lion. She would ask Hannah if she knew her. The area was small; most people knew at least half the population. Yes, she thought, with a small smile. That was a very good idea.

Chapter Thirty-Five

Alanna was waiting in the yard, Punch and Cascade already tacked up.

'Oh! You're taking Cascade out!' Libby beamed at the white pony. 'You know, I shall never be able to call him a grey. Now, Punch *is* a grey.' She stroked the pony's nose and he whiffled at her.

Alanna smiled and brought over the wooden stool for Libby to mount from.

'I'll have to practise,' she said, settling herself in the saddle. 'I was a bit stiff last week.'

'You don't ride since you were young.' Alanna nodded wisely. 'It will get better.'

'Of course it will,' said Libby. 'Is Stella out on the farm?'

'In the office,' said Alanna. 'You want to see her?'

'No, I'll pop in when we get back.' Libby smiled at her escort. 'Where are we going? Lead the way!'

They went out onto the Flats, and to Libby's surprise turned right towards St Cuthbert's church and Yew. She wasn't sure how she'd feel about going that way, as the last time she had, she'd been attacked, but at least this time Punch could make a run for it if they got into trouble.

Alanna led her right down to the beach, where the tide was out, leaving a firm, flat surface of sand, just right for the ponies to have their heads. Ten minutes later, Libby was grinning and breathless,

Punch was wading into the shallows and shaking his head, and Alanna and Cascade were trotting back towards her.

'That was great!' she gasped.

'Good to gallop.' Alanna smiled at her, and indicated that they should continue back along the beach past the golf club.

'Is not their beach,' she said firmly.

'No,' agreed Libby, thinking of the parties that had been held here where once again she had almost been attacked. *I do seem to get into trouble,* she thought. *I hope I don't this time.*

When they'd almost reached the end of the path that led to Colin and Gerry's house, Alanna spoke. 'There was one of Jean's friends.'

Libby waited. Eventually, 'One of Jean's friends who . . .?' she said.

'He told Jean everything would be all right.' Alanna wasn't looking at her, but gently turned Cascade back the way they had come. Libby and Punch followed.

'Do you mean when you were living in the house in Nethergate?'

Alanna nodded. 'Skinner's House. Next to Skinner's Alley.'

'Right. And this friend – he thought it would be all right? What did he mean? That you wouldn't have to leave after all?'

Alanna looked across, her face solemn.

'This wasn't Roy – her husband?'

Alanna shook her head. 'No. He was one of Jean's . . . friends. He said he knew the people who were selling the house. He would make sure it was all right. He said there was . . .' she frowned, 'a . . . a family connection.'

Punch threw up his head and sidestepped, put out by the sudden jab on his mouth.

'Oh.' Libby cleared her throat. 'Well. That was convenient!'

'But it wasn't all right. Not for us.'

'Ah. So this friend introduced Jean to Roy? And she was all right because she married him.'

'Yes.' Alanna nodded again. 'But we had to go.'

'There was another girl who lived near you, I was told,' said Libby, marvelling at how much information had suddenly come spilling out over the last few hours.

'Kayleigh.' Alanna nodded. 'I knew her.'

'Oh – do you still know her?'

'Yes. She lives in . . .' She wrinkled her nose.

'St Mary's – just behind the pub up on the main road.'

'Yes.' Alanna beamed. 'I go there sometimes.'

'Nicer than Jean, then!' laughed Libby.

'Oh, yes. Not . . . what did you say?'

'Up herself,' suggested Libby.

Alanna let out a peal of laughter and Charade pricked his ears backwards.

'Come on,' she said. 'We gallop again.'

They arrived back at Brooke Farm at almost half past twelve. Stella came out to meet them.

'Good time?' she asked.

Libby dismounted inelegantly.

'Lovely,' she said. 'How much do I owe you?'

'Oh, don't be daft. Any time. You can rub him down and put the tack away.'

'And don't forget the bit!' warned Alanna.

Libby managed to remember how to do both, and then asked Alanna if she had Kayleigh's phone number.

'Why?' Alanna was wary. Libby decided to be honest.

'I wondered if she could tell us anything about Jean,' she said. 'Especially now you've told me about Jean's friend.'

Alanna looked thoughtful. 'Perhaps,' she said, and sat down on a hay bale. 'I will phone her.'

'All right.' Libby leant against the tack-room door and waited.

It wasn't very long before Alanna's face broke into a smile and she was jabbering away so fast Libby could barely understand her.

She made out the names 'Jean' and 'Libby' once or twice, but that was all. Eventually Alanna held the phone away from her ear. 'Kayleigh says you can talk to her at the pub.'

'The Red Lion?' Libby's eyebrows shot up. 'When?'

'She works there today. Now.' Alanna beamed again. She spoke briefly into the phone once more, then put it away. 'We go in to Stella now,' she said.

Stella was extremely interested in this new information, although she looked a little concerned at the thought of Alanna going to the pub.

'I won't go,' said the girl. 'I'm not old enough.' She smiled at them both. 'I shall have my lunch with my mother.'

'Now there's a sensible child,' said Stella, watching her fondly out of sight.

'Sensible and incredibly helpful,' said Libby. 'Do you want to come with me?'

'No, you go. Just let us know how you get on. Do you seriously think this could help find Marsham's killer?'

'I certainly think it's going to help,' said Libby.

She was not unduly surprised when she entered the main bar of the Red Lion to be greeted by the same bright young woman she had seen before.

'I know who you are!' Kayleigh said with a broad smile. 'When Alanna said your name, I remembered it and asked George.'

'Who told her to have nothing to do with you at any price,' said George, appearing from the door behind the bar.

Libby grinned and heaved herself up onto her usual bar stool.

'Want a coffee?' George indicated his coffee machine, which got hardly any use as far as Libby could see.

'I'll have a tonic water, please,' she said. 'Are you all right to answer a couple of questions for me, Kayleigh?'

Kayleigh shot a look at her employer, who nodded cheerfully.

'Always glad to help the police,' he said with a wink. Kayleigh's mouth dropped open.

'Don't worry,' said Libby. 'I'm not actually the police. I just help out sometimes.'

George placed her glass of tonic in front of her and retired to his own stool at the other end of the bar.

'Now, Kayleigh.' Libby leant on the counter. 'You knew Jean, didn't you?'

Kayleigh nodded.

'And did you know what she did for a living?'

Kayleigh opened her mouth, then chewed her lip. 'Not to say *knew*,' she came out with at last.

'But guessed?'

'We-ell, I don't know if it was her actual *job* – you know? But it was a bit obvious.'

'Yes, I gathered from Alanna. And one of Jean's "friends" said he knew the people selling the house?'

Kayleigh sniffed. 'It was Roy who was selling it – the one she married. Both as bad as each other, I reckon.'

'Do you know who the friend was?'

'No, but he was around a lot. Always creeping about.' She sniffed again.

'Have you seen him since Jean and Roy got married?'

'Oh yes.' Kayleigh nodded. 'Going to their house, wasn't he?'

'Oh.' Libby swallowed. 'And it wasn't Roy's brother? Or was it?'

'Old Dickie Marsham? Nah!' Kayleigh laughed. 'Saw a picture of Dickie online – when he died, you know? It wasn't him. Tall, this other bloke was. And thinnish.'

'And my friend Lewis at Creekmarsh said you were talking to Jean when they had a Round Table do there. So you still talk to her, then?'

Kayleigh shrugged. 'Can't ignore her. That was a while ago, though. She didn't even speak when they came in on the night of the quiz. You saw her, didn't you?'

'Only briefly,' said Libby, wondering what else she could ask.

'Tell you who you should talk to,' said Kayleigh, meditatively polishing a beer pump.

'Who?' Libby leant forward eagerly.

'That other woman who goes to see Jean sometimes.' She frowned. 'Dunno who she is. Bit younger than you, got that snooty look.'

Libby sent a quick glance towards George, who nodded.

'I think she means Ruth,' he said.

'Ah. Ruth's Roy and Dickie's sister,' she explained to Kayleigh.

'Oh, right.' Kayleigh stood looking – brightly – at Libby.

'Well, that's about all, Kayleigh.' She looked again at George. 'Can I buy you both a drink?'

'We'll put it in the wood,' said George, leaving his stool and coming forward to take Libby's bank card. 'Any help?'

'Oh yes,' said Libby. 'I'm beginning to make sense of things now. But I would like to talk to Ruth again.'

'You've met her already?'

'Yes, through a friend, but I don't like to ask *her* again, and I don't know where Ruth lives. I tried her office number, with no luck.'

'Well, I know where their house is.' George pointed at the old-fashioned map of the area on the wall behind the bar. 'See there?'

'That's the really narrow road that leads from our main road to St Aldeberge,' exclaimed Libby.

'That's where they are, just outside the village. They've got a big 1930s double-fronted place with a five-bar gate. And Veronica lives the other side of the creek.'

'Oh!' Libby was surprised. 'I wonder why Ruth didn't tell me that? We were talking about St Aldeberge and mentioned that we knew the vicar.'

'I don't know, but there must have been a reason. Wanted to keep her privacy, I expect.' George looked up as the door opened and two elderly men entered. 'Geoff, Jack! Morning!' He turned to Kayleigh, still standing – brightly – by his side. 'Off you go, girl. Two pints of bitter.'

Libby grinned as she watched Kayleigh serving the customers. 'I bet she's an asset.'

'She is. And knows her business, too. Doubt if she'll stay, though. Too good for the likes of us.' George sighed. 'Ah well. Anything else we can do for you?'

'No, thanks, George. I'll come and tell you all about it when we know whodunnit!'

And Libby, driving back from Heronsbourne, past Nethergate and on towards St Aldeberge, began to think that soon, she might actually know who *had* done it.

Chapter Thirty-Six

Things were falling into place, and her vague suspicions of Ruth were beginning to have more substance. Thanks to Alanna, and now Kayleigh (thank goodness Lewis had mentioned her), it looked to Libby as if the tall, thinnish man could possibly be Quentin, who was now revealed as one of Gina Marsham's 'friends'. At least, Libby thought so. Which accounted for Ruth's antipathy towards Gina, in part, anyway. Although it wasn't exactly a motive for killing Dickie.

She turned up the narrow road just outside St Aldeberge. This led, she knew, to their friend Rosie's former home. And there, only a few yards into the lane, was the big 1930s house with the five-bar gate. She parked in front of it and hoped nothing bigger than a bike would come past, and that the two cars on the drive would not wish to leave the premises.

Now she was here, she wondered why she had come. It was a Tuesday afternoon. Ruth was unlikely to be at home – surely she would be in the office in Felling. And would she really be prepared to speak to Libby about her husband's affair, if affair it was, with her brother's wife? Although it would appear that whatever it was, it had happened before Roy's marriage had taken place. And, in fact, that Quentin had probably introduced Roy and Gina – or Jean, as she was then.

Libby sighed. It had all looked so good when she was driving here, but in fact, it didn't make any sense at all. She heaved another sigh and was just reaching for the ignition when the front door of the house opened. Ruth Baxter emerged, looking slightly pink and flustered, and turned to usher out a stocky middle-aged man with a pronounced tan.

Libby tumbled out of the car.

'Ruth!' she called, fixing a bright smile to her face. 'I'm so glad I caught you! And this must be Anthony!'

The pair stopped dead between the house and the cars. Ruth gaped, cod-like, and the man frowned.

Libby squeezed through the gate and held out her hand.

'Hello, I'm Libby Sarjeant. I was so sorry to hear about your friend.'

The man's face cleared and he took her hand briefly. 'Anthony,' he said. 'How did you know?'

Hell! How *did* she know? Apart from some inspired guesswork.

'I knew you were in the area, so seeing a man with a tan with Ruth,' she gave an unconvincing laugh, 'I guessed it was you.'

'What can I do for you, Libby?' Ruth had regained her composure. 'We were on our way out.'

'I can see that,' said Libby, her mind racing at a rate of knots. 'Are you going to see Roy?'

The two people in front of her could have been turned to stone. Then the man stepped forward.

'What do you know about it?' he grated out, and shot a furious look at his companion.

'About Roy?' Libby hoped her voice was level. 'I know he's not at work at the moment.' She hoped he wasn't.

Anthony glanced at Ruth. 'I'll go on my own,' he said, and turned back to Libby. 'If you'll just get out of the way.'

Libby decided not to argue. She got back into her car and reversed into a hedge, then watched as Ruth swung open the gate and Anthony Leigh (she assumed it was actually him) drove a small black hatchback out and away towards the main Nethergate and Heronsbourne road. She then shot out of her car and managed to catch Ruth up as she reached the front door.

'Just a minute, Ruth.'

The woman turned her no longer pink face towards her. She was crying.

'Don't you think you'd feel better if you tell me all about it?' Libby asked gently, wishing she'd had the sense to do her leaving-the-phone-line-open-to-the-police-station trick.

Ruth, shoulders slumped, led the way into the house. The panelled hall was dark, but the room beyond looked bright enough. Libby took Ruth's arm and led her inside.

'Is Anthony here because of Roy?' she asked, when they were both seated. 'Or because of Dickie? I know he was at Dickie's house the other day.'

Ruth looked up sharply. 'How do you know?'

'The police know,' said Libby. 'And that he called Alan Farrow. Why did he want to know about Dickie?'

'I thought you knew?' Ruth glared at her. 'You said Roy . . .'

Libby didn't want to admit that this had been a dive into the mist.

'Something to do with Dickie – Richard – *and* Roy, then?'

'Dickie was helping him,' Ruth barely whispered.

'Helping Roy?'

'Anthony helped too.' Now she crumpled in her seat and began crying in earnest.

'Tea?' muttered Libby. There was no answer, so she got up and went into the adjoining kitchen, where she found kettle, teabags, and milk in the fridge. While the kettle was boiling, she went and stood over Ruth, who continued to sob quietly. Eventually, two mugs of tea made and delivered onto the coffee table by Ruth's chair, she had the sense, belatedly, to send a text to Ben, Ian and Fran telling them where she was. Just in case.

'Now tell me, Ruth,' she said, taking a restorative mouthful of tea. 'What were Dickie and Anthony helping with?'

Ruth made an effort to sit straight and picked up her mug.

'How did you know?' she asked eventually.

'I don't really know anything,' Libby admitted. 'You told me.'

Ruth turned woebegone eyes towards her. 'It was all Quentin's fault,' she blurted out.

Libby thought about this for a moment.

'Presumably you don't mean that he killed Dickie?'

Ruth shook her head, looking vaguely scornful.

'So was it because he had an affair with Gina?'

'Affair?' screeched Ruth, suddenly becoming animated. 'He *paid* her!'

'And then,' Libby went on, 'he introduced her to Roy.'

'What was he thinking?' Ruth sank back down and sniffed.

'I'm not quite sure what happened next,' said Libby, piecing things together as she went. 'Was it something to do with selling the pubs?'

Ruth threw up her hands.

'But what, Ruth? The money would have gone to the business. You're on the board, you'd know about it if it was being stolen.'

Ruth just stared at her hopelessly. Libby remembered what she'd said.

'Quentin?' she said slowly.

Ruth nodded.

'Oh Lord.' Libby closed her eyes. 'Quentin fixed the books?'

Ruth nodded again.

'So that Roy had money . . . for his gambling debts?'

Ruth gazed down into her lap. 'Dickie asked Anthony to help.'

'Ah.' Libby frowned in concentration. 'Hang on, I think I've got it. Roy got into trouble with gambling debts, and Dickie asked Anthony to help because Anthony had . . . um . . . contacts?'

Another nod.

'And then they needed paying. So Quentin fiddled the books. Have I got it right?'

'Anthony's friends aren't very nice,' muttered Ruth.

'Was it them who killed Dickie?' Libby was puzzled. 'But why?'

'I don't know!' Ruth wailed.

261

'No.' Libby sat back and shook her head. 'It doesn't make sense, does it? I can see now why you were so cross with Gina – she encouraged Roy, didn't she? And between them they've put the brewery in jeopardy. No wonder no one will speak to the landlords.'

'It'll all come out now,' said Ruth. 'The police are in there.'

'But why did Anthony come over here?'

'He wanted to help. I know he went a bit off the rails a few years ago . . .'

'I think that's putting it mildly,' said Libby.

'. . . but he's always been fond of the family,' Ruth went on, taking no notice. 'He wanted to talk to Roy – make him own up, I think.'

'Can't see that happening,' said Libby. 'Not if what I've heard about Gina is true.'

'Why didn't he stay with Trisha?' moaned Ruth. 'This would never have happened.'

'No, and her dad might not have lost his pub,' added Libby.

'We wanted to give it back to him.' Ruth's eyes were overspilling again. 'Dickie and me.'

'Oh my Gawd, what a mess!' sighed Libby.

'Can you do anything?' Ruth suddenly clutched Libby's arm.

'How?' Libby stood up. 'The only thing I can do is tell the police. I'm sorry, Ruth, I really am. I just wish you'd told someone when things began to go wrong.'

Ruth stood up and flung her mug at the wall. 'What – when Quentin started seeing that tart? Or when Roy started gambling? When, exactly?' She was shaking, and Libby began to get worried.

And suddenly the door burst open.

Libby and Ruth both jumped backwards and fell into their chairs as they were confronted with a screaming Medusa.

Libby sat watching open-mouthed as the termagant raged round the room, throwing pictures and ornaments to the floor to join the

262

remains of the tea mug. Ruth was openly howling now, and the noise was incredible.

Eventually, a brief silence fell for breath-taking purposes, and Libby seized her moment and stood up.

'Gina Marsham, I presume?' she said.

Her reply was a stream of invective, as Gina picked up a small photo frame and aimed it at Libby's head. Libby ducked, and at last it all came together.

'That's what you did to Dickie, isn't it?' she said. 'Only I guess it was something heavier. My, you've got a temper.'

Gina was coming at her again, but Libby, with years of panto-mime slapstick behind her, stuck out a foot. It was unfortunate that the wooden table was in the way, and proved somewhat harder than Gina's head, and while she was still trying to get back to her feet, two more arrivals appeared on the scene.

'Hello, Rob!' said Libby, with relief. 'I'm so pleased to see you!'

Inspector Rob Maiden grinned at her and indicated that his accompanying officer should assist Gina to her feet.

'How do you do it, Libby?' he asked admiringly.

Libby grinned back. 'Just lucky, I guess,' she said.

Epilogue

After having expressed himself forcibly on the subject of interfering bystanders who should know better, Detective Chief Inspector Ian Connell agreed to a private meeting in the Coach and Horses on Wednesday evening, after, as he put it, he had wiped the floor with Mrs Sarjeant.

Said Mrs Sarjeant, driven home in her own car by a gleeful DC Mark Alleyn, who reported the flurry of activity caused by Libby's text message, was suitably penitent when faced with her seriously upset partner. Ben did not seem at all appeased by the information that the visit to Ruth was on the spur of the moment, and she hadn't expected anything to come of it. He did, however, field the anxious, or just plain nosy, calls from their wider circle, informing them that Mrs Sarjeant was prostrated by shock, something none of them believed.

Fran, predictably, was the first to arrive on Wednesday evening, along with Guy and their overnight bags.

'I'm not going to tell you now,' said Libby. 'Or I'll have to do it all over again in the pub. And I've already told Ben and Ian.'

'But why didn't you call me before you went to Ruth's?' Fran asked. 'I could have come with you!'

'You haven't seemed that keen to come with me recently,' mumbled Libby into the scarf she was winding round her neck. 'And I thought I was just going to have a look at the house.'

'Oh yes?' Fran gave her a knowing look. 'You knew I'd disapprove.'

'We-ell . . .' said Libby.

Tim had obligingly put a 'Private' notice on both doors to the small bar, and to Libby's surprise, Edward and Alice, together with Ian, were already seated.

'John and Sue are babysitting,' said Alice. 'We thought Alanna was too young to stay overnight, and the kids love John.' She clutched Edward's arm and gave him a kiss on the cheek. 'So I got a night off!'

'And Stella and Alanna are desperate to hear all about it,' said Edward, 'so you're going to have a second post-mortem over there.'

'Don't make her into too much of a heroine,' warned Ian, 'or she'll be impossible.'

'She's already incorrigible,' said Ben.

Patti and Anne arrived ten minutes later, followed by Peter and, surprisingly, Harry.

'Left 'em to get on with it again, did you?' asked Ben.

'Can't miss the old trout getting told off, now, can we?' asked Harry, giving the old trout a buffet on the arm.

'Right,' said Guy, when they were all seated, 'I'm not sure what's been going on, so I need everything spelt out in words of one syllable.'

Everyone looked at Ian.

'Before you start,' said Libby, 'I've got a question. How did Gina turn up right at that moment yesterday? Anthony hadn't been gone long enough to get to her house and then for her to get to Ruth's.'

'He made the mistake of calling her to say he was on his way,' said Ian. 'I gather she thought she could cut him off somewhere. Instead, she landed up with you.'

'Thank you,' said Libby. 'Just so's I know. Carry on.'

'OK,' he said, picking up his pint. 'It all started with the body in the doorway.'

'Which was Dickie Marsham,' said Anne.

'And one of the first confusing factors was that the doorway belonged to the widow of a London gangster.'

'Who had nothing to do with it whatsoever,' said Libby.

'And then there was the investigation into the local force, which had been found to have some unsavoury elements. I was supposed to be running that while my team – Rob Maiden –'

'Who's he?' whispered Alice.

'Inspector Maiden,' explained Ian, 'and DS Rachel Trent, among others – looked into the murder. The investigations got rather muddled up, especially as we had a superintendent overseeing everything, so Libby was asked to help. With Fran, of course.'

'And the first thing we had to do was look into the sale of the pubs by Marsham's brewery,' said Libby.

'But although we found several, none of them had anything to do with Dickie Marsham.'

'But they all had something to do with his younger brother, Roy,' Harry said.

'We know all that, though,' said Peter. 'What about this Gina – Roy's wife? And the sister, who you went to see yesterday.'

'And nearly got into trouble again,' Ben reminded them.

'The full story,' said Ian, 'as pieced together from Ruth's, Quentin's and Anthony Leigh's testimony . . .'

'That's the Marsham sister, her husband and the brother's friend from Spain,' amplified Fran for Alice's benefit.

'. . . is that Gina Marsham, when single, worked as a sex worker in Skinner's House in Nethergate, a property owned by the Marsham family. A legal migrant family also lived there – that's Alanna, Alice – and when the Marshams decided to sell the property, they were all to lose their homes. However, Quentin Baxter, husband of Ruth Marsham, was a client of Gina's, and introduced her to Roy, hoping he would save her from homelessness, which he did, by marrying her and dumping his fiancée Trisha, the daughter of one of Marsham's landlords.'

'Blimey, it's complicated!' said Harry.

'It gets worse,' said Libby.

'What happened next, then?' asked Anne.

'Gina encouraged Roy in his gambling habits and he began racking up debts to some very nasty characters. So you can see why we looked at the gangster's widow.' Ian took another sip and got more comfortable in his chair. 'At that point, apparently, Dickie rode to the rescue, and solicited Anthony Leigh's help. Leigh, as I once said to my assistant here, is an old-fashioned Costa criminal, who was able to raise some money for Roy to pay off his debts. However, his friends wanted their money back.'

'What a tangled web we weave,' said Peter.

'Indeed. So, Gina, who still had Quentin on a string, persuaded him to help. Her idea was to sell a few pubs – she'd seen how much they made when the sale was legitimate – and pocket the money. Quentin, who had access to the brewery accounts, managed to hide the profits from at least four pubs. God alone knows how. Sorry, Patti.'

'But not Stan's?' said Fran.

'Stan?' asked Alice.

Libby explained.

'No, not Stan's, for some reason,' said Ian.

'Ruth told me she and Dickie wanted to give that back to Stan,' said Libby. 'Do you think they'll be able to?'

'No idea.' Ian smiled at her. 'It would be a great gesture, but the lawyers and accountants will have to sort that out.'

'So now we've got Gina and Roy pocketing the profits and Quentin helping them,' said Patti. 'So which of them killed Dickie?'

'Gina.' Ian looked round the table. 'A nastier piece of work I've yet to meet. As far as we can work out, Dickie called at the house in Links View to try and talk some sense into the pair of them. Only Gina was there, and according to Roy, when he got home from the golf club she was sitting there with Dickie dead at her

267

feet, laid out with something very heavy. We haven't found the murder weapon yet, and I doubt we will. Roy helped wrap the body up and drove it into Canterbury. He had no idea who owned the place where he dumped it; they only found that out later, from the media. And then dear little Gina had the idea of sending some anonymous letters, and finally of ransacking the flat, just to avert suspicion. And by the way, they had no idea Mrs Vaughan wasn't there at the time.'

'Bastards,' muttered Guy.

'What about the attempt on Roy and Gina's house?' asked Libby. 'Was that genuine?'

'No.' Ian shook his head. 'They called the police before Gina had even put the petrol soaked rag through the letter box. We – and the fire brigade - were very puzzled that there was so little damage.'

'Did Gina confess to that?' asked Libby, amid expressions of disbelief from the company.

'No, Roy told us. He's facing multiple charges, of course, and goodness knows what's going to happen to the brewery, but that, ladies and gentlemen, is that.' Ian concluded. 'The mystery of the body in the doorway.'

'Except that Libby got a bit too close for comfort,' said Harry.

'Not just me,' said Libby. 'Fran as well.'

'Not so much,' said Fran. 'And you found Alanna and . . . what's her name?'

'Kayleigh,' said Libby. 'Yes, we couldn't have done it without them. If only we'd talked to them properly at the beginning.'

'I feel so sorry for Ruth,' said Patti. 'She was caught up in it without being guilty of anything, wasn't she?'

'She was,' said Ian.

'And that's the trouble with murders,' said Libby, finishing her red wine and waving the glass hopefully at Ben. 'People think they're exciting, but the reality is very different. It's the fallout. So many people are hurt, devastated, in fact. It isn't just the victim. It's everybody else. It's really a horrible business all round, not cosy at all.' She looked round at her friends and sighed. 'I don't know why we keep getting mixed up in it, do you?'

Her friends looked at one another, then back at her.

'Because we're Libby's Loonies,' said Harry.

Acknowledgements

Thank you to the many pubs and publicans of my acquaintance who helped, not necessarily knowingly, with this book, and to my son Miles, who accompanied me in many of my researches. And thank you to my other offspring, Leo, Phillipa and Louise, who have been carers, shoppers and drivers over the last few years. Thank you, as always, to my fellow Quayistas, Jenny, Liz, Evelyn, Linda, Melanie and Janet (names on request) for huge support and keeping me going. And to Toby and all at Headline, and to Jane Selley, editor extraordinaire, who made sense of the manuscript, corrected my mistakes and reminded me that not every reader would have read all the previous Libby Sarjeant books. Lastly, of course, apologies to all police services in the UK.

Discover more from Lesley Cookman . . .

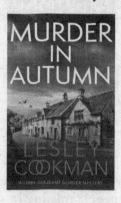

**With Shakespeare on the stage, there's danger waiting in
the wings for super-sleuth Libby Sarjeant . . .**

Libby Sarjeant is proudly hosting an original production of *Much
Ado About Nothing* at the Oast Theatre, which features a daring
twist on the classic play. But an old acquaintance of
Libby's – irascible director Constance Matthews – is outraged by
the show, stirring strong feelings throughout Steeple Martin.

When a body is subsequently found in the woodlands of a grand
estate, the community is shocked by the prospect of murder. But
the case is far from straightforward, with dark secrets lurking
beneath the surface. With the help of friends and family, can
amateur detective Libby – and her friend Fran – unravel a truly
perplexing puzzle?

Available to order

ACCENT

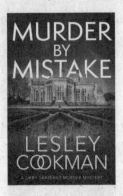

Super-sleuth Libby Sarjeant returns with a baffling new case . . . two people missing in a single week.

When a homeless man from the old-fashioned English seaside town of Nethergate appears to go missing – and the police are not available to investigate – amateur detective Libby Sarjeant and her psychic friend Fran are called in to search for him.

But it seems the case might be far more complex than they anticipated – and when a second person disappears without trace, Libby suspects there must be a sinister connection between the two.

Following a murky trail to uncover the truth, Libby and Fran find themselves uncovering secrets hiding in plain sight.

Can they solve a puzzling mystery before anyone else suddenly vanishes?

Available to order

ACCENT

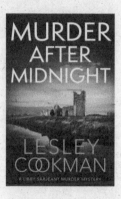

A new year dawns over the sleepy coastal town of Heronsbourne and brings with it a brand-new case for amateur sleuth Libby Sarjeant.

When a woman's body is found on the local golf course after an illicit New Year's party, news quickly spreads, and Libby finds herself being tracked down by locals desperate to share information about the victim, Jackie Stapleton.

But things are never that simple in Libby's world. Whilst everyone had an opinion on Jackie, it seems nobody really knew much about her. Libby's chum DCI Connell is being more tight-lipped than usual, and even with her friend Fran Wolfe's help, discovering a motive for the killing is frustratingly difficult.

Is the murder linked to some distinctly dodgy dealing, a dispute with the local golf club, or something far more sinister – a ghost from Libby's past?

Available to order

ACCENT